THE MISSIONARIES

Norman Lewis has written twelve novels and seven non-fiction works. *A Dragon Apparent* and *Golden Earth* are considered classics of travel and *Naples '44* has been described as one of the ten outstanding books about the Second World War. Apart from writing books his main interest lies in the study of the cultures of so-called primitive peoples. He regards as his principal achievement the world reaction to an article by him entitled *Genocide in Brazil* published in the *Sunday Times* in 1968 which led to a change in the Brazilian law relating to the treatment of Indians and to the foundation of Survival International.

Norman Lewis

THE MISSIONARIES

ARENA

An Arena Book
Published by Arrow Books Limited
62–65 Chandos Place, London WC2N 4NW

An imprint of Century Hutchinson Limited

London Melbourne Sydney Auckland
Johannesburg and agencies throughout
the world

First published in Great Britain by Martin Secker & Warburg Ltd 1988
Arena edition 1989
© 1988 Norman Lewis

Phototypeset by Input Typesetting Ltd, London
Printed and bound in Great Britain by
The Guernsey Press Co Ltd,
Guernsey, C.I.

ISBN 0 09 959960 0

My thanks are due to Luke Holland of Survival International for invaluable assistance in tracking down most of the quotations selected from missionary accounts of their activities featured in this book.

THE MISSIONARIES follows *Voices of the Old Sea* and *Jackdaw Cake* to complete a trio of autobiographical books. It is thus called because while remaining not only an autobiography, but also in a sense a travel book, my experiences of missionaries and their work play in it an increasingly prominent part. At first such contacts were accepted as an inevitable ingredient of travel in tribal areas. Later, as I encountered so many abuses and saw so much damage to the human environment inflicted behind a pseudo-religious front, I found it impossible to remain silent. In the space of a mere thirty years so much has been swept away. The great human tragedy of the missionary conquest of the Pacific is being repeated now in all 'untouched' parts of the world. In another thirty years no trace of aboriginal life anywhere will have survived.

1

In 1767 the English navigator Wallis discovered the island of Tahiti. His visit was rapidly followed by those of the French explorer de Bougainville, and Captain James Cook. Between them these men opened up the Pacific. All three captains were overwhelmed by their reception at the hands of the people of Tahiti, and by the gifts showered upon them. Bougainville renamed Otaheite—as it was then called—New Cythera after the island in Greek legend where Aphrodite had emerged from the sea. When Cook left Tahiti at the end of his second mission he wrote in his journal, 'I directed my course to the West and we took our final leave of these happy islands and the good people on them.' Some years later he was to write, 'It would have been far better for these poor people never to have known us.'

Captain Bligh of the *Bounty*—that stern judge of men— was if possible more impressed. It had been noted back home that the physique of the people of Tahiti was somewhat superior to those of Europe, and the conjecture was that the breadfruit forming a large part of their diet might have contributed to this fact. Bligh spent five months in Tahiti gathering shoots from the breadfruit tree for transportation to the West Indies in the hope of improving the condition of negro slaves. In Tahiti he has become a kind of folk hero, and the memory of him was that he spent much of his spare time playing with the local children. When he finally sailed he wrote: 'I left these happy islanders with much distress, for the utmost affection, regard and good fellowship was among us during our stay . . . their good sense and observations joined with the most engaging disposition in the world will ever make them beloved by all who become acquainted with them as friends.' A few days later the famous mutiny on the *Bounty* took place, due to the determination of members of his crew not to return to

England but to remain and settle on the islands where they had found so much happiness.

The accounts given by the great navigator, and by the lesser sailors and adventurers who followed them of the civilization of the South Seas produced a deep and even dangerous effect in Europe. Certain thinkers, above all Jean-Jacques Rousseau, who wrote of the Noble Savage, seemed inclined to argue the opinion that man had not—as has been so commonly preached and accepted—been 'born in sin', but in his primeval condition was naturally good, and that this original goodness had been concealed due to subjugation of corrupt societies.

A counter-attack by the religious orthodoxy of the day was inevitable. In 1795 the London Missionary Society was formed, its immediate attention focused upon the Pacific; two years later a convict ship bound for Australia put the first missionaries ashore on Tahiti. They, too, were overwhelmed by the warmth of their welcome and since the Tahitians were clearly disposed to give things away they asked for the Bay of Matavai, where they had landed, to be given to them. The request was instantly granted by the local chief, who had no conception of private property in land and was later disconcerted to learn that he and his people were to be debarred from the area.

The evangelists were a strange assortment, picked by the Society on the score of their probable usefulness to uninstructed savages, and they included a harness-maker, bricklayer, farmer, weaver and a butcher and his wife. None of them had ever left England before and few had left their native villages. It was four years before any of them learned enough of the language to preach a sermon to a puzzled though sympathetic audience. The Tahitians built their houses, fed them, and provided them with servants galore, but after seven years not a convert had been made. Children called upon to line up and repeat over and over again this simple verse in Tahitian did so obligingly and with good grace,

10

No te iaha e ridi mei ei Jehove ia oe?
For what is Jehova angry with thee?
No te taata ino wou no to'u hamani ino
Because I am evil and do evil.

But another seven years of such attempted indoctrination produced no results, then suddenly the great breakthrough took place.

The device which eventually established the unswerving missionary rule is described in a letter to home by one of the brethren, J. M. Orsmond. 'All the missionaries were at that time salting pork and distilling spirits . . . Pomare (the local chief) had a large share. He was drunk when I arrived and I never saw him sober.' Orsmond describes the compact by which Pomare, reduced to an alcoholic, would be backed in a war against the other island chiefs on the understanding that his victory would be followed by enforced conversion. Since Pomare was supplied with firearms to be used against his opponents' clubs, victory was certain. 'The whole nation', Orsmond wrote, 'was converted in a day.'

There followed a reign of terror. Persistent unbelievers were put to death and a penal code was drawn up by the missionaries and enforced by missionary police in the uniforms of Bow Street Runners. It was declared illegal to adorn oneself with flowers, to sing (other than hymns), to tattoo the body, to surf or to dance. Minor offenders were put in the stocks, but what were seen as major infringements (dancing included) were punished by hard labour on the roads. Within a quarter of a century the process by which the native culture of Tahiti had been extinguished was exported to every corner of the South Pacific, reducing the islanders to the level of the working class of Victorian England.

J. M. Orsmond crops up again on Moorea where he is remembered with anguish until this day. After their mass conversion it was hoped that the Tahitians might be induced to accept the benefits of civilization by putting them to work growing sugar cane. A Mr Gyles, a missionary who had formerly been a slave overseer in Jamaica, was brought

11

over, along with the necessary mill to set the industry up. 'Witnessing the cheapness of labour by means of the negroes he thought the natives of these islands might be induced to labour in the same way.' He was mistaken. The enterprise failed, and Mr Orsmond, believing that 'a too bountiful nature on Moorea diminishes men's natural desire to work', ordered all breadfruit trees to be cut down. By this time the population of Tahiti had been reduced by syphilis, tuberculosis, smallpox and influenza from the 200,000 estimated by Cook to 18,000. After thirty years of missionary rule, only 6,000 remained. Otto Von Kotzebue, leader of a Russian expedition into the Pacific in 1823, long before the decline had reached its terminal phase, wrote: 'A religion like this which forbids every innocent pleasure and cramps or annihilates every mental power is a libel on the divine founder of Christianity.' The Tahitians, he said, were by nature 'gentle, benevolent, open, gay, peaceful and wholly devoid of envy; they rejoiced in each other's good fortune, and when one received a present, all seemed to be equally gratified'. It grieved him that 'every pleasure should be punished as a sin among a people whom Nature destined to the most cheerful enjoyment'.

John Davies, one of the pioneer missionaries, wrote a history of the Tahiti Mission which he finished in 1851. It was never published in full, probably because it was considered unpublishable by his superiors in the Society, who spoke of 'those facts which it would be advisable to expunge altogether'. Only in 1961 were a number of chapters, put together with selections from missionary correspondence, published under the imprint of the Hakluyt Society. Davies wrote frankly, and from his account the missionaries could hardly have claimed to be saints. They were the sons of an age that has become a byword for hypocrisy and secret indulgence. Behind a sternly teetotalitarian façade the senior missionaries, Messrs Scott, Shelley, Hayward and Nott, wrote Orsmond, ran a still. 'From it the King always drank freely.' Mr Bicknall, a missionary leader, traded in spirits. Despite the Society's written instructions to the missionaries to 'avoid to the utmost every temptation of the Native

Women', several of the weaker brethren defected to set up house with them. Mr Simpson, a royal adviser, was charged with fathering a daughter on the wife of a Tahitian judge, and even John Davies had to face accusations of philandering.

Nor were the possibilities of financial gain overlooked. Missionary police being paid from fines (what remained was divided between the missionaries and the judges) were anxious to secure convictions, if necessary, as Mr Davies says in his History, 'by placing both the guilty and the suspect in the stocks'. The brethren also benefited from 'a system of organized tribute to the London Missionary Society'. In all, they seem to have done fairly well for themselves. Coming in most cases to Tahiti as poor men and receiving no financial support from London, they had become not only all-powerful but affluent. Mr Davies died the possessor of flocks, herds, an orchard and a plantation, 'having', as a fellow missionary described him, 'an abundance of wealth'.

Their power base firmly established in Tahiti, the missionaries moved swiftly to the outer islands. They were at first accompanied by the drunken and ferocious Pomare ('a beastly creature', Orsmond calls him). The methods employed were as before. A local chieftain would be baptized, crowned king, presented with a portrait of Queen Victoria, introduced to the bottle, and left to the work of conversion. In Raratonga chieftains, who opted to carry on as before, abruptly changed their minds at the approach of the missionary forces. In a matter of days huge numbers of islanders were baptized. Hitherto there had been nothing to compare with the success of the Gospel here. It took days to baptize the 1,500 who had chosen Jehovah. Mr Davies wondered if they had been true converts, admitting that Mr Bourne's sermon had been in Tahitian, a language the people could not understand. However a party of idolators continued to hold out and one man in ten of the islanders was conscripted into the missionary police in order to deal with them. A moral code of such strictness was then enforced that a man walking with his arm round a woman at night was compelled to carry a lantern in his free hand.

13

On the island Raiatea a man who forecast the weather by studying the behaviour of fish was treated as a witchdoctor, and put to death.

In this campaign conducted by Pomare and the missionaries it is clear that a process of mutual brutalization had gone on. The missionaries had succeeded in infusing Pomare with a wholly un-Tahitian lust for power, and stupefying him with spirits. But having at first expressed their horror at his many human sacrifices, they were in the end able to overlook these. When he died of an apoplectic fit, John Davies wrote: 'December 7th, 1821 King Pomare departed this life to the great loss of the Islands in general, and the keen regret of the missionaries . . . whose steady friend he had been for many years.'

By 1850 the conquest of the Pacific was complete. With the French and British's formal annexation of the islands, references ceased to what *The Times* had called the missionary protectorate. The colonial officials of both countries who took over were indulgent, and with the development of immunity against imported disease, island populations were on the increase. Breadfruit trees, cut down 'to incite the people to industry by reducing the spontaneous production of the earth', sprang up again everywhere. All-enveloping European clothes, both ridiculous and insanitary in the tropics, would soon be thrown away, and bodies once more exposed to the sun. Peace had returned at last after the wars of religion.

Nevertheless the islanders had changed and would never return to what they had been. Once the lives of the Polynesian and Melanesian people had been intertwined with the processes of creation. They seemed under compulsion to decorate everything, from pieces of odd-shaped driftwood, which they twisted into human and animal shapes and inlaid with mother of pearl, to the enormously tall prows of their canoes into which they carved such intricate designs. But now the mysterious compulsion of art had left them. Of the innumerable masterpieces of carving turned out by the Pacific islanders, only a few examples had escaped the general destruction to become museum pieces. The desire to produce beautiful things has gone—possibly through the long association, transmitted by the missionary teachings, of beauty with evil. Island dances, reduced to grass-skirts and swaying hips, are for tourist consumption, and the islanders' songs seem lugubrious as if they have never freed themselves of the influence of the gloomy hymn-chanting in which they are based.

Missionary effort slackened off by the end of the last century, because for a while the movement had run out of feasible objectives. In the Pacific, hundreds of islands had been reached and overrun with such ease, because they had not only become accessible, but because when reached there were no natural obstacles by way of mountains and forests to delay occupation. Assuming no resistance was encountered, a native 'teacher' supported by a half dozen missionary police could take over almost any island in a week. Suddenly the Pacific had become full of the whalers of all nations, and nothing was easier than to take a passage on one of these promising a harvest of souls.

The Pacific operation at an end, there was—at least by comparison—nowhere left to go. Much of the interior of Black Africa remained closed except to the intrepid explorers. In South-East Asia three-quarters of the vast islands of Borneo and New Guinea remained to be explored. South America contained an area larger than Europe covered by Amazonian forests and swamps. Such regions were known to be peopled by numerous tribes, many of which no one had even set eyes on. There were no maps. In South America the evangelists, who had persecuted Catholics in the Pacific, were not made welcome by the Catholic authorities. In South-East Asia, where they faced Muslim competition, whatever work could be done remained slight and peripheral.

2

After 1945 all the barriers began to fall. The resourcefulness of war had invented the means of conquering the jungles. A miscellany of light vehicles were now fitted with the caterpillar tracks that had permitted tanks to roll over all obstacles. Bulldozers and colossal earth-moving machines smashed roads through the trees, and pre-fabricated surfaces could be laid over swampy surfaces and used to build airstrips. Above all, short take-off and landing planes were developed that could be put down in many jungle clearings, even without previous preparation. Immediately the blank spaces on the map began to be filled in, and the exploration teams, pushing on into the jungle while the trees were crashing down only a few hundred yards ahead, moved steadily towards the sources of unexplored wealth.

Many surprises awaited the pioneers of such penetrations of the unknown. Stark-naked Indians surrounded by their children appeared softly among the trees to watch wonderingly and perhaps with concealed sorrow as the great machines devoured their environment. In these first good-natured contacts the clearance crews gave the children sweets, and sometimes opened tins of meat for their parents, and often the Indians presented them with superbly feathered handicrafts in exchange. When the time came to claim their villages and plantations in the transformation of the forest into ranching land, they sometimes showed resentment at the loss of livelihood and homes. The original smiling contacts were at an end, and the men on the bulldozers might from time to time be received with a flight of arrows.

Resistance was punished. Indians attempting to impede development were shot down out of hand and on sight. Later, agencies not only in Brazil, but in the US and in this country, offered patches of 'safe' jungles for investment or 'fun ranches', and in the short-lived fad for such acquisitions a number of these were bought by the personalities of the

16

day. Some of these would have been cleared of their original Indian population—as it was later learned—by such methods as aerial bombardment, poisoning by mixing arsenic with gifts of sweets, the production of local epidemics by the distribution of clothing infected by the microbes of deadly disease, or more commonly by armed expeditions of mercenary gunmen. All these things were eventually made public in a White Paper published by the Brazilian government. Action, however, came late and it will never be known how many thousands or tens of thousands of Indians perished at this time.

With the opening up of the previously sealed-off jungles in all parts of the world (although at first more particularly in Latin America) the second great historical upsurge of missionary activity was under way. In 1797 it had taken the London Missionary Society's first ship, the *Duff*, six months to reach Tahiti, and to do so it had sailed 13,800 miles—believed to be the longest voyage ever undertaken—out of sight of land. Now the savannahs and forests of Colombia, Peru, Venezuela, Bolivia and Paraguay had been brought within days of the new airborne race of missionaries, and they began to pour into these countries. Previously the English had always been first in the missionary field, but now they had withdrawn into the background to tend their flocks in such places as Singapore and Hongkong, where proselytizing effort was largely at an end, and it was the Americans who took over.

Within a decade of the war's end it was reported that more than 300 foreign religious sects, most of these originating in the USA, were in operation in South America alone. Although many of these had some pretension of missionary endeavour real power was divided between the Summer Institute of Linguistics and the New Tribes Mission, who virtually shared the continent between them. The SIL and NTM were interested only in tribal societies and were specially welcome in 'backward' Latin American countries governed under dictatorial regimes. Here missionaries were

17

accorded the status of government officials and the missions given large tracts of land and contracts to 'settle and civilize' Indian tribes. Between these two organizations, with ample funds at their disposal, an airforce, and the smoothly efficient organizations of a multinational corporation, several thousand missionaries could be put in the field. By comparison the penurious London Missionary Society of old, with its few hundred missionaries at most, who were obliged to trade in order to live, appears as an evangelistic pigmy indeed.

As an average churchgoing village child I had heard missionary endeavour praised from the pulpit, and I had probably been persuaded to contribute a tiny additional amount to a collection for their funds when occasionally the vicar called for some special effort. Thereafter I lost track of their doings. It was many years indeed before I heard of their exploits of old in the Pacific, and only in 1946 that I began to realize that they remained an active force in the religious world. This came about when Doña Elvira, an imposing matriarch I came to know in Guatemala, Central America, happened to mention that she was very happy with the Indian servants she employed through them.

When the war broke out I was living in Cuba with my wife Ernestina. I returned to England in order to join the forces. In response to the British government's urging that all families resident and able to support themselves overseas should remain where they were, she stayed on. In the army I went to North Africa, Italy, Iraq, Italy again, and Austria, and letters from America trailed after me from one theatre of warfare to the next and took as long as seven months to arrive. Another year was added to our separation by the delays of demobilization, and the re-establishment of normal communications between this country and the rest of the world.

When I met Ernestina again in the winter of 1946 it was in Guatemala City to which she had moved soon after my departure. Slowly we had both entered different worlds, and a great divide of time and unshared experience separated us. She was now living in Guatemalan colonial fashion in a house with five patios, the first occupied by its owner Doña Elvira, and the rest shared by family members, visiting relatives and friends, servants and permanent hangers-on. Ernestina was the companion of this elderly, powerful widow, whose natural genius was slowly being invaded and consumed by the cancer often concealed in great inherited wealth. I settled in the old Palace Hotel.

Doña Elvira claimed to be a member of the 'fourteen families' élite, and could prove her descent from one of the mass-murderers sent by Spain to conquer the country, but like so many of her kind she had been ensnared in habits of indolence, spending too much of her day seated in a throne-like chair on a wide balcony over the street. Here she waited for President Ubico, preceded, flanked and followed by his numerous escort, to roar past on his Harley Davidson. Sooner or later he usually did. Doña Elvira studied the way the President crouched over the handlebars of his machine or sat confidently bolt upright, convinced of being able to pick up valuable hints from these minutiae of behaviour. In the changing membership of his *cortège* she would identify shifts in political power. It was an activity that epitomized the watchful lethargy of the country. The preoccupation of Guatemala City, as ever, was with the possibility of this or any other regime coming to a peaceful or violent end, and with the improvements to be fought for, or—in the case of the privileged ladies with whom Elvira played canasta on most evenings—the deprivations to be endured.

This process of looking on, the torpor, the eternal canasta, the incessant parties organized in celebration of trivial events, the ritual of overeating (Doña Elvira consumed five meals a day), the ever-present sensation of lives drifting towards a bloodbath: all this took its toll in Guatemala. Life expectation among the ruling classes, despite their high standard of living, was relatively short. The nervous and indolent five per cent at the tip of the social pyramid were the victims of heart, liver and stomach diseases reaching almost epidemic proportions.

In addition they were prey to numerous other ailments, less easily diagnosable, which were seemingly fostered by the intellectual and emotional climate in which these people passed their lives. In a single week Doña Elvira, for example, had complained to Ernestina of pounding headaches, a persistent itch in an inconvenient place, a tendency to burst into unreasoning and uncontrollable laughter, tingling in the extremities, reduction of the field of vision, the feeling that she was 'somebody else', and a lunatic urge when in the most strait-laced company to shout out the word *cojones* (balls)!

The thing that most impressed one was the number of her Indian servants who were among the first Indians I had ever seen. They were small, fresh and silent girls of 14 or 15 in meticulous highland costume, who went barefoot, flitting from room to room, continually dowsing water on the tiles which, as they dried, gave off an odour not unlike that of rain falling on warm soil. Doña Elvira was fond of them in her way, but worried by the fact that they never laughed and only smiled as if to please her. Sometimes she stopped one to ask if she was happy, and the girl told her that she was.

Her servants came from a mission that had established itself among the Indian tribes at Quetzaltenango where the largely Indian population lived in distressed conditions. Quetzaltenango in the impoverished north was Guatemala's second city; whenever Doña Elvira decided to add to her staff, she had herself driven there, stopping one day *en route* at Lake Atitlán to sketch lakeside scenes. At the mission she placed her order for one or more girls from clean and respectable families whose backgrounds the missionaries assured her they had investigated. I was a little surprised that missionaries should run an agency for domestic servants, but no more than that. Doña Elvira undertook to pay the girls twenty quetzals—the equivalent of five pounds a year—contributing an equal amount to the mission funds. Part of the bargain was that people for whom the missionaries acted as agents should provide their servants with religious instruction. Although Doña Elvira agreed, she made no attempt to keep her promise, and the devotional literature handed out went straight into the fire. 'It's we who need the religious instruction, not them,' she said. 'They're better Christians than any of us.' When Ernestina commented that the wages seemed low, she said, 'Why give them more? There's no point. They haven't the slightest idea of the value of money.' At Christmastime she took her girls out to see the shops and the Christmas decorations. She once bought a girl a doll, but the girl pushed it away in terror, crying out that it was a demon.

Whenever Doña Elvira suffered a severe *crise de nerfs* she would gather Ernestina up and take off for a day or two in the mountains, to be soothed by the cool air, staying for a day or two in Momostenango, Huehuetenango, or Cobán, with one of the numerous distant relatives she possessed, scattered about the country. On these jaunts she made it a matter of religious duty to call on any of the Catholic missionaries working in the area. She and her friends treated such men as if they were members of the deserving poor, never failing to arrive with some gift in the way of food to relieve a normal diet of maize gruel, such as pig stew with aubergines and tortillas, together with a generous handful of medium-grade cheroots. Doña Elvira said they had to be warned in advance of such visits to give them time to remove any Indian 'housekeeper' from the scene.

The evangelists drifting in from Mexico and El Salvador provided a new and enlightening experience. All I could remember of the missionaries described by the vicar of our parish church was that they had chosen to lead uncomfortable lives to rescue the souls of those living in darkness, in savage and often dangerous parts of the world. Guatemala, referred to in its national propaganda as the Country of Eternal Springtime, was not at all like this. The Guatemalan ladies were a little surprised that the missionaries should have involved themselves in trade and commerce, claiming as they did that all profits derived in this way would be put to the service of God. The one in Momostenango ran the filling station. They all seemed to Doña Elvira to have an iron of some kind in the fire. She found it a little shameful

21

that the man in Cobán had organized a trade in exotic birds. The word had gone round that, among those exported to rich collectors and foreign zoos, had been several examples of the exceedingly rare quetzal, symbol of the Guatemalan nation—and for this reason protected—which had by far the longest tail of any small bird in the world. It was sad, too, she said, because not a single case had ever been known of a quetzal surviving in captivity.

Whatever their occasional lapses, the lifestyle of the Americans never ceased to amaze her. Although the aristocratic ladies of Guatemala City might occupy houses with three, four, or even five patios, they were in reality living in the past. Doña Elvira's kitchen was a smoke-filled cave in which half-a-dozen female hangers-on struggled for access to charcoal fires, and the drains in her enormous house remained blocked for weeks on end. Having taken her order for maids-of-all-work, the missionary showed her round the first labour-saving house in northern Guatemala, set a dishwasher churning for her benefit, and smiled with quiet pride. She found it impossible not to be impressed. She told Ernestina that the rumour was that as a young man in El Salvador he had given valuable aid to the authorities when they had suffocated the rebellion of the Pipil Indians, back in 1932. On the whole she thought it a good thing that he and a number of his friends had come to Guatemala. If ever a communist threat should develop they might be useful people to have around.

'So many revolutions, so many assassinations,' she said, 'I can't remember them all. Who was that president who sold out to the American Fruit Company? They took him to Miami, gave him a ride on a circus elephant, stuffed a half million dollars into his travelling bag, and he was their man. They say the missionaries are in with Arevalo, and a good thing, too, if they are to help him to keep this place in order.'

Ernestina herself, in the former years robustly devoid of neurotic symptoms, had been unable to escape the contagion of her surroundings. Now she was troubled by a mysterious constriction of the throat that made it difficult to swallow, and within a few days of my arrival came up with the remarkable suggestion that I should take her to the small town of Chichicastenango, in the mountains some hundred miles away, for treatment by a *brujo*—as witchdoctors are known in Guatemala.

The Guatemalans had become devotees of fringe-medicine, of acupuncture, homoeopathic remedies, faith-healing and the like. Now, after the centuries of contempt, the Indians, long suspected of being experts in this field, were in the public eye. Many claimed to have experienced almost miraculous cures at the hands of the *brujos*, and the pilgrimages to Chichicastenango had begun.

We hired a car and set out northwards through a landscape copied from China: bamboos brushed in on mist; the grey lace of precipices hung from mountain outlines in the sky; Indians dressed in coolie straw under the slant of rain; a stork in silhouette transfixed in a swamp; soft, melancholic water-washed colours.

In Chichicastenango a big church had been built on top of a great pile of masonry with a flight of steps up to its doors. Its echoes of the Mayan pyramids of old, it was hoped, would attract the Indians. Otherwise the town was a rigmarole of low rain-stained houses, general stores selling candles and rope, and slatternly *cantinas* where it was possible to get drunk and stay drunk indefinitely on very little indeed. Behind the face of Christianity the Indians remained stolidly pagan, but a comfortable arrangement had been reached some twenty or thirty years earlier with the priest of the Church of Santo Tomás: before entering the church they were permitted to build their altars, burn incense and invoke their gods on the steps; thereafter they would go through roughly the same devotional procedures in favour of the Christian god and the saints. Almost within memory of the oldest grandfather the Indians had been forcibly baptized, compelled to live in houses without windows, debarred on pain of death from riding a horse, forbidden the use of their twenty-day calendar, prohibited from taking astronomical measurements to work out the dates for sowing their crops, and flogged publicly in the square for failing to produce a child within a year of marriage. Yet now the ancient civilization of the Maya-Quiché, for nearly five centuries buried in secret in the mountains, had stealthily re-emerged, and there were aloof and dignified men in their Indian finery in the streets of the town: the *regidores* and *principales* of the old pre-Colombian hierarchy, to whom more than a shadow authority had returned.

The *brujos* were to be contacted in a slightly shamefaced way through an Indian on the staff of the Mayan Inn, the town's one hotel. We explained to him what was wanted, then settled down for a wait of uncertain length. The powerful and mysterious figures who were the repositories of the ancient culture were extremely poor and obliged therefore to live by raising crops in tiny and remote mountain clearings. From these they returned with ceremony—having let off rockets to announce their imminent arrival—after absences often lasting a week. The hotel go-between promised to enlist the services of a *brujo* regarded by the Indians as an incarnation of the god Zoltaca, Mayan guardian of the dead. This *brujo*, he assured us with some pride, was the poorest and most prestigious of them all.

Several other guests were here, obviously on a similar errand, but only one was prepared to admit that such was the case. She was the owner of the country's leading antique business, a graduate in social sciences who had come to believe that the earthquakes persistently afflicting Guatemala City, and which had brought her ceilings down on several occasions, resulted not from geological but supernatural causes. It was her hope that the same *brujo* as we expected to see would persuade her that this was not the case.

Beyond the spectacular rites performed on the church steps, Chichicastenango offered little by way of entertainment. Indian groups from all over the mountains came here to conduct their special ceremonies. They wore long indigo capes, sometimes great winged hats modelled on those of the Spanish *alguacils* of the sixteenth century, and were otherwise clad in garments woven with symbols proclaiming

24

not only the social, religious and marital status but also the sexual potency of the wearer. They capered in pious frenzy to the music of drums and flutes, burned copal incense, swung their censers, let off fire-crackers and banished the lurking spirits of evil with furious gestures—oblivious of the tourists who little suspected that according to local Indian conviction they were no more than ghosts who had succeeded in taking possession of the world.

In the evening a tiny flea-pit of a cinema functioned in a haphazard fashion, invariably showing some instalment of the old B-movie series *Crime Does Not Pay*. The cinema could only operate when two policemen were available to control the audience. There were always a few for whom this was a first-time experience, and they were prone to violent intervention, in the belief that what they were viewing was an episode from real life. Whenever the policemen were called away to deal with some emergency the cinema closed until their return.

After the adventure of the flea-pit, the evening's last option was a visit to a *cantina* called 'I Await My Beloved', which was dark and full of charcoal smoke and insanely drunk Indians, and whose *décor* attempted to attract custom with a vast collection of dried snakes—some of extraordinary length—dangling from the rafters, their jaws fixed open to show their teeth, and red glass-beads set in their eye-sockets. Whites, up from the City, attacked by boredom and *nostalgie de la boue*, would sometimes slip in here to try the sinister and legendary *boj*. This, brewed illegally by the mountain Indians, and originally sipped only by the officiating priest-hood on sacred occasions, was sold here at some risk, since its possession or sale was punishable by a stiff spell in gaol. The *boj*, frothing and bubbling, released a faintly animal smell, and was kept in a great earthenware pan in a cavern haunted by hairy spiders which leaped from the walls upon intruders, into which a customer practically had to crawl to be served. It was made from sugar-cane juice fermented with certain pounded-up roots and, although the first mouthfuls tasted no better than slightly sour beer, it filled the body with fire and the mind with benign visions, and fostered in

25

the drinker the impulse to give his property away. It was for this latter reason that labour recruiters hung about Indian mountain villages—on the lookout for happy soaks who, having handed over their possessions to anyone who seemed to be in need of them, could easily be cajoled into putting their mark on a contract committing them to three months' labour on a plantation for a dollar a week.

By a curious accident the mission house, run by a fervent American evangelist, was next door, and Mr Fernley, the missionary—a simple and straightforward man—must have been one of the few inhabitants of Chichicastenango who had no idea what was going on in the *cantina* practically under his nose. Nor did he realize that he had *boj* to thank for the regular evening attendance of a handful of softly smiling Indians, who reeled into the mission from the *cantina* in search of a quiet place to sleep—which, if left alone, they were able to do in almost any posture.

Mr Fernley's presence in the town was not viewed with enthusiasm by the local authorities, or by the management of the Mayan Inn Hotel, which depended heavily for its revenues upon American tourists for whom the Indians were a prime attraction. The missionary furiously disagreed with the local Catholic Church's policy of 'doing a deal with the devil', as he was said to have described it. He had no power to put an end to the pagan ceremonies that set so many shutters clicking, or the spectacular and dangerous performance of the Palo Volador, in which the Indians attached themselves to ropes at the top of a revolving pole and were then swung out centrifugally in mid-air. Nevertheless, he set out to disrupt such entertainments in every way he could—often with some success. Mr Fernley's scouts kept him informed of fiestas when these things occurred, and he would hurry to the spot carrying a movie camera on a stand, and start close-up filming. This was often enough to frighten the performers into taking to their heels. He had not the slightest hesitation about discussing the mission's motives in such interventions. Whatever Don Martín Herrera, the priest of the Church of Santo Tomás might claim, he said, the mission would not accept that the souls of these Indians had been

26

saved. Nor would they be saved until every vestige of the customs linking them to a hopeless pre-Christian past—including their dances, music and dramatic entertainments—had been abolished.

The missionary was both ingenious and persevering. He had opened the first tourist shop outside Guatemala City, displaying in its window the finest collection of *huipils*—the blouses worn by the Indian women—that Ernestina had ever seen. These were of a classic design, now hardly obtainable, woven from cotton threads dipped in dye obtained from molluscs, snails, the bark of trees, insects and the excrement of certain birds, and at best they were examples of pure Mayan art surviving only here in Guatemala. Now they were rapidly disappearing, or suffering degradation through the introduction of trade textiles and aniline dyes. Mr Fernley's collection, woven with symbols providing biographical information about the wearer and sometimes a potted history of her tribe, was impossible for collectors to resist. Ernestina, not knowing at that time with whom she was dealing, asked to be allowed to go through the stock, and Mr Fernley smilingly agreed.

'All these wonderful things are disappearing,' she told him, and he nodded in sympathy. She was taking an extra-mural course in the City on the interpretation of Mayan symbols, had been on an archaeological dig to the ruins of Tikhal, and had personally known Pedro Flores, the last Indian able to interpret all the designs, who had died some four years previously.

'A tribe needs above all to retain its identity,' she explained to Mr Fernley. 'For example, a pattern of ducks in flight means something quite different to the Indians from its meaning to us. It means migration. In other words the tribe has migrated from one area to another, and allied to other symbols it may signify that it actually needs to migrate in order to secure its seasonal supplies of food.'

Mr Fernley listened attentively and nodded in sympathy.

Ernestina was on the look-out for a Tzutuhil *huipil* from Lake Atitlán for her collection, but Mr Fernley shook his head. He had obtained several, he said, but the designs included 'representations of horses', by which he meant horses copulating. These, Ernestina was stunned to hear, he had destroyed. She knew of no livelier or more evocative demonstration of the primitive mind at work than a Guatemalan stallion covering a mare, surrounded by gesticulating human babies which had been brought magically into the world through this vast outgushing of the creative urge. Who, she demanded to know, could be offended by such supreme examples of tribal art? Mr Fernley explained that most of his customers were Americans, whether individuals or museums, and he found the *huipils* with these representations of horses too ugly for their approval.

In removing from circulation these masterpieces of Mayan art, Ernestina admitted, Mr Fernley was doing no more than accelerating a process that had been going on for years. Parties of women from the city went out into the mountains, equipped with ordinary good-quality blouses and skirts and a reserve of new dollar coins. Whenever they spotted a woman wearing an exceptional *huipil* they would force five dollars into her hands and persuade her to change clothes on the spot. Either from fear or not wishing to appear ill-mannered, the Indians rarely refused. Mr Fernley agreed that it was the method his own agents adopted, except that instead of paying cash they were instructed to offer a metal bowl of good quality as part of a barter arrangement, in the hope that these would eventually come to replace gourds decorated with figures from the pre-Colombian legends, which he found repellent. As we later discovered, Mr Fernley had gone a step further than the enthusiastic collectors from Guatemala City, for on the blouses he gave in exchange for *huipils* the symbols of old had been replaced by Disney ducks, mice and rabbits. Women wearing these were beginning to appear in the streets of Chichicastenango.

This town's season of Indian pageantry and fiestas began in December, but now a month earlier the rains were already slackening off with one bright day in three, and the restlessness of the coming spring driving people out of the town in search of fiestas. When the further news was that the *brujo* would be detained on his *milpa* for a few more days, we followed the common impulse and drove out to Totonica-pán, reputed to be the best place to witness Indian goings-on.

When it rained in one part of the country it was dependably dry in another, and it was said that there was not a single day in the year when a fiesta was not happening somewhere in Guatemala, all of them conducted remarkably enough by a people notable for their aloofness and taciturnity and their disdain of the outward indications of joy. Some of these featured dance-dramas that went on for days. Whites turned up in small numbers to watch them for an hour or two in a rather bewildered way. Their complaint was that nothing happened. At a fiesta for *ladinos* and whites at Nahualá and other such towns they staged exciting rodeos, and bullfights of a crude and formless kind, but the most exciting sport of all was the race by horsemen at a full-gallop under a line from which chickens dangled, tied by the legs; the winner being the first past the post with a ripped-off chicken's head in his fist. Entertainments of this kind were avoided by the Maya-Quiché.

The greatest of all the Indian dance-pageants was the Rabinal Achi, which must have been extraordinary, with a whole valley as its stage and a cast of a thousand plumed and painted Indians; the Jaguar Men, the Eagles, the Bear Men, the antler-wearing sorcerers, the priests with obsidian knives under their capes, who took a week to present this savage and poetic epic—a detestable and even frightening affair, one would have supposed, to their white masters.

The heroic figure holding the centre of the stage was Quiché Achi, valiant chief of the Chahul people captured in a war with the Rabinaleros, and condemned, at the appropriate phase of the moon, to be sacrificed to their god. Meanwhile the captured prince is treated as an honoured guest, to whom nothing is denied except the privilege of a farewell visit to his native land. In the final scene Quiché Achi joins the Rabinalero bodyguard of Twelve Eagles in a dance before the throne. After this he ascends the high altar where, for the first time since his capture, he sees his far-off country again in the moment before the sacrifice.

29

A German traveller in Guatemala of the last century saw the last performance in 1856 and found it overwhelmingly impressive. The official reason given for its disappearance was that costs of its production were too great for any Indian community to support, but it seems strange that in the days of outright slavery this should have been possible. It was the only example of many ancient plays that had survived without change. Six other dance-dramas remain: the Deer Dance, the Dance of the Jesters, the Dance of the Devils, the Dance of the Snakes, the Drunkards' Dance, and the Dance of the Conquest, but the Church has been patiently at work upon them, hacking away at the pagan significance, grafting on episodes from the lives of the saints—and in one case a moronic sub-plot of bullfighters and betrayals stolen from *Carmen*.

The one dance that had escaped mutilation was the Dance of the Conquest invented by a priest in the sixteenth century. Astonishingly enough, since it portrays the defeat and subjugation of the Indian peoples by their Spanish conquerors, it remains immensely popular and was being performed at Nahualá on the day we went there.

Totonicapán was the scientific and cultural capital of the ancient civilization, and it was in this area that a series of battles were fought between the Indians and the invading force led by Pedro de Alvarado, sent by Cortès to conquer Guatemala and described by one of his sergeants, Bernal Diaz de Castillo, as 'cheerful, frank-hearted and a good loser at cards'. Indian chieftains taken in these battles were charged with deceitful resistance and burned at the stake, and the rest of the survivors were branded and enslaved. There was some quarrelling among the Spanish officers over the share-out of the women, and the rejects, whose modest attractions it was thought might encourage the soldiers to acts of indiscipline, were run through with the lance. The traditions handed down by illiterate people by word of mouth are long-lived, and a trace of memory of these events may have survived, ingrained in the surly resignation of the Indian attitude to whites. There was a feeling of utter abandonment to nature here, where the greatest blood-lettings of old had taken place. Clumps of flowering trees were sheeted with mist drawn up by the sun. Little flocks of grazing sheep attested to a human presence somewhere. Each flock was encircled by small, tripping deer inspecting them with perhaps nervous interest.

At the fiesta the dance had been going on in its leisurely way for two days and another full day would be required to complete all the numerous episodes of the drama. A dozen or so masked dancers traipsed backwards and forwards, watched by a gathering of Indians in silence and utter concentration. The movements of the dance seemed haphazard and unplanned—although we were to learn that this was far from the case—and the dancers' costumes were a fancy-dress collection of martial oddments often worn with freakish effect. A dancer might wear the coat of a Victorian admiral's dress-uniform with a restoration dandy's fringed and heavily embroidered breeches, completing the effect with a great piratical hat. Decoration was laid on everywhere in the way of spurious medals, coins, fragments of mirror-glass and odd shapes cut from tin and stitched on the cloth. Victors were distinguished from the vanquished by the blond locks roping down over their shoulders, the great upswing of their yellow moustachios, and the crimped and beribboned beards stuck on the painted wood of their masks. The effect was absurd, yet in some way sinister. This was not a dance, and certainly not the theatre as we understood it, although every shuffling step and every stiff gesture had been rehearsed, as we were assured, for weeks on end, and was being performed before the most critical of audiences.

We had arrived in the middle of the dramatic episode when Pedro de Alvarado, having sought out the Indian leader Tecu Umán, engages him in single combat in which the Indian is slain. We stayed for about fifteen minutes of this, although the whole episode takes an hour to perform. The action was extremely slow and devoid of incident. Both men in recognition of their importance to the plot had clearly been chosen for their sheer size, being enormous by Indian standards and, laden as they were with military accoutrements and decorations of every kind, they seemed to have

31

achieved a kind of monstrous dignity. Teco Umán's mask frowned in token of his mobility. Alvarado's was carved with the ferocious leer by which he is always to be recognized in such entertainments. The two champions advanced and retreated and took an occasional swing at each other with their tin swords. Excitement spread from the Indian onlookers like an electric current, but not a muscle moved. So huge is the fascination of this dance that villagers walk up to a hundred miles over the mountains to see it performed, and in Chichicastenango it easily held its own with the rival attraction of *Crime Does Not Pay*. Of the story-line of the episodes on offer in the latter case, the Indians are likely to have understood little more than we did of the Conquest.

There remained the question of what seemed the inexplicable collapse of Indian taste in their presentation of such entertainments. How could a people with their outstanding sense of colour, and the artistry and the restraint shown in their weaving, descend to such outlandishness in costuming their performers for a dance? The likely answer is that in their traditional crafts they are concerned only with function and meaning. The symbols and colours employed in their designs are not decorative by necessity, but imbued with magic or religious purpose. Decoration for its own sake is alien to the Indian traditions and character. It is a principle applicable both in Central and South America where outside influences have not been deprived entirely of their magic function. In this case pointless and banal decoration pours into the vacuum left by the eradication of art. Mr Fernley, in some ways a simple man, understood these things so well.

At all times Guatemalans from the City were rare enough. It was reasonable to suppose that Mr Fernley suspected that such visits as ours had something to do with the new approach in the capital to problems of health, and that this was what provoked his call at our hotel within hours of our return. Up to this I had only seen Mr Fernley at a distance, patrolling the streets without evident purpose, as if walking an unseen dog. Meeting the missionary face to face I was taken by surprise. From casual reference to the evangelists I had come to suspect them of fanaticism, but the homeliness of Mr Fernley's presence seemed incompatible with such extremes. He was about forty years of age, a native of Minnesota, with a twinkling eye and a soft, reassuring voice. Back in his small home town where as I imagine first names would be in general use and the protocols of common decency strictly observed, I would have suspected him of selling insurance. There was a whiff of cheerful domesticity about him. He did the odd jobs about the house and the shopping, his wife engaged in translating the Epistle to the Romans, being of delicate physique. 'I felt obliged to come in the hope that you would talk with me,' he said. 'You'll have heard of our work here. There are two of us against so many. So far we're holding the line, but it's quite hard.'

I told him we were there to see a *brujo*, and he nodded understandingly. It was clear that he knew already.

'We discussed the trip with our doctor and he had nothing against it,' I said. 'He hadn't been able to help, and he took the civilized view that there was nothing to be lost.'

'Yes,' he said. 'Yes. I suppose that's a point of view.' He sighed. 'Could you not bring yourself to give the doctor one more trial?'

'I don't think it matters so much as all that to either of us. The doctor has a very up-to-date attitude and he's probably quite happy to be associated with what he sees as an experiment. There's no doubt at all that the Maya have a great inheritance of medical knowledge, much of which we've never bothered to investigate. There was a recent article in *La Prensa* claiming they're able to cure cancer.'

Mr Fernley smiled with ineffaceable patience. 'Whatever they may do here is without God's sanction,' he said. What set Mr Fernley apart from us was that he knew God's mind.

He took his departure, squeezing both of us by the hand, with a final smile and a little shake of his head.

I told Ernestina he seemed fairly sincere.

'That's the trouble,' she said. 'Imagine translating Romans into Maya-Quicho.'

'It's supposed to be the easiest of them,' Ernestina said.

'She'll keep at it for a few years then give it up. They always do.'

She had much less patience with missionaries than I. It was sad, I thought, that they were beginning to spoil the charm of one of the world's most charming countries.

The next day a small boy arrived at the hotel to say that the *brujo* was back, and to summon us to his presence. He took us to a shack in a lane on the edge of town, and just as we arrived a shining black Cadillac swung away from its door. Ernestina recognized the man at the wheel as one of the country's great landowners, with a *finca* in Nahuala so vast that only recently an unknown tribe of Indians had been discovered there living in some caves. Like Doña Elvira, this man suffered from a sense of lost identity.

A slatternly Indian woman let us in and we found ourselves in a single room divided by a curtain, behind which a fairly large family busied itself with domestic routine. In the foreground the *brujo* awaited us, providing yet another of Guatemala's many surprises. We had been prepared for an encounter with a dignitary in full regalia, the kind one saw so often on the steps of Santo Tomás, but instead the incarnation of Zoltaca was a small barefoot peasant in frayed trousers and shirt, with stained, deep-set eyes, fine hairs at each corner of the mouth, and an expression that could have been sullen, and was at best indifferent. Here there was no altar smoking with incense, no magic figures chalked in white on the floor, no prancing image of Tzijolach, messenger of the gods, no candles, no coloured tapes to keep the spirits in their places. Children scuffled and mewed behind the curtain; a parrot squawked; a hairless dog invaded the *brujo*'s privacy, then backed hastily away. Smoke from an open fire beyond the curtain drifted up and was trapped in a hole in the roof that was the only source of light. Strangely, although the day was warm, I felt as though a cold breeze were blowing through the room.

Ernestina described her symptoms and the *brujo* listened, eyes averted and with apparent lack of interest. Then he reached up, placed his forefinger and thumb on each side of her windpipe and squeezed with some force. '*No hay*

34

nada,' he said, which could have meant, there's nothing there, or, there's nothing wrong with you.

'That's all, then!' Ernestina asked, and the *brujo* nodded.

Ernestina gave him the ritual present we had brought: five cheroots, five eggs, and a bottle of *aguardiente*. These he took, and passed wordlessly behind the curtain.

Thus was the cure effected, for relief was instant and complete. Back in the City Ernestina wrote an account of her experience for the *Bulletin of the Indian Institute*, which aroused some interest. For a year or two people flocked to Chichicastenango to be cured of a variety of ailments. Then in 1954 the big Castillo Armas revolution took place, which gave everyone something else to think about, other than small-scale personal problems.

It was the biggest to date of all the many Central American revolutions, when an obscure colonel, backed by the CIA in the frankest possible way, put an end once and for all to any pretence of democracy in Guatemala. For motives that will remain inscrutable several leading families had managed to involve themselves with the two preceding régimes that had been actually elected to power—a repeat performance unique in Guatemalan history. To describe them as democratic would be to exaggerate—one might argue that no purely democratic government has ever come to power in Latin America. Nevertheless these two elections were extraordinary because at least no one shoved a gun into an elector's ribs and told him where to put his cross—which more or less is what has happened since. Ernestina, of whom it might be said that few people were further from communism, had been heard to speak in favour of the second Guatemalan pseudo-democracy and was a marked woman thereafter. Castillo Armas was a notable Indian-hater, which meant that the whites of Guatemala City soon dropped the fashion of going to Chichicastenango for miraculous cures. Although I could not see why this should automatically follow, he favoured the missionaries, and in his short reign of some two years before his assassination by one of his palace guards, the number of missionaries allowed to work in Guatemala doubled.

35

3

Travels in South-East Asia in 1950 proved to be no more than an oriental interlude; a project undertaken in pursuit of a journalistic livelihood. Even before departure I had made firm arrangements for return. In Guatemala I had been ensnared by the fascination of the great Maya past, and by the stubborn survivors of their race: the Indians forming one half of the population to this day. I hoped on my return to be able to include Mexico in my travels and to visit all I could of the monuments left behind by a succession of great civilizations. There was a further chance that here, too, a few Indian tribes might have been able to retain the old culture in remote mountain places. At the back of my mind the hope was born that one day I might even come to write a book on these countries which, despite the assault of our century, had not yet been overwhelmed.

I went to Cambodia, Laos and Vietnam for a total of some three months, spending the most interesting, yet in a way most depressing part of this period in many journeys in a nebulous area of South Vietnam marked on the map as Les Populations Montagnards du Sud Indo-Chinois.

Legally Indo-China as a whole was a French protectorate in which subject populations enjoyed certain rights. This however was an enclave of undiluted and absolute French authority in which a variety of tribes having only recently emerged from the Stone Age were ruled if necessary with a rod of iron.

Although the capital, Ban Méthuot, was only 125 kms as the crow flies from Saigon, to reach it overland meant traversing one of the least explored areas in South-East Asia, using in my case a track only opened up by the Japanese troops some six years before. In Ban Méthuot I received the maximum hospitality and co-operation from Monsieur Doustin, Acting Resident, who claimed to be very bored at being stranded in the middle of a largely impenetrable jungle. He passed me on to Doctor Jouin, head of medical services of the province, and Vietnam's most distinguished anthropologist, and to two genial, if pessimistic, young French colonial servants; Ribo who administered 118 villages, and Cacot an inspector of schools. They were about to set out on a tour, and volunteered to take me along.

I spent most of my first day in Ban Méthuot with Doctor Jouin, who was one of the most interesting and impressive men I have ever met. He was white-haired and gentle, his face permanently illuminated with the Buddhistic peace generated by complete absorption in an urgent and valuable task. He had managed to delegate his medical responsibilities and now spent at least twelve hours a day working to learn and record all he could of what he believed to be one of the most attractive civilizations on earth, before it disappeared completely, as he said it was certain to do. In the beginning his task had seemed simple enough, and in any case he had not intended to probe too deeply. But then he had made exciting discoveries and had been lured on into unknown country where the horizons continually receded. Every attempt to clear up some limited aspect of his subject had uncovered endless others. And now he found himself in a trap. He had committed himself to labours which could never be finished, and time and the conditions of the country were against him. The Moï tribes, having survived in their present location for at least 2,500 years, were about to be destroyed by our merciless century. It needed a dozen workers like himself to occupy themselves with the still enormous volume of material available, which was melting away and in a few years would be lost for ever.

There were supposed, Jouin said, to be about a million Moïs, belonging to some thirty tribes, distributed over the mountainous areas of South Vietnam. The exact number was unknown as a few remote valleys had not even made their official submission. Whatever it was, it was dwindling rapidly, as in the areas most affected by Western penetration some villages had lost half their number in a single generation. They were a people of Malayo-Polynesian stock, related to the Dyaks of Borneo, the Igoroths and Aetas of the Philippines and the various tribes inhabiting the hinterlands of such widely separated parts as Madagascar and Hainan Island, off the coast of China. Above all, for the purpose of this account, it is of interest to record the present view that it was from these areas of South-East Asia that the Polynesian islanders of the Pacific set out on their great voyages of discovery. The Bahnars, Rhades, Jarai, Nonos and Bihs we visited had remained in all probability as the Tahitians' ancestors had been before they sailed out to discover the Pacific over 1,000 years ago. The Moïs hunted with the crossbow, being particularly noted for their skill in the capture and taming of elephants, which they sold as far afield as Burma. The doctor had been able to identify the area of their culture's diffusion through the sap of the Ipoh tree in the poisoning of arrow tips.

Doctor Jouin considered them one of the most handsome and best-formed of all races, and found that a certain mental liveliness, and a pleasant happy-go-lucky temperament accompanied this attractive physique. They gave little thought for the morrow and, except where under extreme pressure, led gay and sociable existences much occupied with gluttonous feasting and the consumption of rice spirit. This hearty manner of living depended upon, and was proportionate to, the tribe's inaccessibility. Unless compelled to do so, the Moïs refused to work for wages. They were art collectors and wealth consisted in the possession of gongs, drums and jars, some of which were of ancient Chinese or Cham origin and of great value. Most interesting of all, the doctor thought, was the Moïs' unique racial memory. Their great speciality was the oral saga, recited over countless generations without the slightest modification. This, despite great interpretational difficulties arising from words and phrases that had lost their meaning, constituted a treasure-house of information relating to the remote past.

I was interested to learn from the doctor that from the sheer multiplicity of their rites, all of which required alcoholic consumption, the intriguing side-issue emerged that respectability and drunkenness were allied. The upright man provided evidence of his ritual adequacy by being drunk as often as possible, respected by all for his piety, and a pattern held up to youth. The words *nam lu* (as I was to experience), uttered in grave welcome to the stranger in a Moï village and meaning let us get drunk together, carried all the weight of an invitation to common prayer. Moï villages were one of the few places in the world where the domestic animals, dogs and pigs and hens, having fed on the fermented mash from the sacred jars, could be seen in a state of helpless intoxication. Conviviality (and this, too, I discovered for myself) was the rule, a norm of polite conduct. Passers-by were begged to join in Moï orgies of eating and drinking, and it was bad taste—and worse, offensive to the spirits—to eat and drink less than provided by the fearsome hospitality of the hosts.

'And they're a doomed race?' I asked the doctor.

'Beyond hope of recovery.'

'Why should that be?'

'Because their economy works on a knife's edge, and the order's gone through that every man must work 50 days a year as a coolie on a plantation. Saving up for a rainy day doesn't come into their calculations. It would be irreligious. They've no reserves. Besides which the missionaries have moved in.'

'The missionaries?'

'They're in with the plantation owners. Part and parcel of the same thing. Sabatier* was always able to keep them out until we went under in 1940. Now he's gone and when we took over again they came in. Get Ribo to tell you what happened to the Bihs.'

I stayed for several days with Ribo and Cacot in Ribo's bungalow on the nearby Dak Lac. There were Moï villages belonging to several tribes on or near the lake and we visited

* Sabatier had been Governor of Indo-China until the Japanese occupation.

39

most of them, being invariably submitted to the amiable ritual Dr Jouin had described. In one case there were serious matters to discuss, but for the Moïs sociable drunkenness came first. There was a formidable possibility, too, that our hosts would insist upon offering us food, and I was warned that I must consume with what pretence of relish I could manage anything that happened to be served, as failure to do so would involve my friends in social, even political, disaster. 'It could be anything,' Ribo assured me. 'They catch rats here and preserve them for several weeks in sections of bamboo. Luckily for us they only bring them out for the most important feasts.'

The village, Buon Plum, was to become a model settlement, and an object lesson to all its neighbours, and Ribo who had arrived to announce this project to the assembled notables asked for the ceremonies preceding the palaver to be cut to a strict minimum. These entreaties appeared to have no effect; we were led up into the common room of a long-house that could have been 50 yards in length, where my friends' misgivings deepened at the sight of the lined-up alcohol jars with their drinking tubes in position, and boys had already been dispatched to fetch water from the nearest ditch to top up the levels.

There was no way out. The Moïs had a way of measuring the amount each participant sucked from the jar and no business would be conducted until this befuddling minimum had been consumed. When we had fulfilled our obligations the villagers joined in, led—since the Moïs were matriarchal—by aged and socially powerful women. While we drank, the Moïs summoned their household spirits with a frenzied beating of gongs. It was correct at this point to spit copious libations to them through the loosely woven bamboo floor, and these were received with acclamation by eagerly guzzling ducks which, attracted by the din of the gongs, had placed themselves in position directly under the jars.

After an hour or so of this, when all present were considered to be adequately mellowed, Ribo hauled himself to his feet to deliver his speech. He began by pointing out to them that, since the first census had been taken twenty years before, the population of the village had declined from eighty-six adult males to forty. Ribo told them they were being killed off by malaria and went to great lengths to prove that this was so, and to explain the measures that should be undertaken to combat the disease. Unfortunately for him, as he had previously explained to me, the model village project, in which he had been compelled by his superiors to involve himself, was little better than a charade. Why should these people who had occupied the areas where they now lived for at least 2,500 years have so suddenly fallen victims to malaria?

It was a case where the rice wine worked well for us all, including the Moïs. They held each other upright, smiled and nodded their agreement, assuring Ribo through his interpreter that they would grow vegetables and fruit to raise the money to buy mosquito-nets and quinine, and agreed that all would be well. Afterwards the interpreter took us aside. The men sent to work for the statutory fifty days on the rubber plantation had not returned, and the Moïs feared that they had been forced or tricked into signing on for a further five years, in which case the villagers knew they would never see them again.

These were the hard facts of life in colonial Vietnam and no one realized them more bitterly than Ribo and Cacot, both of them liberals, much attracted to the teaching of Jean-Paul Sartre, the existentialism and the philosophies of post-war France of the Left. They had taken their degrees in philosophy, politics and social studies at the Sorbonne and come out here with high hopes in their hearts, to face the naked truth of French colonialism at bay and fighting for its life. France had to have rubber at whatever cost and while I was there in Bon Méthuot a deputy arrived from Paris charged with the mission of stepping up its production. The Moïs on the nearby plantation worked a 13-hour day, and it was general knowledge that they were flogged or even tortured if production fell behind. Those released from the plantations were sick men who came home to die. The Resident told the official from Paris that at the rate things were going the whole Moï population would be exhausted

41

in five years, pointing out that many of them had been conscripted into military service. With the outposts of the advancing Vietminh only thirty miles down the road from Ban Méthuot, the deputy's unreasonable order was to take all the conscripts out of the army and send them to the plantations.

Buon Choah, principal village of the Bihs, spoken of by Dr Jouin as the most interesting family branch of the Moïs, was only a few miles down the road and this and all the other Bih settlements had fallen under the control of Mr Jones, one of the eleven evangelist missionaries who had disembarked with the first of the French troops to return to Vietnam after the defeat of the Japanese.

Monsieur Doustin, the Acting Resident, had spoken of him with cool distaste. At their first meeting he had politely hoped that they would be able to work together, to which Mr Jones had blandly replied that he only needed the coop-eration of God. Mr Jones had soon demonstrated his total independence of Doustin's authority. Doustin had received orders from Paris to see that he was appropriately lodged in Ban Méthuot and he had requisitioned the largest villa there—considerably grander than the Residence. Jones was provided with two cars, and the latest executive Cessna aircraft.

He then set to work on the conversion of the Moïs, making a start with the Bihs. Their only previous contact with West-ern religious belief had been through the ministrations of a charming but ineffectual old Roman Catholic missionary, one of a number who had been withdrawn by the authorities after averaging less than two converts per head over a period of five years.

Making enquiries Jones found out that the Bihs still retained ancient burial customs which they shared with the Horas of Madagascar. For two years the dead were exposed in open coffins in the trees. After that the bones were taken down and thoroughly cleansed, and before burial the skull was carried round the fields by an old woman of the family, and offerings were made to it. This rite, Jones told Doustin, he had decided was the cornerstone of the Bih system of beliefs, and he asked for it to be suppressed. When Doustin declined to do so, Jones went over his head to the Quai D'Orsay and received their backing. Police arrived from Saigon and stood guard over the missionary while he pulled the coffins down from the trees and had the contents thrown into a common grave.

Conversion had been instant. A Bih spokesman told Ribo that their spirits having deserted them they were resigned to extinction. The Bihs had paid their rice tax punctually, supplied their menfolk to plantation or army without protest, but had ceased to produce offspring. We had been spotted on the outskirts of Buon Choah, and had probably been taken for evangelical missionaries, for by the time we walked into the village an extraordinary spectacle was taking place. Women were scrambling in lines down the stepladders of the long-houses, like cadets coming down the rigging of a training ship. They formed up in two rows—one on each side of the path, dressed in navy-blue calico blouses and skirts, and standing fairly smartly to attention. The chief came hurrying to meet us carrying in one hand the usual diploma of meritorious service to the Japanese (who the Moïs could not tell from the French) and in the other a copy in English of the Gospel of St Mark.

Ribo asked them if all the Bihs had become converts and the chief told him, every one. Where were the gongs and the jars? Ribo asked, and he was told that they had been removed. 'By the missionaries?' 'By the missionaries.' 'Some of them were hundreds of years old. They were priceless,' Ribo told us.

'At least tell the women to take their missionary blouses off while we're here,' Ribo said to the chief.

The chief rapped out a word of command and the women began to strip to the waist. In a few seconds the reception parade was ready and we made our way to the chief's house between two score or so of freely and splendidly displayed torsoes. Cacot supposed that in the circumstances we would be spared the necessity of drinking more rice-wine, but Ribo disillusioned him.

43

'Not a chance of it. Be sure he'll have a jar hidden away somewhere for use in emergency.'

And he had.

I went to see Mr Jones, realizing immediately how far in the four years since my first encounter with Mr Fernley in Chichicastenango the evangelicans had progressed. In Chichicastenango Mr Fernley had held the thin red missionary line. Here Mr Jones was in reality in command. He was a large, spare, basically happy man, never deserted by a confident smile, and devoid I would have said of the slightest shadow of doubt. Every action he took was covered by justification, and explaining his activities in Bon Méthuot he smilingly pre-empted criticism. One or other of the French he had come into contact with must have commented on his lavish lifestyle, and he was ready for that. Referring to the luxurious appointments of his villa, Mr Jones went out of his way to assure me that they were normal by French colonial standards. He added the information that he had imported several tons of canned food—enough to last his family for the length of his tour—'to avoid imposing a strain on local resources'. In reply to my inquiry after the progress of his labours, the pastor said they were making headway under some difficulties. He supposed I would have heard that the whole Bih tribe had recently conducted a ceremony in which he had presented them with a harmonium and they had witnessed for Christ down to the last man, woman and child. He put a book into my hand. It contained, said the title page, thirty hymns, a section on prayer, an explanation of twenty-six religious terms, a short summary of the Old and New Testaments and a Church manual with the duties of preachers, elders, baptism, the Lord's Supper, dedication, the marriage service, churching of women, and the Apostle's Creed. All this was written in Rhadès—the principal Moï language—despite the fact, he said, that about one-third of the words employed in the holy text were missing in local tongues.

I asked him how he viewed the fact that up to a half of

his converts had been carried off for forced labour on the rubber plantations, and that this naturally prevented them from attending Divine Worship.

Mr Jones was ready for this, too. He was concerned only with the natives' spiritual welfare and their material conditions were of no interest to him whatever. A thought occurred to him and he brightened. One thing that could be said in favour of the plantations—which he saw as much maligned, surprisingly even by the French—was that a man working there was at least put out of the way of temptation. He had already mentioned the matter of biblical instruction for the plantation's coolies and the owners had made no objection to his conducting a short weekly service for them, and this he proposed to do.

Jones was completely unselfconscious, in his simple fanaticism, as he spoke with modest pride of his close and daily contacts with the Almighty and the free discussions on a range of subjects that took place between them. All his actions were designed with the single end in view, to use his own phrase, 'that God should get more glory for Himself', and God responded by easing Jones's missionary work with the provision of regular small miracles. He mentioned a recent one in which he had to fly back to the States and God's providence had delayed a plane for an hour and a half, which otherwise he would have missed.

Towards the end of this encounter his wife came in. She was a strapping woman with big hands and feet, brisk almost impatient movements, a sun-bonnet of a kind I had not seen for many years, and a woman's version of the pastor's imperishable smile. She described the errand on which she had just been employed, involving the baptism of several converts in an area where control was divided between the French and the Vietnamese enemy. She had gone there contrary to the advice of the French, and had carried out the baptisms in an inflatable child's paddling pool with the sterilized and consecrated water the missionaries carried in their specially adapted jeep wherever they went. On the way back she found that a Vietnam patrol had sneaked in and blown up a bridge, leaving her and her car stranded across the river. The experience had not bothered her in the slightest, for the Lord 'in His faithfulness' had instantly provided a boat. She had left orders with the Moïs for the bridge to be repaired, and next day she would go back for the car.

When I left the Moï area I had been hoping to be able to find my way across country to the west to Stung-Treng in Cambodia and was passed on by Doustin to his colleague Monsieur Préau at Pleiku, the next town along the route. Monsieur Préau, saying that he would be glad of the excuse to get away from it all for a couple of days, gave me a lift in his Citroen through jungle tracks to Cu-Ty, about a third of the way. Excluding Kontum it was the last village in central Vietnam where the French had a representative of any kind—in this case a huge grinning villain, a Moï Henry VI, whose name, Prak, meant money. He was supposed to have committed three murders, possessed five elephants, a number of wives, and a jeep given to him by a planter who was supposed to pay him ten piastres (40p) for every man supplied to the plantations, in addition to the government bounty of a half a piastre per head.

We sucked up the minimum of rice wine in his long-house, into which—an interpreter whispered—Prak, spotting our arrival, had ordered a quart of French brandy to be tipped. Préau, yet another liberal, oozed guilt as he passed on the deputy from Paris's demand for the supply by the Jarai tribe, of which Prak was chief, of another 300 able-bodied men. One of his servitors wound up his gramophone and put on a samba and Prak staggered round the common room to the rattle of maracas, before settling again for a fresh intake of rice wine. Leering ferociously, he agreed to do what he could. We were then taken to inspect the village school where the children had so far been taught only controlled breathing exercises and to say 'Bonjour Monsieur. Merci Monsieur.' Préau asked what the chances were of getting through to Stung-Treng, and Prak told him none at all. Bandits had taken over Bo-Kheo, the next village along the road, where a good deal of shooting had been heard on the

46

previous day. 'What could you expect?' he asked. 'All the menfolk have been conscripted.'

On our way back Préau asked a favour. Would I agree, if invited, to have dinner with Mr Wheelock, the evangelist pastor at Pleiku? When I asked what on earth for, he said that Wheelock complained of his loneliness and was always on the look-out for someone to talk English to. Besides this he had just returned from Kontum, for which Préau was responsible, and which was the last of the Moï villages to the north. Kontum was now virtually cut off—accessible only by air, and only Wheelock in his light plane could slip in and out at will. Préau said that he was anxious to obtain up-to-date information about the situation there. He found Wheelock hard to approach, and contact between them was made all the more difficult because, although the missionary claimed almost to have completed the translation of one of the gospels into the local Bahnar language, he spoke little or no French.

The expected invitation was received and accepted. Pleiku was a smaller and less important town than Ban Méthuot, in reflection of which Mr Wheelock's living style was less imposing than that of Mr Jones. He was tall, spare and restless and in constant motion, as if in an attempt to burn up energy. He came from Amarillo, Texas, and had worked there in oil until he had been called 'to assist in the finishing of God's unfinished work'. Unlike Jones who had referred continually, with his unquenchable smile, to his belief of being shielded by the Almighty's special protection, Wheelock, appearing naturally prone to indignation, seemed inclined to reproach God for abandoning him in this place.

In a way it was not to be wondered at. There had been a touch of Alpine Switzerland about Ban Méthuot with its deep, protruding eaves and decorated gables, intended to convince those who lived there that they were enjoying a cool climate. It possessed an eight-hole golf course, a *cercle sportif*, a nursery playground, and a good restaurant. The war remained not quite real—an excitement if anything on the periphery of comfortable lives. Pleiku was very different. There were no distractions, but instead food shortages, frequent power failures, and night alarms. On the evening of my arrival enemy infiltrators had ambushed and killed three French soldiers in a jeep within a few hundred yards of the *place centrale*, and no one had dared an attempt to recover the dead before dawn, by which time the corpses had largely been devoured by the tigers infesting the area. Pleiku was not a place where small, reassuring miracles were so easily experienced.

Wheelock clearly detested it, saying something to the effect that its only possible advantage was its liberal provision of the adversity by which the Christian virtue of fortitude was strengthened. The lighting came and went, sometimes being so dim that I could hardly make out the details of the pastor's face across the table, and gecko lizards scuttled about the walls, stopping from time to time to utter their powerful startled outcry. A plague of moths had put the air-conditioning out of action. Wheelock apologized for the locally grown, earth-flavoured rice, forming the basis of the meal, saying that priority shipments of war supplies to Pleiku had put an end to deliveries of the canned food on which he normally lived. He was worried, too—justifiably in my opinion—about the water supply, believing it to harbour dangerous organisms that even resisted boiling, and as soon as one sterilizing tablet had ceased to release its minute bubbles in the flask standing between us he was ready with the next.

The pastor admitted that he did not much care for the French who reminded him of what he had read of the pagan Romans of old. He was less than enthusiastic, too, about the Moïs among whom he laboured—even those who had agreed to become converted. When the first arrived he had been pleasantly surprised at their eagerness to possess crucifixes, which he had handed out in all directions only to discover that what interested them was the technique of what they saw as a new and possibly more effective form of animal sacrifice. He had cut off the supply when he found that one had been tied round the neck of a buffalo he had been unable to prevent them from slaughtering in their ritual fashion. Like Jones he felt that as soon as they had gone through the motions of conversion it was better for them to be out of harm's way. In Pleiku they grew tea on the largest plantation in Vietnam, on which a thousand Moïs toiled—a steadily increasing number of them becoming what Mr Wheelock called 'my Christians'. He spoke with approval of the plantation's Algerian owner—who, Préau informed me, was notorious for the tortures he inflicted on his workers, and who had supplied all the furniture for Wheelock's house.

The time had come to ask Mr Wheelock for news of Kontum, and his expression of repressed anger strengthened. 'Kontum is primitive,' he said. 'Just primitive.'

Weren't all these places primitive in their way? I suggested. What could be more primitive than Pleiku, with a native civilization on the edge of obliteration, and a raw Western replacement that had not yet found its feet.

'Kontum offers nothing to gratify any of us,' the missionary said. 'Pleiku is growing towards the light. Kontum remains in darkness.' He suggested I should visit Kontum and discover for myself how truly backward it was.

We talked on and I found that Wheelock was describing an almost completely unspoiled community—perhaps the last of its kind—that I had hoped so much to see, and I knew now I never would. The long-houses (described by Wheelock as the natives' evil abodes) were, with their majestic, steepled roofs, the longest and most spectacular in Vietnam. The Bahnar subdivision of the Moï peoples had been among the last to be subjected to French rule, and by some happy freak of soil and weather it had been thought inadvisable to establish the usual plantation in the vicinity of the villages to batten upon their manpower. Wheelock said that he had wanted to build a mission house at Kontum, but the Bahnars had declined to co-operate, and the French were too busy with their war. A few Bahnars from Kontum had been sent down to Pleiku to the tea-picking estate, but had been rejected as unsatisfactory.

'Why was that?' I asked.

'They were communists,' Wheelock said. He agreed that they had never heard of Russia or Karl Marx. It was something bred in them, and ineradicable, like original sin.

49

And what form did their communism take? I asked, and the missionary said that they were crazy about sharing. If, for example, fifty of them inhabited one of their evil dwellings, they divided everything by fifty. Each man or woman owned a fiftieth of the house itself, and a fiftieth of each pig they kept. If a man went out and shot a jungle fowl with his crossbow, it had to be divided up into fifty parts. By Wheelock's understanding this was communism carried to its most unacceptable lengths.

He seemed to brighten up at the memory of an incident of his stay with the Bahnars. The basic reason for the trip had been to visit one of his Christians there who had been put in prison for failing to notify the French of the presence of the Vietminh in the vicinity of his village. Quite casually Wheelock added that this Christian who had been locked up for three months, couldn't use his arms yet. I asked him why, and Wheelock said, as if it followed as a matter of course, that they'd been disjointed in the interrogation. Were there any more than his Christian involved? Why yes, about eighty had been arrested of which he guessed that no more than twenty had been strung up.

It seemed hard, I said: if the Bahnars informed on the Vietminh to the French, the Vietminh burned their village. If they failed to report the Vietminh presence the French wrenched their arms out of their sockets.

Mr Wheelock shrugged his shoulders. 'It must be that affliction comes,' he said, 'but woe unto him by whom affliction cometh.' He sipped his chlorinated water and grimaced. 'Whatever happens they are all doomed to disappear shortly from this earth.'

I understood that he was speaking of the Moïs in general, and I was sure that he was right.

4

Free of Vietnam I returned in haste and with some relief to Guatemala. At the time of the first visit I had formed a friendship with Dr Morales of the Indian Institute. We had exchanged letters and, when I had raised the project of the book with him, he had been full of encouragement and help. Ernestina's advice had also been valuable. She was now an expert on the subject of the fast-disappearing Mayan textile designs, and anxious that a study of them should be published before it was too late. We had a great deal to say to each other on the topics of history and art, but little on personal matters. Back in 1947 it had been instantly apparent that the marriage was at an end, however a correspondence that was always friendly—and for my part hugely entertaining—continued over the years. I saw a great deal of her in 1951, when she told me that she had formed a relationship with a local politician, although at that time she did not wish to marry him. Politics in Guatemala are a dangerous business. Both of them were in the shadow of official displeasure following the success of the Castillo Armas revolution in 1954. It was decided that it would be safer for them to leave the country. Ernestina got a Mexican divorce, and they went off to live in Haiti.

My third visit to Guatemala was within weeks of this hasty departure. My friend Dr Morales had prepared an almost overwhelming programme of scholarly activities: ancient Mayan sites to be visited, experts in various fields to be consulted, books and manuscripts in private collections to be read. Slowly I was beginning to experience Dr Jouin's quandary when, as he plunged deeper and deeper into his study of the Moïs he understood with widening and ever-receding horizons of knowledge, the task was one that would never be completed.

Doña Elvira came into this. I called on her, finding her still as bored as ever, but still very much mistress of her

51

labyrinthine house with its five patios, its communal kitchen, its small, silent Indian servants fluttering with jugs of water from room to room, and the familiar hordes of relatives and spongers of all kinds. She spent much of her day, as ever, looking down from her wide balcony on the disorderly Guatemalan scene and had actually, with barely repressed joy, witnessed the crash in which the new president (who had revived the ceremony of the motorcade) had fallen from his motorcycle and flattened his nose.

The so-called democratic interlude which had left all white Guatemalans in a state of abject terror had done wonders for Doña Elvira's nerves. For two years she had worried happily about the possibility of a few thousand acres of Quetzaltenango estates she had barely seen being handed over to the Indians. Further stimulation had been provided by the building of a bunker in one of the patios in which she and her immediate family would gather to fight until the last bullet. Now, with the stagnation of peace re-imposed by the dictatorship, life had gone flat. Her headaches and her itches were back, she told me, and sooner or later she would be unable to prevent herself shouting *cojones* in the face of the Monsignor who visited her once a month, to renew his blessing on her work as patroness of the charity known as La Gota de Leche.

Doña Elvira did not care for Castillo Armas, her dislike arising largely from his treatment of the Catholic fathers, some officially missionaries, and some not, who had gone to live in the villages, and whom she had come to regard as her protégés. She had gone to the Palace to speak to the President on their behalf, and was much offended by his neglecting to dismiss the sycophants with whom he surrounded himself during this meeting. Castillo Armas was winkling the Catholics out of the villages as fast as he could get the North American Protestants to replace them. Doña Elvira made a last attempt to arouse some admiration for men who had chosen not only to live with the poor, but to suffer the same hardships and share the same sicknesses. The President assured her that the Catholic fathers had all his sympathy, but that they were ineffectual.

Doña Elvira had heard about the projected book and my search for local unpublished material and she now astonished me with the news of her possession of a family heirloom in the form of a holograph letter from Hernan Cortès, conqueror of Mexico, to Pedro de Alvarado, his commander in Guatemala. This she was anxious to show me and made no objection to my taking along a young American curator from the National Museum, who I hoped might help with the archaic Spanish.

We found that Doña Elvira kept the letter on display in a case in a room devoid of other furniture in the rabbit-warren of the central part of her house. In this, the illumination was provided by a single low-power electric lamp, as she was of the opinion that exposure to normal wattage would produce instant and terminal fading. The occasion was dignified by the arrival of an Indian maid, barefoot as ever, but wearing an apron and white gloves to serve sweet sherry in Bohemian glasses, and by the background presence of an old servitor dressed like a town-crier who nodded and winced when anyone looked in his direction. Wheezing prideful noises, Doña Elvira pulled back the flap covering the glass and we looked down upon two frayed, yellow worm-eaten sheets, covered with some ancient and wholly indecipherable writing that might have been Pali as far as I was concerned.

'I've always refused to allow it to be photographed,' Doña Elvira said. 'I even turned President Ubico down. The writing's on both sides, but the paper's in no state to be moved. You're welcome to glean anything you can from what you see. As for the rest, it's anybody's guess. There's nothing to stop you using your imagination.'

We thanked the old lady most profusely for the great experience she had provided, and Robinson from the museum asked if he could possibly bring a friend shortly arriving from the States, who was an expert in early sixteenth-century Spanish calligraphy, to help with the interpretation. Doña Elvira graciously agreed that he could bring anyone he liked.

'Could you make anything of it?' I asked him as soon as we were outside.

'No,' he said, 'but why bother? It's only another eighteenth-century fake. They used to turn them out by the dozen.'

A few days before the time came to leave Guatemala Dr Morales suggested a trip to Chichicastenango and I accepted with alacrity. Morales said it was the best place to go to look for Mayan antiquities. The principal form of sacrifice in the old days had been to throw ceremonial vessels—always of great artistic value—into the Lakes Amatitlán and Atitlán, from which divers had recovered them by the hundreds. The cellars of the National Museum were full of outstanding examples stacked away to await cataloguing that would take years to complete. Morales mentioned that the villas built by rich Guatemalans round Amatitlán, which was only 20 kms from the capital, used Mayan altars as hat-stands. No one in Guatemala placed much value on such things, and the reason for going to Chichicastenango to look for them was the presence there of several junk shops. Tourists rummaged in such places for souvenirs and could occasionally be induced to pay a few dollars for a polychrome chalice or beaker from the classic period which a Guatemalan would have ignored.

As our acquaintance ripened I had come to realize there was nothing the doctor enjoyed more than a piece of truancy of this kind disguised by serious purpose. The moment he was freed from the dignified surroundings of the Institute he became a changed man, proclaiming this to the world by changing his well tailored suit for a belted Norfolk jacket of the kind favoured in the twenties by George Bernard Shaw, worn with a black felt hat. No one knew why but this had become the male uniform of several of the highland tribes, but the hat and jacket were always worn with breeches woven with designs of ducks and stags. This, even Morales could not bring himself to do.

It was seven years since I had been in Chichicastenango but since that time it had undergone little outward change.

It turned out that Morales was a connoisseur of *boj*. Under the democracy it had been brewed and drunk openly in a number of *cantinas*, but now once again, with the re-establishment of authority, clients were obliged to crawl once again into the spider-haunted cavern of 'I Await My Beloved' to relieve illicit thirst. It had remained open under the protection of addicts among the police. We went there, but were the only customers. The skeins of spiders' webs, daily renewed, were stretched as ever, like grey paper-chains across the dark ceiling, and the *boj*, working in its vast pan under its crust seamed and cracked like an elephant's hide, emitted the smell of a dog fresh from the river, and occasionally the faintest of gurgles. A hunchback in a Norfolk jacket like the one worn by Morales served us a mug apiece, and the familiar glow began to spread its consolation from the pit of the stomach. We went out, hoping to find a collection of the Indian regulars of old, sleeping in Fernley's mission house next door, but this was closed and shuttered.

All Morales' friends were absent from these scenes. The story was that there had been a crack-down on them by the new government. Jacobo Arbenz, the latter of the two elected presidents, had distributed extremely small patches of uncultivated land in the neighbourhood, and the new government, waiting until the crops sown on them had begun to grow, sent teams of horsemen to trample them down, and to burn whatever would burn.

On the missionary front, the fairly mild and conciliatory Mr Fernley had gone to be replaced by a man of sterner stuff, from one of the new, more politically inspired missions operating with government approval. The new missionary, given the green light to stamp out paganism, was determined to put a stop to picturesque displays of Indian religious fervour in, and at the approaches to, the Church of Santo Tomás. Whip in hand, and accompanied by two nervous policemen, he dashed through the celebrants on the steps and up into the church shouting that he had come to drive the money-changers from God's temple. As ever, there would have been less than a hundred Indian worshippers kneeling on the bare floor before their lighted candles, and the missionary, slashing out in all directions, kicked as many candles over as he could before the Indians grabbed him and threw him down the steps. Following this a government order placed all Indian ceremonies under a ban, until with the foreign visitors ceasing to come, and the hotel about to close down, the pressure of the tourist lobby proved irresistible and things slipped back to what they had been.

In search of absent faces Morales dragged me on a pilgrimage from saloon to saloon full of the thunder and crash, and the wild, flickering lights of jukeboxes and of half-breed desperadoes. Forcing *aguardiente* on us, they watched through narrowed eyes as we gulped the spirits and licked the ritual salt from the palms of our hands. Their hope was to be able to pick a quarrel. Such off-beat terrain in Guatemala was the homeland and citadel of *machismo*. Men like this, who lived on raw spirits and air, killed one another or an unknown stranger on the slightest pretence, or none at all.

In that very year in the railway station *cantina* in Guatemala City one bored man had said to his friend, 'I bet you're not man (*macho*) enough to shoot the next person who comes through that door.' 'You're on,' said the friend and shot the next customer through the heart. 'A reprehensible impulse,' said the judge, sending him up for three years—a sentence which would be automatically reduced by one third in case of good conduct.

The police tolerated the *machos* because they could be rounded up, if required and put to sinister use. They studied us with some contempt whispered behind their hands. When a fresh bottle had to be opened a man would draw his machete like a Japanese swordsman and with a single twist of the point, scoop the cork from the neck.

What the *contrabandistas* were on the look-out for was what they called *falta de urbanidad*—discourtesy—likely to include refusals of invitations to drink, as well as failure to offer hospitality in return. They were punctilious themselves and expected it of others in the frequent use of such phrases as 'do me the favour', 'by your permission', and 'you were most gracious'. My feeling while we were there was that we teetered on the brink of offence. It was a relief when Morales called it a night and we could retire to the sleazy security of our boarding-house room, which we shared with a travelling salesman of false teeth.

Two days in Chichicastenango proved unproductive in the matter of ancient artifacts, but it had made a pleasant outing. Having in the past been my principal source of information on the subject of Mayan history and culture, Morales now made an attempt to guide me through a maze of current politics.

Politics was the game of Guatemala, and people played it with the ardour devoted elsewhere to ball-games of various kinds. Every white Guatemalan belonged to one of the many political parties, most of which possessed only a few hundred adherents and none, so far as I could see, with any power or hope for it. Morales was inscribed in the URD (Unidad Revolucionaria Democratica) which he cheerfully admitted had nothing whatever to do with revolution, and which I also assumed had little to do with democracy. The UDR had some 200 supporters and returned one member, its leader, Licenciado Adolfo Mihangos to Congress, which itself, under the fist of the iron colonel Castillo Armas, was little better than a fiction. Morales favoured this tiny group of politically impotent men because Mihangos had once made a speech saying that something ought to be done to help the Indians, numbering exactly one half of the total population of the country, most of whom lived in conditions of destitution.

Despite the strong element of make-believe pervading the Guatemalan game it was exceedingly deadly. I hardly knew of a single sizeable Guatemalan family that had not lost a son in the labyrinthine wars fought between the many groups jockeying for power. Morales, an unworldly academic incapable of hurting a fly, was in trouble soon after this and, feeling obliged to flee the country, took refuge in Costa Rica.

In 1970 I was in Guatemala for the last time and on 10

December of that year I called on Licenciado Mihangos to enquire what news there was of his old supporter. Mihangos turned out to be an agile, vivacious cripple in a wheelchair which he manipulated at great speed through the cluttered spaces of his office. I had arrived at a bad time. Heavy guerrilla fighting had broken out in the mountains of the north. The guerrillas were not as one would have supposed, the downtrodden Indians themselves, but boys from middle-class families who saw no future for them in a corrupt and subservient society. Mihangos had just come from the funeral of a friend, González Juárez, assassinated he supposed because sixteen years previously he had been secretary to Jacobo Arbenz, the final democratically elected president. 'He was on the elimination list,' Mihangos said. 'I am, too.'

The army, he said, had taken over. The colonels in control of the President had fallen in with the US plan of using national armies to do their police work for them. These men had been indoctrinated into a belief that a Third World War was inevitable and they had been chosen to defend the values of occidental culture.

I asked him if he had a bodyguard. He laughed the suggestion off and I got the impression that this man in this fear-stricken city was incapable of fear. 'It wouldn't make any difference,' he said. 'You never know where the bullet is coming from. Every time I leave home to go to my office, my wife wonders whether it's the last time we shall see each other. One hopes for a quick death, that's all.' He added in a matter-of-fact, unemotional way that Juárez was tortured, but the papers couldn't print the details. 'In my case,' he added, 'perhaps it's not quite the same. After all, I'm a cripple. They may not think I'm worth bothering about.'

Mihangos was wrong. Three weeks later a machine-gun volley, fired at him from a taxi as he was being wheeled through the door of his office to go home, put an end to his life.

5

In the autumn preceding this fateful year for Guatemala I went to Mexico. It happened almost by accident. I was in California writing about the grape-pickers' strike (eventually successful) that had been going on for five years, and had by then reached a stage when grapes were no longer to be seen on American tables. I saw the imported Mexican and Filipino workers living in conditions that came close to slavery, and the grapes rotting on the vines, wrote the story, then prepared to return to England. It occurred to me that this offered a splendid opportunity to see something of Mexico, and instead of flying straight to London I changed direction and went south. I promised myself that I would see all I could of the ancient sites scattered throughout the country, including recent excavations considered to be of great importance. Here was more potential material, I attempted to convince myself, for the book that had been ten years in the making, and was now further than ever from completion. Apart from the journey itself, none of these plans came to fruition.

Buses penetrated every corner of this vast country, crawling through the valleys of the Sierra, chasing the wild horses from the desert roads and briefly shattering the peace of hollow-eyed, sleeping towns. The de luxe *rápidos*, Mexican version of the US Greyhound, cover such journeys in a consistent and dependable way, provide certain comforts and enliven the journey with music of a desperate kind. *Regulares*—local buses—also travel great distances but stop everywhere, and do not always arrive at their proclaimed destination. They are great fun, and very cheap. Boarding one of these is like being granted temporary membership of a species of club. Fellow travellers are recommended to bring with them vast quantities of food and liquor, as much for exchange with complete strangers in token of new friendships as to eat themselves.

I joined my bus at Tia Juana on the US frontier, and began the first of several stages travelling with various changes and many delays down the west coast road through Ciudad Obregón, Cuilicán and Mazatlán in the direction of Mexico City. *Regulares*, although often verging on decrepitude with looseness in their joints, bald tyres and uncertain steering, reach dangerously high speeds when driven flat out on the long, straight desert roads. On one stretch a small *zopilote* (vulture), snatched up from its carrion was plastered heraldically over the windscreen, disintegrated hens passed the windows in a snow-flurry of feathers, and an oncoming bus charged out of control off the road and was lost among the cactus. Such incidents called forth a chorus of *chingars* from the men and a ripple of Aztec excitement among the women whose tendency under stress it was to add an Aztec *nahuatll* to the ending of each word.

Travel by the mettlesome but spasmodic *regulares* stopped where the heavy traffic filled the road after the city of Guadalajara and buses such as ours were checked over for canvas showing through tyre treads, and blood stains caused by collisions with animals before the turn-round. Here I found that after 1,400 miles I had nearly worn out the seat of a pair of cotton trousers, and I decided to break my journey and book into a hotel for the night.

Apart from the need to buy more trousers I stopped here because I had seen Indians with painted faces, embroidered tunics and feathered hats on the last stage of the journey, and a group of them had actually boarded the bus at one stop, deposited bows and arrows in the hat rack, and travelled with us a few miles before getting off. When I asked about them the small, fat, restless Mexican squirming at my side let out a hearty oath. They were Huichols, he said, adding in a voice surprisingly free from contempt, that they were really no different from animals, and I suspected him of being a man who was kind to cats. They lived in caves, he said, like the beasts of the field, could run all day without fatigue, caught deer and strangled them with their bare hands, and were lucky to eat a square meal more than twice a week. '*Por ellos,*' he said, '*no tenemos existencia.*' (For them we don't exist.) It was something I had often heard said in Guatemala. The Huichols never looked in our direction, and when occasionally by accident I intercepted a Huichol glance it was quite evident that I was regarded as being of no more interest than the scratched and dented bodywork of the bus against which I was lightly squeezed by bulk of my fellow passengers.

A poster in the hotel advertised an exhibition of Huichol art at the Basilica of Zapotán, a small Mexican version of Lourdes some four miles from the city's centre. A showcase displayed examples of Huichol beadwork and embroidery featured in the exhibition, and these seemed of sufficient interest to make a visit to the Basilica worthwhile, so after my first night's sleep in a bed for three days, I took a taxi and went over there.

The exhibition contained its surprises. Here were the woven designs, the menagerie of symbolic animals—the cats, deer, the cockerels, the turkeys posturing and sparring in courtship display made familiar by Guatemala—and an outsider like myself might even have mistaken these weavings and embroideries for the work of Guatemalan artists. Yet to the Mayan Indian of Guatemala they would have conveyed no message, remaining inexplicable—a foolish enigma. Similarly a Huichol confronted with Guatemalan work would have felt little but bewilderment. To which should be added that neither Indian would experience the slightest admiration for the work of the other, although the non-Indian, where understanding is not necessarily at the base of appreciation, might find them equally admirable.

The most striking component of the exhibition was the collection of *nearikas*—painting in coloured yarns, pressed by the fingers into patterns on a wooden surface coated with beeswax, of the kind which have been placed possibly for centuries as votive offerings to the gods in shrines scattered throughout the western Sierra Madre. The best of those on view were the work of Ramón Medina Silva, principal Shaman of the Huichol people. All Huichol art is devotional,

61

and the majority dealt with the predicaments of the soul after death. They were examples of primitive art in its freshest and most exciting form, and the feeling they gave was of an absence of premeditation—of being the production of a hugely talented child. Works by the Shaman's pupils were also on display, and although equal in technical quality it was clear in these cases that inspiration had failed. The pupils were slaves to the Shaman's vision, but with the Shaman no longer there to guide them they were falling into error, and where the master painted with a simplicity that was almost austere, a softness and over-elaboration appeared in the art of those who followed him. In the case of *nearikas* offered for sale by the Basilica the wooden base of the painting was replaced by hardboard to eliminate the magic inherent in sacred objects, but a trace of this sanctity was always considered to remain, for which reason no visitor to the Basilica was allowed to watch the Huichol artists at work.

These and other facts were set forth by Padre Ernesto Loera of the Franciscan order in charge of the Basilica who had collected and arranged the Shaman Medina's original masterpieces and encouraged the pupils after his departure to carry on in the Shaman's tradition. This enterprise at the Basilica had come to the notice of Peter Furst of the University of California, who had thereafter spent several months with the Shaman and produced a richly illustrated monograph published by the university devoted to the *nearikas*. Dr Furst was enormously impressed not only by Huichol art, but by everything about the Huichols themselves, most of all perhaps the ideal motivating their lives. He quotes the Shaman Medina in his monograph:

> *'Everything we do in life,'* the priest instructs the child, *'is for the glory of God. We praise him in the well-swept floor, the weeded field, the polished machete, the brilliant colours of the picture—of the embroidery. In these ways we pray for a long life and a good one.'*

Ramón Silva Medina [Dr Furst explains in his introduction] *is a mara'akame, combining in his person the traditional shaman, curer, priest and guardian of the sacred chants and traditions of his people. The making of a mara'akame is a long and arduous process of self-training involving much physical and spiritual stamina—above all, a sense of inner balance, of spiritual equilibrium. To be a mara'akame a man must also have participated in at least five pilgrimages to Wirikuta, the sacred peyote country in the desert of San Luis Potosí, and to have proved his ability on those peyote hunts to take complete responsibility for the group of pilgrims whom he leads. On this hunt, he assumes the identity of the Mara'akame Tatewari (Our Grandfather), the deified Fire and principal divine being of the Huichols, who also led the first peyote hunt in ancient times.*

Padre Ernesto seemed to go even further than Dr Furst when he said that he regarded the Shaman as one of the greatest living Mexicans. Speaking in a somewhat roundabout way he hinted that Ramón Silva had been under certain unidentified pressures in the sierra, and that his presence in the Basilica had been almost that of a refugee. Here he had made his *nearikas*, and not only that but had lent a hand with the principal activity of the shrine—the healing of sick pilgrims who arrived by the thousand at the time of the annual pilgrimage. 'He pitched a tent in the quadrangle,' Padre Ernesto said. 'When there were cases we couldn't handle we passed them over to Ramón, and he soon had them on their feet again.'

We were strolling together in the cloisters and a few off-season pilgrims had come limping in, assisted by attendants and friends. The members of a party lowered themselves painfully to their knees, crossed themselves and knelt in prayer for a while, heads bowed; a young Huichol as supple as a cheetah loped by, a skein of scarlet wool dangling from his arm.

'He was a godsend,' Padre Ernesto said. The admission seemed remarkable for it contained a suggestion that a pagan Indian's success-rate in the matter of paranormal cures could be higher than that of the patroness of the shrine. Latin American journeys were great destroyers of the stereotypes and it was already hard to think of the father as a monk. His habit was worn with the easy confidence of a well cut suit, his manner was cosmopolitan and his near-perfect English, laced with anthropological jargon, lent authority to his views on the subject of Indian culture. Padre Ernesto was a photographer of almost rabid enthusiasm, the possessor of three Hasseblad cameras and a vast range of special-purpose lenses and equipment. There was nothing he enjoyed more, he assured me, when his duties permitted than to slip away to the sierra and spend a few days photographing Indian ceremonies. Isolation in the high, almost inaccessible valleys, he said, had protected the Huichols from the contagion of our times. About 10,000—the largest Indian tribe in Central America—had managed to survive, with all the panoply of their ancient religion intact. He mentioned this last fact with what seemed to me something very close to satisfaction.

Padre Ernesto got out his albums of photographs which showed something very close to professional quality, and my enthusiasm for his pictures of leaping, cavorting dancers with their mysterious paraphernalia, their wands and their whips, the deer's antlers and their animal skins, was so clearly genuine that he immediately suggested a trip. 'Why don't we go up there together?' he asked. 'It's an experience you won't forget. You can count on a week on a mule in each direction, and another week for the photography. We could buy a bull for them to sacrifice. They cover themselves with blood,' the father said with relish, 'then they dance.' His face fell. 'I can't make it,' he said. 'The Bishop's paying us a visit next month, and the place has to be tidied up for him.' He thought for a moment. 'Come back in a couple of months,' he said. 'I'll be free by then, and we can go or if you can't manage that you could go now, but I'd have to arrange for you to be with a member of the Franciscans and stay at a mission.'

I asked why.

'Because otherwise you would be killed,' Padre Ernesto

said, with great simplicity. He made it sound like a warning that I might get caught in a shower. 'Up in the sierra it's like a scene from an old Western movie. The bandits will kill you for robbery, and the Indians will kill you because they assume any stranger in their territory must be a bandit.' He went on to assure me that the trip wasn't so bad as it sounded, and only reasonable precautions were necessary to avoid being shot, stripped and thrown over a precipice by a Mexican bandit, or picked off by an Indian bowman waiting behind a tree. All I had to do was to go to the town of Tepic, some seventy or eighty miles away, ask at the airfield there for Padre Alberto Hernandez of the Franciscan Mission, and through him charter the mission plane. This would fly me to a landing strip high up in the sierra in the middle of Huichol country, after which, he said, I would be faced with a short walk to Santa Clara, where I could be put up.

'Don't be put off by the idea of missionaries,' the padre said. 'These aren't the old-fashioned kind you used to see. Quite the reverse. And another thing, don't worry about not paying your way. They won't give you anything for nothing. If you want to go up there you have to fall back on them because there's no alternative. No one's going to ask you to go to church. You'll enjoy every minute of it.'

So far, it seemed, so good. Later I was to learn that from long association with Indians Padre Ernesto had fallen into the habit of vagueness and understatement in the matter of time and distance.

The alternative to the plane trip and the 'short walk' to follow it, was at most nine days on the back of a mule. In this case a bodyguard would have to be hired and provisions for the journey taken along. It could be a rewarding experience, he thought, but on the other hand—he summed me up with the look of a man with a long experience of the realities of life in the Mexican outback and doubt mastered the normal optimism of his expression. 'What sort of shot are you?' he asked.

'Very bad,' I said.

A nod of understanding showed me that I had no more

than confirmed his assumption. 'I always carry two camera bodies and five lenses on a trip,' he said, 'a few pounds of jerked meat and a .306 repeating rifle. On my last jaunt I saw a woman hanging from a tree. I think you had better go with one of the fathers, who knows his way round,' he said, 'to avoid the possibility of running into experiences you might find disturbing.'

I thanked Padre Ernesto for his advice and for his offer to help with arrangements for a visit to the sierra, and took the plane next day back to London, where I saw my old friend David Montgomery, a photographer who was providentially tired at that time of commercial photography, and proposed a mild adventure to him, which he instantly accepted. By the end of the next week we were in Guadalajara again for a final briefing by Padre Ernesto, who went away to telephone Tepic and came back to tell us that everything was fixed up. 'They will be delighted to see you,' he said. 'You are in good hands.' He then asked if we had brought guns, and when I said no, he shook his head.

We took a roaring *rápido* bus down to Tepic, finding the town laid out on the gentle slope down to the Pacific coast. Modernization had advanced in a patchy fashion here, and despite half-finished factories there was still a touch of Dodge City, 1885, about it, with swing-door saloons and streets full of expressionless men on horseback, and an abandoned locomotive with cow-catcher and funnelled smoke stack. On the airfield Indians with eagles' feathers stuck in their hair were fuelling up a plane, a few yards from a burned-out wreck from which a wing was thrust like an imploring arm into the sky. To the south an ancient eruption had dumped glittering coals on a horizon of lively greens. Eastwards a small volcano tilted its crater in our direction, and beyond it the Sierra Madre rose up in a gentle blue swell. Two Huichols had come to catch a plane that might or might not be going somewhere next day and they squatted, faces chiselled with noble indifference, among the gesticulating cactus at the edge of the field, absorbing time through their skin. Vultures were pinned here and there like black brooches on the sky, and presently there appeared among them the glittering insect that soon transformed itself into the mission's plane. Padre Alberto drove up through the wash of excitement created by this arrival in a large American car. He came here every morning for an hour or two to supervise air cargoes flown into and out of the mission in the high sierra at Guadaloupe Ocotán; a neat, quick man in ordinary street clothes and well polished shoes, with an important file of papers under his arm. He glanced at Padre Ernesto's letter, and listened to what we had to tell him, but seemed unimpressed, even wary, giving no indication of having heard of our existence.

Padre Ernesto, remote from such scenes of action, had been ready to promise anything. He had excited David by his dramatic photography. David hoped that he might be able to get pictures of this kind, and the padre had told him that nothing was easier. He was a man radiating optimism. 'If there happens to be a fiesta, all well and good. If there isn't, do as I do—manufacture one. You can buy a bull for nothing. Huichols have no sense of money. Make sure all the young braves take part in the sacrifice, and tell them not to be shy about painting themselves up with the blood.'

I made a diffident mention of this suggestion to Padre Alberto. He shot me an austere glance and a chilling of the atmosphere could be felt. 'Such sacrifices,' he said, 'are strictly reserved for ceremonial occasions. At the moment I'm afraid you would find little to interest you in Guadaloupe Ocotán.' He then exploded his bombshell. The mission's plane was too busy carrying urgent cargo to take us to the sierra. If we still insisted on going all he could suggest was that we chartered a twin-engined Beechcraft belonging to a local company. This could fly us into the sierra to San Andrès, which possessed the only airstrip it could use, and from San Andrès we could walk to Santa Clara where the order had their second mission, and where they would be able to put us up. The trip would be expensive and—it had to be pointed out—chancy, because the weather at the moment was tricky, with high winds, so that even if the Beechcraft could fly us in there was no telling how long it might be before it could return to pick us up.

At this point I remembered the mules. It proved that there was a big trade in hiring them and for journeyings into a hundred and one places in the mountains remaining otherwise quite inaccessible. They were kept in a corral like a small bullring on the other side of the town where, at the time of our arrival, some thirty or forty of them were racing round in what struck us as a state of dangerous frenzy. Until this moment the picture I had always had of mules was of patient, reliable, plodding animals devoid of neurosis or spirit in any form. The Mexican reality was otherwise. These were large and wild, a black apocalyptic version of the horse, who screamed, snapped and kicked out at each other and splashed lather over us as they went rearing and plunging past. The owner, calm and matter-of-fact to the point of lethargy, offered to find the necessary guide and bodyguard to Guadaloupe Ocotán. He took me into a shed and showed me the new repeating German rifle with which the man would be armed, upon which a substantial deposit would have to be paid. I mentioned that the mules appeared to be very lively, and he said, 'It's the feed we give them to keep them going. It's a hard slog up there. You find they quieten down after a day or so. The only thing that may worry you at first is finding yourself on a path a yard wide on the edge of a thousand-foot drop. That's where an animal like one of these comes in. You stop worrying and leave it to them. They take over.'

'Can you ride?' I asked David, and he said no, but he could learn. We went back to the airfield for another meeting with Padre Alberto, who may have heard something after all of Padre Ernesto's commitment to our cause, for he seemed to have relented slightly. He had ascertained that the Beechcraft would in any case be making the flight to San Andrès next morning. This was a Friday and on the Sunday—which was not normally a working day—the mission's Cessna could be chartered as a special concession to fly in and pick us up at Santa Clara, where there was a small airstrip it could use. This solution was accepted with huge relief, although San Andrès was twice as far away as Guadaloupe Ocotán, and we had heard that there were fewer Indi-

68

ans there. A suspicion lingered, hardening to a surmise, that the padre had decided that this was the best way of getting rid of us. Why—it was hard to say. Writers and photographers could be seen as a nuisance in off-the-beaten-track places like this, where it may even have been felt that certain happenings might have seemed unpalatable if presented to the outside world.

On leaving Padre Alberto we called on Dr Ramos, Director of the Instituto Indigenista whose permission was required for a visit to the Huichol region. We found the doctor—himself clearly an Indian—seated beneath a fine *nearika* of a double-headed eagle. I asked whether this was the work of the celebrated Shaman Ramón Medina and the doctor said that it was, adding in a somewhat enigmatic way, 'He has taken refuge with us.' Dr Ramos thought that the Shaman might agree to meet us and allow himself to be photographed. This was a piece of outstanding good luck, because the last news of him in Guadalajara had been that he had disappeared from view, and was said to be living on his family *rancho* somewhere in the remote sierra. A tentative appointment was fixed at the Institute's office for four that afternoon.

The Shaman arrived punctually; a remarkable figure even in Tepic where there were many Indians in the streets and not a few of them in bizarre attire. He was a man in early middle age; short, with a small brown, smiling face and penetrating eyes and, in his cotton shirt and trousers embroidered with deer, eagles and jaguars, and his wide hat decorated with coloured wools and fringed with pendant ornaments, he dominated the discreet environment of the Institute's office.

In previous encounters with the Indians of Central America—in particular the Maya-Quiché of Guatemala—I had found them taciturn, unsmiling and aloof. This I attributed to the long centuries of their subjugation by the Whites. For half this period of domination and enslavement elsewhere, the Huichols had succeeded in retaining their independence, surrendering this only in 1721. Even following this, contact with the outside world remained slight, and the five missions

69

established as part of the treaty, by the Jesuits and Franciscans, shortly disappeared. For this reason, if it was possible to judge from the Shaman's presence and manner, they were in a very different case. The handbook of the National Museum of Mexico described them as light-hearted, outgoing and hospitable. 'They regard it as a matter of pride,' Lumhoetz, an early visitor, had noted, 'to treat strangers with the strict courtesy accorded to their own people.' Ramón Medina fitted this picture. David asked his permission to take pictures there and then in the office. A Maya-Quiché grandee would have turned on his heel and walked away in disdain, but Ramón, remote from small-scale intolerances and endlessly benign, allowed himself to be studied from angle to angle and shifted from position to position while the shutter of David's camera clicked interminably.

He spoke Spanish with a limited vocabulary, but in a slow and precise fashion as if he had learnt the language late in life, and the careful, syllable-by-syllable march of words made for ease of understanding. The director had told him of our wish to visit his country, the Shaman said, and he would be happy to help us in any way. '*Muy feliz, muy feliz*,' he assured us, and he squeezed our hands and nodded and smiled. It would be very convenient for all concerned if he went with us, he added, as he had urgent business in the sierra. Moreover if we went alone we would see nothing. The Indians lived on isolated *ranchos* which no stranger would ever find, coming down to their five villages only for ceremonial purposes. He was as free as the air to come and go where and when he pleased, he told us. The suggestion naturally delighted us, and it was instantly agreed that we leave together on the next day's plane.

At 5.30 in the morning we went in a taxi to find him in a glum little street on the outskirts of the town where his neighbours were waiting with their lamps lit to see him off. Besides the three of us two other passengers were waiting at the airfield: a young Huichol and his exceedingly pretty wife aged about fourteen. She had the small-boned elegant features of an Andalusian dancer, without Mongoloid traits

70

and her cheeks were flamboyantly rouged in the local style. She and her husband sat well separated, backs turned to each other in demure Huichol fashion, while the plane, trailing its dust-skirts came lumbering in.

The plane was a little discouraging, with significant patches in its fuselage and a small oil-drip from the engine, and the American pilot lopsided like an old arthritic horseman, due as he admitted to crash-landing in the remote past. His method now, he said, was to circle while over the valley until he had made enough height to be able to put the plane down if anything went wrong on one of a dozen flat tops throughout the sierra. He threw in the dismal information that he himself was obliged to do what maintenance was necessary to keep the plane in the air.

'Suppose we decide to put this off. Could you fly us into Guadaloupe?' I asked.

'If the missionaries say OK. Sure I could. You have to remember the weather.'

'What if the missionaries don't say it's OK?'

'It's their strip. What's wrong with San Andrès?'

'We want to see Indians, and I hear there aren't many about.'

'No,' he said. 'There aren't. They're on their way out.'

'Why's that?'

'For one thing they act like they own the sierra. Take for example the mining companies. They want to send exploration teams up there and the Indians might get in their hair.'

'Do they give you any trouble?'

'They did, but not now. Something had to be done.'

The engine started, shaking us with its vibration and starting a landslide of the many small objects left in the aisle. We took off, and within moments a dramatic landscape had been spread beneath us, tilting and rocking gently as the air currents buffeted the plane. We stared down into the green-baize-lined crater of the small volcano, and—despite the fact that Nayarit is supposed to be devoid of archaeological

71

interest—a neat construction of concentric rings that was unmistakably an ancient pyramid appeared, then slid away. Ahead, the sierra threw itself in grey waves against the horizon, and the Beechcraft, thundering towards them, bucked like a horse. Apart from such convulsions it seemed, after the years of air-travel in jets, hardly to move in space, but to be suspended, shuddering in each trough of the mountains, before the struggle up to clear the edge of the next shattered Crusaders' castle of rock. At these moments of maximum effort the fuselage flexed gently and the pilot reached out to make an adjustment here or tighten a wing-nut there. The Rio Chapalanga, drawn in its gorges like a flourish under a signature, appeared and vanished again. The Shaman, remote in his aura of dominance from preoccupations and perils, said that the fishing in this river was good, and pointed to locked-away valleys where jaguars abounded. Elsewhere, Huichol protocol had collapsed under the strain of the experience, and the young wife buried her face in her husband's neck.

At last a tongue of tableland appeared with a patch of green fabric glistening among its trees that was the landing strip, and the plane banked to come in and bounce along the strip to a halt. We clambered down and looked around us, finding ourselves in a forest of sparsely planted oaks; bromeliads knotted with their thin daggers of blossom among the branches. Harsh sunshine shattered itself in facets of jade and quartz on the rocks beyond the runway, and a freezing wind hissed down. Saying something about worsening conditions, the pilot hoisted himself back into the cockpit. The engine started with a cough and a great belch of blue smoke, and the plane shook itself like a wet dog, went fluttering its wings down the runway and took off. A group of Huichols who had appeared from nowhere and squatted in contemplation of this miracle got up and trotted away, vanishing instantly among the trees. There was no path; no indication of the direction in which the mission might lie. The short, spiky grass ended at a frontier of trees, all equally spaced and of equal height. The silence was measured at intervals by the abrupt, melancholic hooting of an invisible

72

bird. Loneliness seemed to lie in wait, yet it was likely that the Huichols were keeping watch on us from behind the trees for shortly two drooping, apathetic-looking women drifted into sight. The Shaman pounced upon these and immediately enlisted them as porters, inducing them to take charge of two of our valises, which they carried in Indian style, suspended from headbands tied across their foreheads.

At this point a matter arose that underlined certain realities of our situation. The Shaman took a battered-looking automatic pistol from the splendidly ornamented satchel he carried. 'I brought this for you,' he said. He wanted me to try it, which I felt reluctant to do. When he insisted, I slipped out the charger, cocked it, but found the action so stiff that it was almost impossible to pull the trigger. I handed it back, and he seemed both surprised and disappointed, indicating by unmistakable gestures that we had to be on our guard. He said that one still ran into the occasional wolf, bear or jaguar in this area, but I sensed from his tone and manner that it was not wild animals we had to fear. Once again I excused myself from the responsibility of carrying the gun—for which there were only four bullets—telling him that it was too stiff to be fired with accuracy, and that in any case I was an impossible shot. The proposition had come as a slight shock. I could accept that the urbane and worldly-wise Padre Ernesto should arm himself to go on such an expedition, but I had divorced the Shaman in my mind from the necessity of such expedients, and I found it hard to think of a man of such authority and spiritual power as the possessor of a murderer's tool.

We set off in single file, spaced about thirty yards apart, and this age-old precaution against ambush could only be seen in a disquieting light. The Shaman went first and, carrying David's massive tripod, I followed. David came next, and the two Huichol women trailed in the rear. We found ourselves following a narrow track, often along the edge of a steep drop, twisting up through the valley towards a crenellation of grey peaks. The landscape's beauty was of a theatrical, almost premeditated kind. My previous experience of Central America had been among the Maya who had changed all that was cultivatable in their landscape throughout the millennia into a vast market garden. This place had remained untouched since the beginning: pines trained and spaliered by the winds, streams running in shining alabaster beds, the great silver trunks of fallen oaks, waterfalls generating their small rainbows, indigo and orange macaws, and hawks chasing great sulphurous butterflies.

An hour passed and the trail became tighter, steeper and cluttered with immense boulders. We looked down into a gorge; a small Grand Canyon with green, mossy walls, a thread of water in its bottom, and a Huichol rancho wedged in a niche some hundred feet down from the edge, a quarter of a mile from where we stood. The women, who had been calling to the Shaman, came up and pointed to it, and his face changed. I asked what was the matter and he said that the small wooden shack had been attacked, although in this case the attackers had been driven off. 'And who were the attackers?' I asked. 'The people who want to drive us away,' he said.

Three and a half hours after setting out from the airstrip we came in sight of the mission buildings. It had been eight and a half miles of hard going, and only the Shaman showed no signs of fatigue. At this point he dropped back, keeping within the cover of the trees, while David and I found ourselves on a neat path leading to the compound. A moment later we saw a Franciscan padre also bound for the mission, and slightly ahead of us. We caught up with him and introduced ourselves and learned that this was Padre Joaquín, in charge at Santa Clara, who had just arrived from Tepic in the mission's Cessna, in which we were a little surprised to be told he was the only passenger. I explained that we were here at Padre Ernesto's suggestion, and he replied somewhat coldly that he had heard all about us from Padre Alberto, and no great sense was called for to conclude that this was probably the last man in the world to speak to about the possibilities of organizing Padre Ernesto's pagan fiesta. The Shaman was now out of sight among the trees, but the padre had almost certainly caught a glimpse of him.

74

It occurred to us that whatever hope we might have had for the welcome promised by Padre Ernesto had faded at our appearance in these surroundings in the company of what Padre Joaquín would probably have regarded as a medicine man, in all his stone-age trappings.

The padre was a man of extremely few words, and little was said until we crossed a stream in which a large, battered metal object lay half-submerged. This, he told us, was the remains of the mission's workshop, which the Huichols had burned down two years before. Speaking with some emphasis, he added, 'They were hostile to us at that time.'

To further conversational efforts his replies were brief and to the point. The primary function of the mission, he said, was to educate Huichol children. At that moment they had sixty pupils of both sexes—all of them boarders, because their family *ranchos* were too far away for them to return home each day. No charge was made for instruction or board. The children had the afternoon free from study, so we would not see many of them about. He evaded a question as to the subjects taught, and made it clear without saying as much that he had no intention of showing us over the mission, nor indeed beyond short answers to specific questions of entering into any discussion of missionary work in general. Despite the hospitality promised by Padre Ernesto, it was clear, for reasons we had no way of knowing, he was nervous and put out by our arrival in Santa Clara. What was most important to him was that there should be no mistake about the arrangements for our departure. The plane from Tepic would come on Sunday morning—early he said, to avoid the high winds—and he quoted the price for its charter. He then showed us the hut on the edge of the compound where we were to sleep, and quickly made an excuse and hurried away.

We went off to sit with Ramón among the trees out of sight of the mission. Nature here worked to a timetable and woodpeckers with fiery crests had suddenly appeared, and scuttled up and down the trunks all round in search of their evening meal. The talk was on the conflict between the mission and at least a faction of the Huichols, made evident by the ruin of the workshop, remaining in sight from where we sat. The missionaries, he said, were attempting to steal away the Huichol soul. They persuaded Huichol families who feared for their children's safety in the lawlessness of the sierra to place them in the care of the mission. This the parents sometimes brought themselves to do, taking comfort in the belief that once an Indian always an Indian, and that a Huichol soul could not be 'caught' by the Christians. Whatever the shortcomings, the errors or the backsliding of this life, he saw, he, the mara'akame would come for it at death, conducting all the ceremonies necessary to ensure a safe passage past the many perils to be faced beyond the gate of the underworld, and thereon on its progression towards the sun. Thereafter, if after five years it craved return to earth, he would build for it the grass shrine to be placed in the family house where it would live on throughout eternity in its earthbound form as a rock crystal.

All this, he said, Huichol parents understood, but the great betrayal they now faced was the Franciscans' plan to turn their race into *mestizos* through the mixed marriages among the mission children which they were doing all they could to encourage. The offspring of such marriages would be lost to the Huichol people, their blood diluted with that of strangers who had lost their past.

A little later the Vespers bell rang, and the *mestizos* came riding down the trails to attend the service; men, as Lorca would have said, with their mouths full of flints, slender and saturnine and dressed in cowboy style, with big sombreros, silver spurs and leather chaps. They doffed their hats as they passed, and the Shaman gave them the easy smile that hid an implacable contempt. These men were nothing, he said. They had the souls of the mules they rode.

Early evening came, with the woodpeckers gone to roost or in their holes, and a sky full of toucans and parakeets and soft lemon light. The *mestizos* came swaggering out of the mission. They waved their hats to us, leaped into the saddle and rode away. Children appeared on the slopes, both Huichols and *mestizos*, dragging up firewood on sledges for the fires. When the firewood had been stowed away they reappeared and began a cautious movement in our direction, the girls in head-shawls, demure little extras in a sentimental old Hollywood film about Mexican life; the boys in their sombreros with crisply up-curving brims, and carrying guitars and Huichol violins. These were a sketchy version of the original European instrument, made up for a few pesos in Tepic. It was clear that their intention was to serenade us, but, despite the encouragement of the girls who kept up a vigorous pentatonic humming, the musicians were too shy to do more than strum a few bars. It was hard to tell from their faces, whether boys or girls, dressed as they were in the Mexican national style, were pure Indians with what the Shaman called Huichol hearts, or of mixed parentage—and therefore belonging wholly to the modern world. Thus in the missions had the process of assimilation begun.

The Shaman had withdrawn to sit apart from this scene. He was always kept busy even when on the march with the magical formulae with which he guided the sun in its rising and going down, and the invocations and rapid ceremonies with which he shaped the Huichol destiny and precipitated the gods of fire and of rain. Whenever we paused to rest he occupied himself as he did now with sketching designs for incorporation, as I supposed, into his *nearikas*.

Somebody had given him a notebook and a ball-point pen, but after experimenting with these he threw them away and went back to a scroll of cheap paper he always carried, already partially covered with ideographs, on which he wrote with a piece of charcoal. The Shaman drew innumerable human figures, small strutting manikins with slightly birdlike faces, although sometimes, when shown as engaged in a ritual hunt, the nostrils and jaw were elongated into a muzzle, and then they became half-man and half-deer. There was something pathetic and childlike in these figures, and as a drawing progressed it was clear that they were always caught up in a predicament in which it was evident that the Shaman felt himself to be vicariously involved. They were under attack by scorpions, poisonous spiders or

77

centipedes larger than themselves. Sometimes the aggressors were Ant People having the power to transform themselves into affable and persuasive humans who accost a defenceless Huichol on the pretext of leading him to a cache of maize. Then, when he falls asleep, they revert to their ant form to rob him—by nibbling away clothes, hair, even eyebrows—of everything he possesses.

After death the Huichol soul passes through five successive levels in its journey to the underworld and it is the alleviation of this passage, beset with perils, that calls for the exercise of all the Shaman's magic and artistic skills. On leaving the body the wandering soul is instantly confronted with two paths. One, reserved for the offender in this life against important taboos, provides a series of painful experiences. The offender is temporarily impaled upon a huge thorn, subjected to purifying fires, crushed between moving rocks that close on him, and immersed in a stinking quagmire. The virtuous march down the straight and narrow alternative, protected by powerful animals, a black dog, a crow and an opossum to the lake of pure water in which they cleanse themselves in preparation for the onward journey.

The four remaining stages feature their own hazards and problems, and these are diversions from the main route for special cases for which exemplary castigation is prepared. The Huichols are remarkable among the Indian peoples in their possession of the concept of retribution—inherited possibly from their inflexible ancestors, the Aztecs, who linked pain with moral regeneration. They also experience sexual guilt, and the arrival in the underworld of the soul who has offended taboo through intercourse with a non-Huichol is delayed while he is led away to a corral, there to be trampled by mules. The symbolism of the mules is double-barrelled. As the animal of the *mestizo* and the white, it is an alien, while its sterility brands it as contemptible. In the Huichol view it is fitting that punishment for race-defilement should be inflicted by this aberrant beast. However correction is strictly limited, and after a few kicks the soul is released from the corral and set upon the right path to the next stage in its journey and its accompanying hazards.

Sometimes the Shaman drew girls. They were more cheerful and animated than his manikins, and there was something strangely modern and non-Indian in their stance, their excited arm-waving gestures and in their invariably long pony-tails swept into the air by a lively breeze. He was sorry only to be able to show these spirited maidens, the five daughters of the maize, in his black-and-white sketches, assuring me that when the *nearikas* with their brilliantly dyed wools were done and the girls prepared in their five symbolic colours—black, red, white, green and blue—I would be captivated by their beauty. I asked him to try his hand with the missionary. This at first he seemed reluctant to do but in the end made a hasty sketch of an outsize Indian with the usual Huichol parrot-face and an insane grin. After I had inspected this result he tore the piece of paper from his scroll and burned it on a palm leaf, then blew the ashes into the air. I was reminded of the Maya-Quiché's memory in the masks they created of Pedro de Alvarado, as the man with the eternal smile, although this caricature seemed unfair to Padre Joaquín who was not only a dignified but a somewhat solemn man.

Two adult Huichols were at work on the foundations of a building on the outskirts of the compound and the Shaman went off to enquire from them what were the possibilities of our witnessing interesting ceremonies in this part of the sierra. He had already assured us that the chances were slight. Apart from the fact that the Huichols seemed to be slowly withdrawing from the area, it was a bad time of the year. People everywhere who live off the land can best find the resources and the spare time for celebrations when the harvests are newly in—and in the Sierra Madre this is in the months of October and November. Thereafter food supplies begin slowly to diminish, no rain falls in the mountains and the grass withers away. In bad seasons—and this was one— maize stocks soon run out, and the family eats once a day, and then every second day. Apart from any pressures of a new and sinister kind they might be experiencing, food shortages might have the temporary effect of forcing the able young men and women into trekking down to the coast-land to grow a cash crop of tobacco.

Watching the Shaman in his confabulation with the builders it was clear from his gestures that his somewhat unpromising view of our prospects had been confirmed. When he returned he was exceptionally silent, seeming at first disinclined to reply to questioning. He then produced a disquieting piece of information. The builders had told him that four days before—on the Monday—bandits had broken into a Huichol *rancho* just out of sight in the fold of the hills from where we stood, robbed the owner, and then murdered him by hanging. Having passed on the news the Shaman went off and sat alone some way away, among the trees.

Some time later, one of the boys came out to summon us to supper, to which we had been invited by Padre Joaquín earlier in the evening. He had waved aside an offer of payment for food, saying that this would be included in the hire charge for the plane. David and I ate at the far end of a long table in the mission dining hall in conspicuous isolation from Padre Joaquín and several nuns, where we were served bowlfuls of *atole*—sweet cornflour gruel—followed by tortillas and bean stew, all of it delicious. Despite Padre Joaquín's aloofness the opportunity arose for a brief conversation with one of the nuns in the course of which she made casual reference to an occasion during the padre's absence when she and the other sisters had to fight off an attack. By whom? I asked, and she said, bandits. As this appeared to be the only instance of the sisters being involved in a shoot-out it was hard not to wonder whether this could not have been the episode which caused the destruction of the workshop, blamed by Padre Joaquín on the Huichols.

The Shaman, preferring not to be included in the meal, remained outside. We had brought with us a large can of processed ham, which he told us he could not eat, and, apart from that, several packets of biscuits. He took one of these, which he said would satisfy his needs for twenty-four hours.

The night was cold. David and I slept fully dressed under what we could find in the way of blankets but were awakened at about three by a chill that made it impossible to sleep longer. This was the hour, too, when the Huichol day starts, and we could hear Ramón praying, then shuffling about in the darkness, and finally the door opened and closed behind him as he went out. At about four, activity outside became general, and the mission children, irrepressibly musical, came and went about the morning's business, strumming their guitars and playing their violins.

There was nothing for it but to face the gelid air, and we dragged ourselves stiffly up the mountainside in the direction of a fire. Here we found the Shaman who had been joined by a semi-circle of *mestizos*—silent and motionless pyramids of blankets, beyond which nothing showed of them but their eyes and the toe-caps of their boots. Presently we heard the sound of music and voices chanting 'Silent Night' and saw the flicker of torches among the trees of a procession winding down the hill. This proved to be the boys who had been for a swim in the freezing lagoon. Joining us they removed their hats in deference and asked permission to play a few bars *para saludar el alba*—to salute the dawn—which, being granted, they did. The Shaman found little but self-indulgence in their exercise and of the softening fostered by the mission environment. Three in the morning was the Huichol hour at which to take one's dip, not dawn. This he mentioned was the habit of any woman worthy of consideration. Such dousing increased the natural sexual coldness that the Huichols appreciated in their womenfolk. He added the interesting information that any Huichol who had intercourse more frequently than at intervals of ten or fifteen days was regarded as a debauchee. This ideal of sexual conduct, he said, had been established by the nation's divine ancestor, the deer, who limited sexual activity to a brief, yearly season. Later, as the first rays of the sun touched our faces, and the *mestizos*, bowing to each of us in turn and whispering a soft *adios*, had gone their way, he added the opinion that apart from the fact that they had no souls, the main cause of their inferiority was their over-indulgence in intercourse by which they wasted their blood.

The sun came up with reluctance, although assisted by a

seemingly perfunctory waving of the two small feathered wands the Shaman carried for the purpose of setting it on its course across the sky. David and I went off, at the beckonings of the child who had conducted us to table on the previous night, for more tortillas with *atole*, and the Shaman nibbled a rich tea biscuit, and, having dealt with the sun, now turned his attentions to the rain god to whom in the dry season it was necessary to address prayers five times a day. When these priorities had been accomplished we set out on a 17-mile walk, for the Shaman had decided to go to San Andrès, the ceremonial Huichol village located hardly more than a mile from the airstrip at which the plane had put us down on the day before. He explained to us that Huichols were deserting (or perhaps being forced out of) the area of Santa Clara, and that it was only at San Andrès that there was any hope of seeing any. It seemed also likely that he'd some personal business to conduct in the village, although perhaps through linguistic difficulties that sometimes arose, or even through certain evasions, the nature of any such business was never made clear. A little of the high good humour with which the Shaman had begun the journey back to the place of his birth seemed to have evaporated. He smiled less readily, and his expression was sometimes clouded, even wary. Above all he seemed eager, as soon as possible, to free himself from the mission surroundings.

The day had made a lively start. We trudged through great palisades of shadow thrown down by the morning sun. Birds chuckled and hooted. A deer started up and raced away into the mist. Tiny, scarlet flowers had opened everywhere overnight in the close grass, and beads of watery condensation sparkled among the quartz seams of the rocks.

Once again, as the sun rose we stopped to rest and look down into the frenzied depths of the Nautla Gorge. The Huichol who had survived the assault on his *rancho* was doing something in his garden very close to a 500ft drop to the river. Down there close to the bottom, and out of sight from where we stood, the Huichol idols were stored in the cave of Te Kata. It was located, Padre Ernesto had said— tempting us to further adventure—only a half day by mule from Santa Clara, and no white man had ever been there. But with the tight time-schedule Padre Joaquín had imposed, it was a temptation we were obliged to resist.

Soon after, the Shaman, detecting an omen in the call of a bird, decided on a change of direction, and we branched off onto another trail where shortly the landscape opened up in a cataclysmic vista of tumbled rocks, chasms and ravines, across one of which a small mountain, cracked in half, seemed about to fall apart. This scene of ruin suggested the epicentre of an earthquake—in all likelihood a recent one—for nearby in another direction a landslide had picked up hundreds of trees, smashed them into firewood and tipped them into the valley. A Huichol came up through the wood then made a detour to avoid us. The Shaman called to him when he came level, although by this time he was a hundred yards away. He stopped and we saw that he was carrying a yellow-painted rifle. A brief, shouted exchange followed, after which the man went on, and the Shaman stood watching him until he was out of sight. He seemed more than ever subdued, and when we started off again warned us to keep well to the rear of him, studying the ground carefully as he walked, as if in fear of stepping on a snake. After a while he stopped. Two branches had been laid to cross over the trail, and the Shaman bent down to study them and warned us not to pass. He then announced that this was a *travesía*—a matter of witchcraft—the intention being to debar entrance to the area. Picking up the branches he threw them into the air and blew after them. After that he wiped his hands carefully as if they had been contaminated with radio-active matter. He then put it to us that it might be safer to turn back, even though he had dealt with the spell, but it was agreed that we should continue.

A *mestizo* on a mule now appeared, riding towards us and the Shaman stood in his path. This man looked the part of a Mexican film villain, with sleepy yet furtive eyes; his mouth on the verge of sneer. A heavy pistol stuck out of his saddle bag. The Shaman started a stern questioning in Spanish, and the man, having to explain his presence there, began to look alarmed. He was going to Jesús Maria, he said, to try to

83

buy cattle. He couldn't say from whom. There was a well-known cattle dealer in the village whose name might have been Pedro or Juan. He couldn't remember. Nor could he supply the name of the *tatouan* (governor) of Jesús Maria. The Shaman asked him if he had any associates in this district, and he said he was the partner of a Señor Adolfo Castañera. He fidgeted and sweated while Ramón interrogated him, but in the end was allowed to go. 'He is one of those who murdered the Huichol at Santa Clara,' the Shaman said. It seemed impossible to ask him how he knew, besides which an imprecision in the charge was favoured by a woolly use of language. *'Uno de esos,'* he said, which might have meant that the man himself had been among the killers, or simply that he was the kind of man who committed such murders.

San Andrès came into view beyond the airstrip. It was not the original village, said by the Shaman to have been dismantled some two centuries before by order of the Jesuits sent to subdue the area. We left the trail for a hundred yards to inspect a few half-buried stones marking its position. The groundplan of the first settlement, conforming to Huichol metaphysical principles, had been circular and the houses built with slight but essential structural variations to denote the status of their occupants, and tenanted according to rules hardly less complex than those governing family relationship themselves. It was sited among the trees, to benefit not only from their shade, but from the many benign arboreal influences attributed to them by most Indians. The Jesuits must have stood here to shake their heads over the puzzling symmetry of this Indian village, and its hidden implications, before ordering the trees to be cut down and the huts dismantled. They had brought with them the plans for the new village, which was to be rectangular in Spanish style with verandahs replacing the shade which the trees no longer gave.

There was something a little sinister about the present settlement consisting of some twenty raw, stone-built square huts. Both the buildings themselves and the rock on which they stood were of a deep and lugubrious red, which seemed to fill even the shadows with lurid light. No vegetation, not even a weed could exist here, and the first thing that drew the attention, in this emptiness and blinding light, was a structure resembling a pillory in the centre of the square, on which a number of withered-looking objects had been nailed. To this post, the Shaman later informed us, deflowerers of virgins were tied to be flogged, and the shrivelled wreaths—as they turned out to be—that still decorated it were crowns symbolizing instances of ravished virginity. Since physical punishment of offenders was not a part of Huichol culture, and the conception of virginity was foreign to almost all Indians, it was to be supposed that this somewhat barbaric ritual was introduced at the time of the Jesuit presence.

At the moment of our arrival the only human form in sight was a single Huichol sprawled motionless against the verandah of what seemed the village's principal building. He ignored us, not even raising his eyes when we approached. This, the Shaman told us was the *topiri*—the police officer—and while the man continued to give no sign that he was aware of our presence the Shaman fingered and explained to us the insignia of his office; the sacred cord wound round his waist, used to tie up prisoners, and the staff of office, with its bunch of ribbons stuck into his belt. The *topiri*, immured in an obsidian reserve, replied with eyes averted, and without changing his posture to the Shaman's questionings. He mentioned briefly that a week or two before a ceremony had taken place that it would have been interesting for us to see. A new *tatouan* (governor) had been elected, and according to Huichol democratic procedure he had not been informed in advance of his candidature. As the office provided for no remuneration but imposed many onerous duties he had been persuaded to accept nomination only after a short period of imprisonment without food. The *tatouan* was now away on his *rancho*, recovering from the experience, and should have returned on this day to provide and pay for celebrations to mark his takeover of office. These had had to be postponed because one of the villagers had had a premonitory dream.

85

A few more Huichols conjured up from nowhere had drifted silently into view and were moving very slowly and cautiously towards a *mestizo* armed with a rifle who had appeared at the entrance to the village. It was a moment of almost over-theatrical impact. The newcomer surveyed the scene, looking down from a slight rise in the maroon earth, gun held ready in both hands, turning his head slowly from side to side while the Huichols, some holding bows, moved step by step towards him. Ravens croaked in the gunmetal sky, one of the Huichols gave a long, shrill whistle. Another raised his bow. The intruder put down his gun, and the Huichols closed in.

The man was accused of being a *malhechor*, the word used locally for bandit, and he protested his innocence, giving the name of Castañera—being none other than the associate claimed by the man on the mule. Not only was he no outlaw himself, he said, but he was one of their victims. As proof of this he took off his shirt to display the scars of a terrible foot-long wound in his stomach, produced by the exit of a dumdum bullet, and we were invited to examine the small white circle in the skin of his back where the bullet entered. He had been shot from ambush, he said, on 22 June of the previous year, on the trail we had just come down from Santa Clara, about five kilometres from San Andrés. The argument that no man with such a wound could but be innocent failed to impress the Shaman who, after performing a small magic ceremony involving the manipulation of a horse's jawbone and intense psychic concentration, pronounced him as the murderer of the Huichol found hanging in his *rancho* near the mission. Now, while the Huichols covered the man with their drawn bows, the *topiri* came forward to tie his hands with the sacred cord, and a messenger hurried from the village to find the *tatouan* on his *rancho*, and bring him back to preside over the trial.

There seemed no end in this village to the complications of violence and terror. A house had been kept locked up for some months, and the Shaman, saying that he sensed the presence of death in the village, ordered it to be opened and went in. He came out instantly in a state of some

86

agitation to tell us that he had found the body of a murdered man. We followed him and went in at the moment when the Huichols were lifting the corpse down from a space into which it had been crammed between the rafters and the roof. There was an intense reek of putrefaction, and David, called upon to photograph this grisly episode, and who had never seen a dead body before, said that he felt faint. The dead man, identified as Miguel García had been killed by a gunshot wound in the right side of the chest. García, in his splendidly embroidered trousers and his new sandals, his woven Huichol belt and the plain blue shirt of the kind to be bought in a town store, was laid out on a palliasse. About a quarter of the area of the shirt, extending down to his right armpit, was crisped and blackened by his blood; his eyes had been bandaged at the time of death and this bandage was left untouched. Four Huichols standing at his feet waved their wands and uttered hoarse prayers to Watakame, Clearer of the Fields. The Shaman moved in the background with suggestive, fluttering motions of his fingers, designed to lure the spirit from the body, and set it on the path to the village cemetery. Trails of pebbles had been laid to guide it thence, and also to confuse any attempt to return. An only sister stood by the body's head to chant and sob.

It was hard to discover just what had happened. The Shaman explained that Miguel García had met his death in the mountains, and then had been carried here to be hidden in this house by six men. It was an explanation that seemed hard to accept as a literal fact. Why should not the killers, we asked ourselves, have left the body where it lay to be consumed by wild animals? In which case all traces of the crime would have vanished within days. It was hard, too, to believe that the assassins would have chosen to hide the body of their victim in his own house, and at this point I began to suspect that we had strayed across the vague frontier dividing established fact from magical interpretation. Truth, in so far as it could be defined by the senses in the Huichol country, conflicted with truth discovered by visions. Thus the Shaman leading his people in search of the sacred peyote cactus undergoes a spiritual transformation into *Tate-*

wari, ancestor of the race, while the peyote becomes a deer, not to be collected but hunted down with bows and arrows. In this maze of symbolism it is easy to see the six men who carried García to his house as the six mortuary assistants of Our Mother Eagle God, the divinity who watches over those who are not truly dead because a Shaman has not induced the spirit to leave the body. Similarly the Huichols may have been only ritually unaware of the presence of García's body in the village, although obliged by custom to utter cries of consternation and surprise as they trooped into the house. 'Death in the mountains', too, may have been only a conventional euphemism for death from unnatural causes.

For all that, this tragedy had taken San Andrès off its guard. At that moment, having painted their faces appropriately, the Huichols should have gathered to drink *tesquino*, their ritual beer, but there was none. There were no candles to be found either, no animal of any kind that could have been decently sacrificed, hardly enough flour even for the five tortillas, one of which would sustain the dead man's spirit in each of the stages of its journey through the underworld. What could be found of García's possessions were assembled for burial, but it was essential to include with them symbolic bodily parts; arms and legs, and a head woven from some sacred material, that would replace the physical body as corruption advanced. None of this could be discovered and the Shaman had to make do with ordinary grass. The atmosphere was one of depressed but frantic improvisation, against which the dead man's sister wailed softly.

The *tatouan* and his officers now arrived, presenting stoic Indian faces to the ritual confusion. Wearing their ceremonial hats, decorated with buzzards' and eagles' feathers, they stalked in slow, solemn procession into the council house to begin their deliberations. A grave 15ft-deep was almost finished, but their decision was that whatever the religious imperatives, the body must remain unburied until all the relatives had been assembled—and some of them lived in *ranchos* a day's ride away.

In this the Shaman, who had called for immediate burial, was surprisingly overruled. The major ceremonies required at the time of burial could not be carried out for we were obliged to leave the village by four in the afternoon in order to reach Santa Clara by nightfall. The Shaman was overruled, too, in the matter of the bandit suspect who, after a short and perfunctory trial, was released—seemingly through insufficient evidence. The man was given back his gun and left the village with a swagger emphasizing victory, and a last, meaningful glance in our direction that was devoid of amity. In a way the verdict came as a relief. Life in the sierra, we now understood, was cheap indeed, and voices had been raised at first in favour of rough and immediate justice—at which moment Castañera's life had probably hung by a hair. There now remained the uncomfortable possibility that somewhere in the forest between San Andrés and Santa Clara a man with a deep grudge against the Shaman might be lying in wait. We set out as before, walking in single file and well-separated to reduce the risks inherent in the situation.

Reaching the Nautla Gorge we joined forces again, and threw ourselves down to rest. The mission was only a half-hour's scramble away down the mountainside, and already the sun had fallen behind the peaks. It was a moment to search for an answer to aspects of the day's happenings that remained obscure, and with what tact I could muster in a foreign language I asked the Shaman how, and at what point he had discovered that García's body was hidden in the village, and whether the *travesía* left on the trail that morning was in any way connected with the tragedy. Here the blunt linguistic instrument of Castilian failed us both. The Huichols, cousins of the Aztecs, speak a version of the Aztec tongue, rich in nuances and undercurrents of allusion that are untranslatable into the basic Spanish of a foreigner, and my categorical questions called for muted and conditional answers for which no words could be found. On one issue the Shaman was definite. I had been unable to accept the story of the body being hidden by casual murderers in a village house. Did he really believe that the Huichol in San Andrés had been killed by bandits?

'No,' he said. 'The man was killed because he wanted to be a shaman.'

And this, in the light of what we had seen, heard or surmised seemed to make sense. All shamans—the guardians of the old traditions—who could be reached by the soldiers of the conquest, or by the officers of the Inquisition who followed them, were resolutely eliminated. To be burned at the stake was the only penalty for those who resisted the imposition of Christianity. Those who had survived until now among the Huichols had only escaped their fate through the ruggedness and inaccessibility of this mountain environment. The Sierra Madre since then had remained too poor in all the old-fashioned resources to attract exploiters. There was no gold or silver to be mined here. Nothing could be grown for the market in this poor, thin soil, nor could animals be raised on these steep slopes and in these narrow valleys except a few scrawny cows for local consumption. But now the planes were flying in bringing the advance guard of missionaries, to be followed by the geologists and mineral prospectors who were discovering everywhere exciting reserves of new wealth, often in areas where in the past nothing but the deepest poverty had existed. For these men the presence of the Indians, prepared to defend themselves against incursions into their tribal territory, presented a dangerous nuisance. I could understand that Miguel García might have invited a violent end by proposing to set up as shaman—in this way associating himself with a traditional resistance. I also understood now why Dr Ramos had described our friend Ramón Medina as having 'taken refuge' in Tepic, and was inclined to the view that Castañera was indeed a hired killer who had followed us along the trail awaiting a favourable moment to shoot the Shaman, and only prevented from doing so by the unexpected presence of the Indians in San Andrès.

It was hard not to suspect that here among the Huichols we were witnessing the very beginnings of a process of extermination now being conducted by all accounts among so many of the tribal people of Latin America.

*

By this time our relationship with the Shaman had become close and affectionate and he chose this moment to create us honorary compañeros of the Huichol people and formally invited us to set out with him on the annual pilgrimage due to start in 25 days' time. For the sixth time Ramón would lead his people, at the head of four captains, across mountain and desert for 20 days to Rial Cartorce in the high desert of San Luis Potosí, where the peyote grew—or, in the Huichol metaphysical sense, grazed. If we joined the pilgrimage we would become ritually Huichols, subjected to tribal discipline, carrying nothing but bows, sacred tobacco and ritual impedimenta, taking part in the many ceremonies to be performed, sustained on the journey—as the Shaman put it—by the virtue engendered by our own austerities. It was a tempting prospect, and much as it sounded strenuous it had already been accomplished by Peter Furst and his wife—the first persons outside the Huichol tribe to have enjoyed this clearly extraordinary experience.

Enthusiastic as both David and I were at the chance of such an adventure, it would have been impossible at short notice for either of us to reorganize our lives to go on the pilgrimage at that time, but it was agreed that we would be prepared to do so in the following year. Some months later I wrote to Ramón care of the Indian Institute at Tepic to learn how arrangements were going but received no reply. A letter addressed to the Institute itself elicited the news that the Shaman had left Tepic and nothing was known of his whereabouts. It was only years later, chancing on an article in a Mexican publication championing Indian rights, that I learned that the Shaman Ramón Medina was dead, murdered within months of our meeting in the Sierra Madre.

6

In the fifties the great extermination of the forest Indians of
South America began. It was the secret operation conducted
behind the world's back in the hitherto largely impenetrable
forests of Paraguay, Bolivia and Brazil, and unsuspected by
the ordinary citizens of those countries.

Due to the involvement of dictatorial governments in control of a muzzled press, no estimate will ever be possible of
the deathroll among the Indians of Paraguay and Bolivia.
In Brazil as soon as news of the nature and scale of the
tragedy leaked out immediate and effective action was taken
against those responsible, and there was no attempt at a
cover-up. It was a different matter to bring the instigators
of such crimes to book, for only too often they proved to
be powerful, even international land-speculators. It was a
time, too, when multinational corporations were joining the
drive to develop the untapped natural resources and to fill
the apparently empty spaces of Latin America. Those who
organized the massacres were in most cases functionaries of
the Indian Protection Service. This according to General
Albuquerque, the Brazilian Minister of the Interior, had
been converted into an instrument for the Indians'
oppression, and had therefore been dissolved. There was to
be a judicial inquiry into the conduct of 134 agents. A full
newspaper page in small print was required to list the crimes
with which these men were charged. Speaking informally,
the Attorney General, Senhor Jader Figueiredo, doubted
whether ten of the Service's employees, out of a total of
over 1,000, would be fully cleared of guilt.

The official report was calm, phlegmatic almost—all the
more effective therefore, in its exposure of the atrocity it
contained. Pioneers leagued with corrupt politicians had
continually usurped Indian lands, destroying whole tribes in
a cruel struggle in which bacteriological warfare had been
employed, by issuing clothing impregnated with the virus of

smallpox, and by poisoned food supplies. Children had been abducted and mass murder gone unpunished. The government itself was blamed to some extent for the Service's increasing starvation of resources over a period of 30 years. The Service had also had to face 'the disastrous impact of missionary activity'.

Next day the Attorney General met the press, and was prepared to supply all the details. A commission had spent 58 days visiting Indian Protection Service posts all over the country collecting evidence of abuses and atrocities.

The huge losses sustained by the Indian tribes in this tragic decade were catalogued in part. Of 19,000 Munducurus believed to have existed in the 1930s, only 1,200 were left. The strength of the Guaranis had been reduced from 5,000 to 300. There were 400 Carajas left out of 4,000. Of the Cintas Largas, who had been attacked from the air and driven into the mountains, possibly 500 had survived out of 10,000. The proud and noble nation of the Kadiweus—'the Indian Cavaliers'—had shrunk to a pitiful scrounging band of about 200. A few hundred only remained of the formidable Chavantes who prowled in the background of Peter Fleming's Brazilian journey, but they had been reduced to mission fodder—the same melancholy fate that had overtaken the Bororos, who helped to change Lévi-Strauss's views on the nature of human evolution. Many tribes were now represented by a single family, a few by one or two individuals. Some, like the Tapaiunas—in this case from a gift of sugar laced with arsenic—had disappeared altogether. It was estimated that between 50,000 and 100,000 Indians had survived.

Senhor Figueiredo estimated that property worth 62 million dollars had been stolen from the Indians in the past 10 years; cattle and personal possessions. He added, 'It is not only through the embezzlement of funds, but by the admission of sexual perversions, murders and all other crimes listed in the penal code against Indians and their property, that one can see that the Indian Protection Service was for years a den of corruption and indiscriminate killings.' The head of the Service, Major Luis Neves, was accused of

42 crimes, including collusions in several murders, the illegal sale of land, and the embezzlement of 300,000 dollars. The documents containing the evidence collected by the Attorney General weighed 103 kgms, he informed the newspapermen, and amounted to a total of 5,115 pages.

In the following days there were more headlines and more statements by the Ministry.

Rich landowners of the municipality of Pedro Alfonso attacked the tribe of Craos and killed about 100.

The worst slaughter took place in Aripuana, where the Cintas Largas Indians were attacked from the air using sticks of dynamite.

Survivors were chopped up by mercenaries employed on an overland expedition.

The Maxacalis were given fire-water by the landowners who employed gunmen to shoot them down when they were drunk.

Landowners engaged a notorious pistoleiro and his band to massacre the Canelas Indians.

The Nhambiquera Indians were mown down by machinegun fire.

Two tribes of the Patachos were exterminated by giving them smallpox injections.

In the Ministry of the Interior it was stated yesterday that crimes committed by certain ex-functionaries of the IPS amounted to more than 1000, ranging from tearing out Indians' fingernails to allowing them to die without assistance.

To exterminate the tribe Beicos-de-Pau, Ramis Bucair, Chief of the 6th Inspectorate, explained, an expedition was formed which went up the River Arinos carrying presents and a great quantity of foodstuffs for the Indians. These were mixed with arsenic and formicides . . . next day a great number of the Indians died, and the whites spread the rumour they had died from an epidemic.

A favourite method employed on several occasions was to shower gifts from a plane over a village then return on a second run dropping similar gifts booby-trapped with explosive devices.

Where the Brazilian government Commission's report left off, the newspapers took up, led by the authoritative if conservative dailies *O Jornal do Brazil* and *O Globo*, and now it was the missionaries who were under attack.

In reality [said the former], those in control of these Indian Protection Service posts [where the majority of the atrocities had taken place] are North American Missionaries— they are in all the posts—and they disfigure the original Indian culture and enforce the acceptance of Protestantism.

Back to the Commission's report.

'In the 7th Inspectorate, Parana, Indians were tortured by grinding their feet in the angles of two wooden stakes driven into the ground. Wives took turns with their husbands in applying the torture.'

But the leading Brazilian newspaper had said that there was a missionary in every post, and this was confirmed by the Brazilian Ministry of the Interior. Where were the missionaries when these tortures were inflicted and their screams must have resounded in the small clearing where both mission house and government hut had been built side by side? Despite the law of every civilized country, including Brazil, that those who witness, or have knowledge of a crime without denouncing it to the authorities are held to be accessories to that crime, there is no record to be found of any such denunciation. 'It was missionary policy,' said *O Globo*, 'to ignore what was going on.'

'What is extraordinary,' *O Jornal* said, 'is the extent to which these people have penetrated, and how they have established dependence.' It quoted the sensational case of the landowner Jordão Aires. A missionary had been able to persuade 600 Ticuna Indians that the end of the world was to take place and that they would be safe from destruction only on Aires' ranch. Here they were enslaved, subjected to fearful tortures and a number became lepers. What astounded *O Jornal* was that when Federal Police Delegate Neves was sent from Brazilia to investigate, she could only reach the area where the crimes had occurred by begging a lift in a short take-off missionary plane.

When *O Jornal* spoke of the disfigurement of the Indian culture it meant the banning by the missionaries of Indian ceremonies of all kinds, of Indian dances, of the playing of native instruments, of the self-treatment by Indians by their own medicinal remedies, of self-decoration in any form, or the wearing of apparel other than of the plainest and inevitably drabbest kind. We were back again to the apparatus for the repression of joy found to be so hideously successful by the grey men of the London Missionary Society sent to the South Pacific.

'They seem to have developed the uncanny knack,' the newspaper said, 'for discovering whatever it may be that is most likely to weaken the Indian and destroy his morale. Like weasels, they go straight for the jugular vein.' The case of the slow destruction of the Bororos was instanced. This was the tribe in Brazil among which the great anthropologist Claude Lévi-Strauss had lived for several years and who had led him to the conclusions of 'structural anthropology', including the proposition that 'a primitive people is not a backward or retarded people. Indeed it may possess a genius for invention or action that leaves the achievements of civilized people far behind.' He had said of the Bororos, 'few people are so profoundly religious . . . few possess a metaphysical system of such complexity. Their spiritual beliefs and everyday activities are inextricably mixed.'

Since Lévi-Strauss had studied them they had been forcibly evicted from their ancestral lands—and removed to the Santa Cristina reserve. Here they were recruited for forced labour by local farmers. They had also fallen prey to the missionaries who had imposed all the usual bans on pleasure.

These the Bororos had accepted with traditional stoicism, but there was a final prohibition against which they continuously rebelled, but in vain.

Most Indians are obsessed by their relationships with the dead, and by the conditions of the souls of their dead in the after-life—a concern reflected by the most elaborate funerary rites—orgies of grief and intoxication sometimes lasting for days. The Bororos, seemingly unable to part with their dead, bury them twice, and this custom provides the central emotional pivot of their lives. In the first event—as in hope of some miraculous revival—the body is placed in a temporary grave in the centre of the village, and covered with branches but otherwise regarded as still part of the living community. When decomposition is advanced the flesh is removed from the bones, which are painted and lovingly adorned with feathers, after which final burial takes place in the depths of the forest.

The Bororos had always done this, and explained that if forced to relinquish this custom they would no longer consider themselves Bororos and would prefer to die. Nevertheless despite the fact that neither the government nor the Catholic Church had ever interfered, the North American missionaries had been able to persuade the local police to enforce this ban, and the suicides had begun.

Of this the newspaper said, 'It is sad to see the plight in which these people have been left. The missionaries have deprived them of their power to resist. That is why they have been so easily plundered. A great emptiness and aimlessness had been left in their lives.' It concluded with a report by a young Bororo girl of her experiences in the reserve.

The Indians worked as slaves. They took me from my mother when I was a child. Afterwards I heard that they hung my mother up all night . . . She was very ill and I wanted to see her before she died . . . When I got back they thrashed me with a raw-hide whip . . . One day the IPS (Indian Protection Service) agent called a carpenter and told him to make an oven for the farmhouse. When the carpenter had finished the agent asked him what he wanted for doing the job. The carpenter said he wanted an Indian girl, and the agent took him to the (mission) school and told him to choose one. No-one saw or heard any more of her . . . Not even the children escaped. From two years of age they worked under the whip . . . There was a mill for crushing the cane, and to save the horses they used four children to turn the mill . . . They forced the Indian Otaviano to beat his own mother . . . The Indians were used for target practice.

There were missionaries within earshot when these things happened.

7

From all the innumerable and mostly critical reports of missionary doings appearing at this period in the Brazilian press the singular fact emerged that the newspapers had little idea of what they were up against. It was a vagueness equally shared by the governmental bodies. Although the US evangelists had been flooding into the country since immediately after the war, they were still seen as individual families, or at most small groups working in isolation to advance their particular brand of the faith. On the whole Brazilians viewed them as harmless eccentrics of the kind to be seen in those days parading the main streets of American cities carrying sandwich boards inscribed with messages of impending doom. It was assumed that, even if they did little good, they caused no damage.

By this time the two major evangelist sects, the Summer Institute of Linguistics, and the New Tribes Mission were virtually dividing the whole of Latin America, where tribal people remained to be reached, into their spheres of interest. I cannot remember a single instance when either of these exceedingly powerful organizations was mentioned by name in the press. I was never able, for example, to discover which of the sects was responsible for sending the missionaries to the Santa Cristina reserve where the Bororos were brought so close to extinction. Missionaries kept as much as possible to themselves, and did all they could to avoid publicity. In reality there was little known about them, and that was the way they preferred it to be.

The policy adopted by the Summer Institute of Linguistics in the concealment of its aims embodies the most successful missionary device since the evangelists of the London Missionary Society manipulated a drunken king to assist them in their conquest of the South Pacific.

Missionaries have many enemies. In Latin America Protestant fundamentalists are rejected by an educated minority, under attack by an entrenched Catholic Church, and at the mercy of suspicious if venal governments. The 'Dual Identity' which helped to establish the SIL as uncontested leaders, with 3,500 missionaries in the evangelical field, was the invention of William Cameron Townsend, founder of the Wycliffe Bible Translators of Arkansas; formerly a Bible salesman in Guatemala. To advance his missionary work and to defend it from enemies and competitors alike, Townsend devised a pseudo-scientific shield behind which it could take cover, and in due course his missionary groups were legally incorporated under the title, the Summer Institute of Linguistics.

For the purposes of his supporters back in the Bible Belt at home, Wycliffe Bible Translators remained the zealous proselytizers of old, concerned only with carrying the Gospel to the heathen. Once overseas, missionaries were at least nominally transformed into linguistic investigators, wholly absorbed in scientific studies of language. To some of his followers, there was a disquieting element of deception in this double posture, maintained even when entering into contracts with foreign governments. In soothing troubled consciences Townsend went so far as to quote divine subterfuge as a precedent. The US anthropologist David Stoll, in *Is God An American?*, describes Townsend's argument that '1. God led us into the policy. 2. Businessmen do the same. 3. SIL's host government thinks it's fine, and 4. There is a Biblical precedent for it. Namely, just as Jesus came out of Nazareth disguised very effectively as a carpenter, Wycliffe Missionaries go into the field as linguists. Asks Townsend: Was it honest for the son of God to come down to earth and live among men without revealing who he was?'

Whether or not the Dual Identity ruse is honest there is no doubt as to its success and its continued employment whenever found necessary until this day. Despite the use of linguistics as a scientific front for less than scientific activities, a huge amount of biblical translation goes on, much as some of it may appear to an outsider of doubtful utility, or devoid of essentially religious content. Missionaries prefer to deal in Old Testament fulminations with little application

100

to our times, or in the Epistles of St Paul. Quotations from the religious founder himself are generally avoided and in particular its central inspiration, the Sermon On The Mount. I have never seen in any missionary writing a reference to the blessedness of the poor, or the desirability of storing up treasure in heaven.

Sent to Brazil by the *Sunday Times* while the great Indian scandal was at its height, Donald McCullin, the photographer, was recommended by the PRO at the Ministry of the Interior, to go and take photographs of the Kadiweus—often referred to as the Indian Cavaliers—a mounted tribe of which the Brazilians were inordinately proud. They lived in a remote place, so he was obliged to travel by missionary plane, and the missionary put him up. At the Ministry someone had clearly blundered, for of the Kadiweus, whose land had been stolen, all who remained were a few sick and starving women and children who rode their skeletal horses each morning down to the mission house to beg for scraps. The missionary seemed indifferent to their plight. He was lost in a single all-absorbing task; the translation of the Epistle of the Galatians into Kadiweu. He had given ten years of his life to this, he told Donald, and expected to finish the work in another ten years. 'But won't all these people be dead by then?' Donald asked.

'Yes, they will,' the missionary agreed.

'Then what's the point of the whole exercise?' Donald wanted to know.

The missionary thought about this. 'It's something I cannot explain,' he said. 'Something I could never make you understand.'

Almost certainly Janus-faced Summer Institute of Linguistics men had been among my early missionary contacts, but none of them had ever revealed their affiliations. When I met a member of the SIL, proclaimed as such for the first time, it was by pure chance shortly after the upheavals in Brazil had settled, and outrage at the genocide practised on that country was now directed at Bolivia and Paraguay. Here, from the little news that filtered through, things went on as before.

Bolivia remained the second poorest country in Latin America, with cocaine as its principal export, and where a high proportion of German immigrants arriving since the last war had remained loyal to the Nazi political philosophy. The attitude to its Indian minorities was such that on my first day in La Paz, a column inch in the newspaper *Presencia* announced that an army special-force trained by the US Rangers had been sent to clear the Indian population from a large estate acquired in the north of the country by the president's wife.

I was there in the hope of meeting the German anthropologist Jürgen Riester who was conducting a study of the migrant cane-cutters brought down annually to work on the estates round Santa Cruz. Almost all of these are debt-slaves, the debts they are induced to incur mounting every year, so that they are bound for life to a particular employer; as their children, legally inheriting the debt, will be bound to him, too.

While waiting for Riester's arrival I decided to fill in time with a visit to the north of the country, taking in if possible the Bolivian First Lady's now notorious estates. To be able to do this, the sanction of the Ministry of the Interior was required, and I went there and saw an Under-Secretary, Dr Guido Strauss. As far as his department was concerned, there was no problem, said the doctor, adding, to my astonishment, that I should also require the permission of Mr Victor Halterman, of the Summer Institute of Linguistics. I told Dr Strauss that I found this astonishing, to which he laughingly replied that he did, too. Not only that, he added with a wry grin, but that even if he as a fairly high-ranking government official decided—which God forbid—to visit such a remote and barbarous part of the country, he would have to go cap in hand to Mr Halterman before this could be arranged. I asked him. 'What's going on up there?' and he said, 'God knows. I expect it's something to do with the CIA.' I never met a Bolivian who did not regard the Summer Institute of Linguistics as the base for CIA operations in Bolivia; possibly in South America itself.

The mildness of Mr Victor Halterman's personality came

102

as a surprise after learning something of his reputation. His reticence and modesty were reflected in his bare office in a ramshackle building. He was engaged on the telephone when I entered, taking a shopping order—from his wife, and there was some problem about finding the bag. Shoved into a corner at the back of the cheap furniture stood a splendid object of carved wood and macaw's feathers, an Indian god, said the missionary, that had been joyously surrendered to him by some of his converts. The other decoration was a coloured photograph of a Chacobo Indian wearing handsome nose-tusks, and a long gown of bark.

The presence of these reminders of the Indians' uncivilized past came as a surprise, because, in the mood of the Pilgrim Fathers, most missionaries frown on all such things; banning personal adornments of every kind, unless produced in a modern factory, as well as outlawing musical instruments, and jollifications of any kind in missionary compounds. Mr Halterman was more liberal in his outlook. Indians might dress up as they pleased and even sing and dance, but only in a 'folkloric' spirit, i.e. as long as such activities were stripped of any possibility of a hidden 'superstitious significance'.

I learned with surprise that Mr Halterman was an official of the Bolivian Ministry of Culture and Education. He had a close relationship with the government, he said, and found them most helpful in their support of his missionary work.

It may be in acknowledgement of this official co-operation that the biblical text that features most prominently in the SIL's well produced promotional literature is Romans 13:1, offered in Spanish and eight Indian translations. The Institute's text is at variance both with that of the English Revised Version of the Bible, and its Spanish equivalent. *'Let every soul be subject unto the higher powers'* becomes *'Obey your legal superiors, because God has given them command,'* while the SIL quite remarkably re-translates *'The powers that be are ordained by God'* as *'There is no government on earth that God has not permitted to come to power.'* General Banzer who seized control of the country in 1971 would certainly have approved.

103

Mr Halterman agreed that the SIL, as well as the two other leading evangelical missions, were religious fundamentalists, and therefore ready with a tooth and nail defence of every line of the Holy Writ, including the world's literal creation in six days, and Eve's origin as a rib from Adam's side.

Fundamentalists also believe that all the non-Christians of this world, including those who have never heard of the existence of the Christian faith, are doomed to spend eternity in hell. As the printed doctrinal statement of the New Tribes Mission—with whose theology Mr Halterman said he was in complete agreement—puts it: 'We believe in the unending punishment of unsaved.' Thus are consigned to hell not only all those millions brought up as Jews, Muslims, Hindus or Buddhists, but all the unimaginable multitudes of good and great men born into this world before the advent of Christ. It was revealed in *Time*'s study entitled *The New Missionary* that a fundamentalist missionary interviewed by their reporter had 'trouble acknowledging Catholics as fellow Christians'. Both SIL and New Tribes made it clear that converts other than those they share are hardly better placed in the salvation stakes than outright pagans.

'He comes,' as the missionaries never cease to quote, 'not that Man shall continue to live in the world, but shall be with Him in the hereafter.' The unimportance of a comfortable earthly life, weighed in the balance against the threat of eternal punishment in the next, inspires many missionaries to gather souls at all costs, often with disregard for the converts' welfare in this world.

'We have a very limited medical programme,' Mr Halterman agreed, and one could be sure he meant what he said.

William Cameron Townsend had invented a kind of pseudo-religious newspeak, by which the onus for missionary activities, which may be seen to the outsider as devious or even immoral, is placed upon God. When Townsend admitted to an underhand re-allocation of funds, contributed for scientific purposes, to church building, he spoke of the 'out-workings of God's unfolding plan for salvation'. This was the way missionaries, who had picked up the habit, still spoke. Not so Mr Halterman, who came straight to the point. 'A number of Indians remain in forest areas designated for white occupation,' he said gently. 'They are a dangerous nuisance as it is, and they must go. Our task is to ease their passage.' He described the method by which the occasional surviving Indian tribe was eased out of its natural environment.

'When we learn of the presence of an uncontacted group,' said the missionary, 'we move into the area, build a strong shelter—say of logs—and cut paths radiating from it into the forest. We leave gifts along these paths—knives, axes, mirrors, the kind of things that Indians can't resist—and sometimes they leave gifts in exchange. After a while the relationship develops. Maybe they are mistrustful at first, but in the end they stop running away when we show, and we get together and make friends.'

But the trail of gifts leads inevitably to the mission compound, and here, often at the end of a long journey, far from the Indian's sources of food, his fish, his game, it comes abruptly to an end.

'We have to break their dependency on us next,' Mr Halterman said. 'Naturally they want to go on receiving all those desirable things we've been giving them, and sometimes it comes as a surprise when we explain that from now on if they want to possess them they must work for money. We don't employ them, but we can usually fix them up with something to do on the local farms. They settle down at it when they realize that there's no going back.'

'Wouldn't something to do on a local farm sometimes amount to slavery?' I suggested.

He considered the word. 'No, not a slavery,' he said. 'But the work can be hard. We do our best to check abuses. Sometimes they occur, but whatever can be done, we do.'

8

A few days later I linked up with Jürgen Riester who had arrived in Santa Cruz de la Sierra, capital of the eastern lowlands of Bolivia. What distinguished Riester from perhaps the majority of anthropologists, preferring to conduct their studies in an atmosphere of scientific detachment, was a habit that compelled him not merely to gather and evaluate data but immerse himself in causes. Among other scientific works he was the author of *Indians of Eastern Bolivia* (IWGIA, Copenhagen) and, with an all too close experience of what happens to those Indians, was prepared to take time from his academic work to do what he could about it.

Riester's account had been largely devoted to the migrant Indian cane-cutters and cotton pickers, some 40–50,000 of whom are imported into the lowlands for a season of up to three months each year. The men worked a 15-hour day, starting at 3 am by moonlight or the light of kerosene flares, except on Sunday when 13 hours were worked. Pay was the equivalent of 50p per day, although this was subject to various rake-offs and deductions. Those we saw were housed in dreadful conditions in airless barracoons, where they slept, sexes mixed, and tightly packed in rows. Where there were children these were just piled on the adults. Being accustomed to the cold, clear air of the high plateaux of the Andes, where they are recruited, these Indians suffered from the tropical heat and the incessant attacks of insects that made life unbearable to them. Many became sick, and watch was kept to see that those likely to die could be shipped out back to the highlands. The only medicine, supplied impartially to those suffering from tuberculosis, enteritis or snakebite, was aspirin. Indians were obliged to buy supplies from company stores where up to ten times normal prices were charged.

Worst of all, these tens of thousands of Indians were locked into a system of debt slavery, from which there was no escape. Any attempting to default would be hunted down and sentenced to long terms of imprisonment. In all these backward, under-developed, missionized, dictator-ridden countries, there was slavery under one guise or another whichever way you looked.

Riester's arrival from Germany with three female co-workers had been strategically timed so that they could be on the scene for the end of the season, within days of the arrival of the ramshackle buses in which the migrants would be transported back to the Andes. This had been arranged so as to defeat the annual practice by which those Indians, who—despite all forms of plunder and extortion—had managed to put aside a few pesos, could be relieved of them.

The only object—the single article of luxury every migrant family wanted to possess—was a chair. This after the long summer of labour was the symbol of survival and reward. To be able to take a chair back to their furniture-less Andean shack and display it proudly to admiring neighbours was the height of Indian ambition. The company store carried a stock of chairs but few families had scraped together the money to pay the company's price for one, and a surrender to the temptation to take one on credit only dragged a family deeper into debt.

At this point Riester and his team of ladies went to work. Riester found a loophole in the company's contract by which he contended they were only compelled to buy provisions from the store. He then went to a furniture manufacturer in Santa Cruz de la Sierra and bought all the chairs required at factory prices. I helped them load up a hired truck with chairs, and they took them back to the estate and handed them over to the Indians. I was dazed with admiration not only by Riester's resourcefulness, but his courage. By this action he made enemies of ruthless men and placed himself in danger. In Santa Cruz hired gunmen worked to a tariff: they would kill someone of slight importance for 100 pesos (£3). An average citizen could be removed from the scene for about ten times that amount, and a foreigner's elimination might cost as much as 3,000 pesos. It was still less than £100. This in Bolivia was the way accounts were settled.

Glancing through the local newspaper, *Presencia*, soon after my arrival, I was struck by an item that read almost as an ugly fairy story in the calm and security of the Santa Cruz Holiday Inn. The story described the kind of misadventure that could befall a group of forest Indians—in this case Ayoreo refugees from a missionary camp—who had wandered away down a long traffic-choked road, finding themselves in the end, bewildered and dazzled and deafened by the clamour, and unable to make themselves understood, in the streets of a boom city. They camped out on a strip of urban garden at the side of one of the busiest roads where the women prostituted themselves, to get food, behind the shelter of low flowering shrubs. It was probable that few citizens of Santa Cruz would have noticed they were there.

One of the male Ayoreos, a young man called Cañe, was washing his clothes one evening when he heard screams coming from a car parked nearby in which two men were attacking a girl. He ran to the girl's aid and the two men drove off but soon returned with a police car. In this, after a thorough beating, Cañe was driven to the police station where, as he was unable to give any account of himself, a specialized piece of machinery was used in an attempt to break his wrists and, when that failed, a policeman simply drew his gun and shot him through the head. The bullet entered the right side of the head, low down, behind the ear, and exited some inches further away, astonishingly without damage to the brain.

What is unusual about this story, presented by the *Presencia* writer with no more passion than if he had been reporting an accident to a bus, was that not only had Cañe survived a bullet through his head, but that he had then been sent to hospital. In Latin America it is almost unthinkable that an ambulance should be sent for an Indian.

I mentioned this case some days later to Jürgen Riester and it was decided that we should go and see if the Ayoreos were still there. Learning that Cañe—now released from hospital—and the rest of the fugitive group were still to be seen on a piece of waste ground outside the Brazil station we took an interpreter and went in a taxi to talk to him.

The taxi driver had some reason to know where the Ayoreos were to be found, because he mentioned that he had had intercourse with one of the women only a few days before. As sexual partners he found the Ayoreos very satisfactory, he said. They were cheap, the price being 5 pesos (13p) a visit, and much more gracious and natural in their manner than the ordinary hard-bitten prostitutes of the city with whom he was normally obliged to consort. On the other hand, whereas girls in the brothels underwent regular medical inspection the Ayoreos did not, with inevitable results. He now awaited with anxiety the possible appearance of dread symptoms.

It was early evening, and to me there was something faintly satanic about the scene outside the Brazil station. A new dual carriageway had been cut through here, and there had been some attempt to dispel the rawness of the environment by plantings of palms and hibiscus, and by decorative street lighting. In between the swish of traffic and the brazen uproar of car-horns the sob and wail of cassette-music came from the double-parked cars. An amphitheatre of electric signs enclosed the lower part of the sky.

We found the Ayoreos as promised, and at the moment of our arrival some half dozen middle-aged women were at work to prepare as many nubile girls, whose bodies would provide survival for them all, for the night's work. The older women and the men were still in the dismal regalia and the sad sacks of the mission camp, but mini-skirts and T-shirts had been bought for the girls—each of them nursing her baby—and one or two of them sported new shoes with bright buckles. Make-up was being applied using tiny jungle tools with breathless concentration and considerable skill, although the attempt to lighten a normal Ayoreo swarthiness by the application of white powder produced a slightly ghastly effect. In the end the girls were ready, kneeling, eyes downcast, the great clamour of the city about them, bright reflections of headlights and advertising signs crawling over their cheeks, babies cradled in their arms at the pavement's edge. There was something profoundly formal about the sight, oriental rather than Indian, an act of submission

109

to destiny. Not one of them had so much as glanced in our direction.

The men busied themselves in small ways among the background shadows of the trees. The younger ones looked extremely strong. Through selective breeding necessary to survive in the daunting environment of the 'Green Hell' of the Chaco, the Ayoreos have developed perhaps the most imposing physique of the Indian races, making a fetish of manly strength. To acquire status and marry well a man had to be prepared to tackle a jaguar at close quarters in such a way that the maximum amount of scarring was left by the encounter on his limbs and torso. Physically the brawny Ayoreos were the antithesis of the nimble, mountaineering Huichols. When Cañe was found we were confronted with a young Samson, and although he spoke nothing but Ayoreo it was clear that he was amused that even with their wrist-breaking machine the police had been unable to break his wrists. They had thrown him into the street at the back of the police station at a time when by the greatest good fortune he had attracted the attention and curiosity of a passing doctor, surprised that a man with such a wound should be not only alive but conscious.

The wound in the back of his head was still raw and suppurating with no dressing on it, and before displaying it he cleaned it as best he could with a wad of cotton waste. A number of ribs had been broken by the beating he had received, but these caused him no trouble. He had been taken by a missionary as a boy from the Chaco during an army attack on the tribe and had seen his father and mother killed by the soldiers. Since then he had slaved for farmers, being rewarded with an occasional cast-off garment and enough rice to keep alive. And then he and his companions could stand no more of the life in the mission camp and wandered away, following first a jungle track, then the railway line, then another road that brought them to Santa Cruz.

Strangely he seemed in no way embittered by this unprovoked attack that had nearly cost him his life but was, rather, smiling and jubilant at his escape—and this was character-istic of the way the Indians saw life.

Now the first customer had driven up, parked and locked his car and was strolling in our direction. The girls knelt as if carved in stone. Cañe wiped a small smear of blood from his head and we turned to go, promising to return with some rubber sheeting of which Riester kept a stock, for the rains were due to start.

The Indians had decamped from a South American Mission station in the jungle near the village of Pailón, some twenty kilometres away. Riester suggested that we should go down there next day and see what was happening, and this we did.

We left before dawn next day in Riester's Land Rover, and found the missionary camp at the end of a jungle track, along which threatening notices had been posted in the hope of keeping visitors away. Nearer the centre of the camp grimed and dishevelled women and children squatted round a fire on which a tortoise was being cooked. Riester, offered a blackened claw, took this and chewed it with every appear-ance of satisfaction, and later tried a bone covered with a furry layer of putrefaction that was being passed round to be gnawed. In the centre of the camp we found a large wooden hut with several male Ayoreos propped against its walls and keeping themselves upright by holding onto the overhanging rafters with their hands. These men were dazed with apathy and unable or unwilling to speak. When some hours later we left the camp their position had not changed, and one of the German girls suggested that they might be willing themselves to die.

While the New Tribes Mission had been allotted the Ayoreos removed from the jungle in the Paraguayan sector of the Gran Chaco, those in Bolivia had become the charge of the South American Mission Society. Of these, 275—a substantial proportion of the survivors—had been rounded up with their jaguar-scarred chief. He presented himself to us in all his dignity, wearing a motorcycle crash-helmet. This was removed for us to inspect a deep cleft in his forehead where he had attempted to commit suicide, using an axe.

111

A commotion began, led by some weeping women, who had broken through to tell us that the camp's water-supply had been cut off as a punishment for some offence, and that many sick children in the camp had been without water for some days. It seemed a matter of urgency to do something to rectify this situation so we went to see the missionary, Mr Depue, whose trim compound was adjacent to the bedraggled camp area. The missionaries occupied a substantial but unpretentious house and one was immediately aware of crated machinery that had arrived or was waiting to be taken away; the radio mast, the generator's throb, the cases of Dr Pepper's empties, and the line-up by the door of sturdy imported toys. Mr Depue and his family were at lunch when we arrived and we were shown into an anteroom within sight of the Depues at their meal, which they consumed slowly and in absolute silence. After Mr Depue had said grace the family rose from the table and marched wordlessly away, and Mr Depue joined us, a lean, shaven-headed man reminiscent rather of the male figure in Grant Wood's well known picture, *American Gothic*.

He unhesitatingly confirmed that he had ordered a collective punishment he believed most likely to be effective to deal with a case in which two or three children had broken into a store and stolen petrol. There was to be no more water until the culprits were found, and brought into his compound there to be publicly thrashed.

'Would you be administering the thrashing, Mr Depue?' I asked.

'That is my intention,' he said, 'although I should not be averse to supervising the necessary chastisement undertaken by another person. But I'm afraid that's unlikely.'

He went on to explain that the situation was a difficult one because in all the many years he had spent as a missionary he had never heard of a single instance of an Indian punishing a child, which was to say that the conception of corrective chastisement seemed to be beyond their grasp. Mr Depue spoke of this aversion to punishment as of some genetic defect inherited and shared by the whole race. It had now come to a trial of strength, a test-case. He hoped as much

112

for his own sake as for the Ayoreos' that it would soon be resolved.

'Why do you say that?' I asked.

'Because we are in the same boat with them. Whatever discomfort they may be experiencing is being shared by us. I have ordered the water to be cut off to the mission house, too.'

It occurred to me that before taking this step Mr Depue might have prudently arranged for a reserve supply, because both water and soft drinks had been in evidence at their midday meal.

Mr Depue happened to have read the newspaper account of Cañe's misfortune, and remembered that he himself had 'brought him in' during a pacification drive in the Chaco. 'Three or four youngsters including this fellow became separated in the panic from the rest of the tribe. I kept out of sight and sent Ayoreo-speaking Indians to offer them a better life, and to persuade them to come in, and they did.'

We stood at the door of the mission house looking down over the scene of Mr Depue's endeavours, over the planning and order of the mission compound, the chapel where frequent prayer-meetings were conducted and a low dais for speech-making, where it was to be supposed the public thrashing would take place. Beyond that the cleared area was strewn with pitiful litter, and the shed was still in sight with Ayoreos clinging by their arms to the roof-rafters. One hundred and fifty yards away the dry secondary scrub forest began. The Indians told our Ayoreo-speaker that nothing lived in it: it had been cleaned out by the dispossessed Indians and not a bird, not a snake, not an edible grub remained. The tortoise eaten that day had been thrown to them by a local farmer who had visited the camp to discuss some business with the missionary.

'And do you still believe that this is a better life?' I asked Mr Depue.

'Yes,' he said. 'I cannot describe to you in words how much better it is.'

'The Ayoreos who left the camp and went to Santa Cruz,'

I told him, 'are living on the women's earnings from prostitution.'

'There would be little alternative,' he said.

'How do you feel about that?'

'I leave it to you to imagine my feelings,' Mr Depue said, 'and I am only comforted by the knowledge that a soul once truly saved can never be lost.'

The first great intervention by the missionaries in the Bolivian Chaco had been led by William Pencille, of the South American Missionary Society, called in when white cattlemen moving into the tribal area ran up against the Ayoreos. Pencille established a friendly contact, persuaded the Ayoreos to give up their resistance, and settled them on a barren patch of land by the side of the railway line, where within a matter of a few weeks 300 Indians died of influenza.

There can be no doubt that it would have been possible for the missionary, who had a jeep, an aeroplane and funds at his disposal, to save the lives of these people. But Pencille was convinced that 'It's better they should die. Then I baptize them (on the point of death) and they go straight to heaven'. (Extract from a conversation between William Pencille and Father Elmar Klinger, OFM, quoted by Luis A. Pereira in *The Bolivian Instance*.)

Mr Depue's successful collaboration with the Bolivian Army, as described to me, was probably the last operation of its kind, after which it is believed that no Ayoreos were left at large in Bolivia.

The once virtually impenetrable jungle of thorn-scrub and swamps, known as the Gran Chaco, sometimes referred to as the 'Green Hell', covers an area of roughly 1,600 square miles and is divided by Bolivia and Paraguay. As far as is known, the last of the Bolivian Ayoreos had been cleared out of the Bolivian sector to the north of the operation in which Mr Depue was engaged, although possibly 1,500 remained in Paraguay. Ranchers and oil prospectors began to move into the area. In 1942 General Alfredo Stroessner, dictator of Paraguay, gave a contract to the New Tribes Mission of Florida 'to settle and civilize' the Indians of the Chaco, later presenting them with 2,500 hectares of land.

It was a task which the missionaries set out to accomplish with considerable vigour and, as one can gather from the accounts of the day, with the assistance of the Paraguayan airforce. In 1943 the first of many Indian hunts by the missionaries in Bolivia had taken place, in the course of which five missionaries were killed.

Missionary descriptions of such operations are often disarmingly simple and direct—all the more so because it has always been NTM policy to recruit young evangelists of limited education, who are not always discreet. *God Planted Five Seeds*, by Jean Dye Johnson, a classic of its kind, is the account of a young missionary wife, soon to become a widow.

When the Johnsons arrived in Bolivia it is not at all certain from the wife's account that they realized that they were in the same continent as the United States. Only once in 213 pages does she refer to Indians, and then in quotes, as if real Indians were to be found only in North America. Otherwise the mission is out to capture 'naked savages', or *bárbaros*.

Mrs Johnson refers in terms of rather dreamlike detachment to the killing of naked savages and a single quotation is enough to convey some idea of what the process of capture and conversion must have been like for those subjected to it.

We did not know then how clever the Ayoreo were at hiding from the very sight of a plane. A captive bárbaro *later explained how everyone threw himself on the ground at the first sound in the air. A mother would prostrate herself over her child to keep him from moving, her brown body blending into perfect camouflage with the jungle browns and greens.*

115

There is no criticism of these happenings. No sympathy for the Indian mother's heart-rending predicament.

We were more than ever determined to win these souls to Christ when the Ayoreos, driven in their extremity out of the jungle, came in.

Mrs Johnson noted that the householders, 'most of whom owned ranches or farms just out of town were shameless in their desire to get their hands on some Ayoreo who would become a labourer without pay'.

Many neighbouring ranches already were using Ayoreos as workers, most of whom had been captured as children. Now the townspeople looked them over calculatingly, picking out likely prospects.

The use in this passage of the adjective 'shameless' is the single example of implied criticism in this book of the servitude imposed on the Indians. For years Mrs Johnson lived among 'captives' and 'labourers without pay', but the word 'slave' is never used. On a single occasion she expressed regret for the murder of an Indian.

He (Paul Fleming, founder and head of the NTM) was troubled by the fact that the second search party had killed a savage.

With this in mind also, Dorothy (one of the missionary wives) answered Paul's letter.

It might only mean that more savages would be killed, and sent into Christless graves. We came down here to reach them not to kill them.

Mrs Johnson's concern here is likely to have been less with the death of a savage, which was a matter of frequent occurrence, than with the mission's responsibility for a soul's condemnation to everlasting hell.

9

Undeterred by world opinion the manhunts have gone on,
the last of these on 30 December 1986, resulting in the
deaths of five missionized Indians of the NTM's 'contact'
force. Following this, newly 'contacted' Indians were carried
off to the NTM base at Campo Loro, where, according to
a report received by Survival International, they all suc-
cumbed to newly introduced diseases. Following this incident the NTM's Director in Paraguay told Survival International:

*'We do not go after people any more. We just provided
transport.' However, at a subsequent meeting with Survival
International in Florida, the NTM's chairman, Macon G.
Hare, confirmed that the NTM remains committed to 'contact work'. He acknowledged that the NTM is currently
trying to 'bring in unreached tribes' in Brazil, Colombia
and Bolivia.*

In a later exchange of views, Les Pederson, the NTM
Field Co-ordinator for Latin America said that he did not
know how many of the newly-contacted Indians had survived. 'We don't keep that kind of detailed record,' he said,
adding, 'they're all pretty mixed up with the others down
there and those Indians all look pretty much the same.'
Contact work, one learns from a study of the missionary
publications, when not undertaken by the missionaries themselves is confined to native 'deacons'. These, in the style of
the London Missionary Society's police of old, carry guns.
At this time some 850 Ayoreos thus contacted are in NTM
camps, and a very large, but unrecorded number have died.
Cultural Survival, a US organization not wholly unsympa-
thetic to missionary endeavour, admitted that inmates of an
NTM camp visited by their representatives were held there

against their will. In the legal sense, therefore, they had been kidnapped.

Missionary accounts of such activities display almost incredible insensitivity. Thus a letter back home from the McClure family dated March 1979 reads:

Dear Prayer Partners,
Early last year we asked you to claim 1978 as the year we contacted the Totobigosode or 'pig people'. The following is what your prayers have effected.

It started the 28th December when Bruce Higham and I took 27 Moro men (mission 'deacons') to a site about 200 kilometres from El Faro . . . It was evident that the 'pig people' were in this area . . . When the El Faro men were close they started shouting their names, and that they had come in peace. To this the 'pig people' shouted back, 'These men are saying that they come in peace but what if it is a trick, because they have done this to us long ago.'

The turning point seemed to come when Cadui, one of the El Faro men, threw his rifle behind him and walked forward. There were 12 men and 8 women. However, they had to wait three days before all the women were rounded up; they were scared to death. One lady was injured when she fell from a tall tree. [She broke a leg in two places, and was obliged to walk back to the mission on it, and subsequently died. In a previous encounter with the mission's 'tame' Indians her right breast had been shot off.] It was a joyous occasion when we arrived at the mission station . . . The El Faro Indians and missionaries are just praising the Lord for his faithfulness in bringing this all about. There were so many little events which could have gone wrong had it not been for the Lord's timing . . . An interesting note to add to all this is that the fierce chief of the El Faro Moro [missionized Indians] Dejai, who had led so many raids against the 'pig people' in the years past, died of old age only two days before 'the pig people' arrived.

Reaching the lost for Christ,
The McClures.

Describing this exploit to Luke Holland of Survival International Lane McClure, its organizer, described the system of 'grabbing'. When El Faro 'deacons' entered the Indian village they 'grabbed' members of the other group and became their owners. A missionary said, 'They're so sold out on Christianity and the Lord that they witness in this manner—by grabbing one of the Pig People. People who are grabbed are in a way slaves of the ones who grabbed them.'

Another missionary said, 'The Pig People who were brought in recently didn't keep many children because it was too hard to run away. They killed many children.' To this sombre account a further missionary report adds in the most casual fashion. 'One woman buried two of her children alive.'

From the modest if violent beginnings in Paraguay the NTM never looked back. In 1945 it expanded into India, in 1946 into Venezuela, and in 1949 into Brazil, New Guinea and Japan. By 1952 there were mission in the Philippines, and Thailand. Expansion followed rapidly in Latin America, Africa and the Far East. At present NTM claims to have about 2,500 evangelists in 24 countries, working with 159 tribes. Most missionary children are sent to MK (Missionary Kid) boarding schools where they are brought up in the fundamentalist faith. The hard-liners of the NTM are discouraged from socializing with 'liberal' missionaries. Marriage with non-Americans is 'strongly advised against'. The sect is authoritarian. Leaders, unlike those of the SIL—which appears by comparison as a hotbed of liberalism—are not elected but appointed to their posts.

Both the SIL and the NTM have met with great resistance in the countries in which they have established missions; both sects have been excluded from a number of these, but have always succeeded in making a return. This strange invulnerability has aroused increasing resentment in countries involved, with complaints of behind-scenes pressure permitting this to happen.

In the matter of the techniques of evangelization, the SIL with a better educated membership is more sophisticated; the NTM more aggressive. It is also persistent. Back in 1972 the NTM—to use its own description of the operation—'was constrained by God to contact the primitive Macu Indians in Colombia . . . Because of the uncertainty of the Indians' moods our men decided to build their house in the middle of a lake in the contact area.' On this island they sat for ten years. Frequent progress reports appeared in the NTM's house journal *Brown Gold*. The Indians, the missionaries reported, showed great fear, as well they might have, for— doubtless through editorial slip-ups—guns came into the picture again. Words were at last exchanged between the missionaries and a Macu group. The journal reports, 'They also remembered the fear that held them in hiding. "Would you have killed us with your shotgun back there?" an Indian cries out.'

The Lord was constantly at the missionaries' side, nevertheless the outcome of the long struggle remained undecided. The missionaries had crossed the lake to reach the shore when the Macu counter-attacked and the retreat was sounded.

> the men pointed their blowguns at us. They moved towards us and started shooting. Banana trees obstructed the view of us as we quickly moved down the bank and down into the water. The Lord had graciously arranged for our canoe to be untied and floating a little distance off-shore. Darts were falling all round us as we swam and dove and made our way to the canoe.

Five years further on, a handful of free Indians are still there.

Over the years *Brown Gold* has reported all the missionary triumphs, and the occasional setback such as this. The magazine offers invaluable insight into the missionary mind and a view of religion which seems often strange to one brought up in a background of orthodox Christian belief. God is personal and close, but the fearful majesty of the

Creator of the Universe has departed. The deity of the old London Missionary Society might well have been a pre-Victorian mill-owner with an interest in the slave trade; here we have a small-town American politician of ultra right-wing persuasion, who can be flattered, cajoled, bargained with—occasionally even deceived.

The missionaries' God is readily available for consultation on monetary matters and direct contacts are promptly made. Henry W. Frost tells how his financial problems were solved. 'God kept asking, "Why do you keep talking about $2,000 when it's $6,000 that is needed?"

"But Lord, how could I ever raise $6,000."
'His reassurance was firm, "I'll take care of it."'

Tim Wayma, writing from Bolivia, recommends unflagging praise, 'If your objective is to glorify God, don't hesitate to interest yourself in the project. It pays handsome dividends in both temporal and eternal perspectives.'

However, May Wheatley, in Indonesia, whose plane had crashed, administered a mild rebuke, 'God's timing is always perfect, although there are times when we are tempted to doubt it.'

The devil, too, is close and familiar in the missionary world, conducting what is presented as a fairly evenly matched struggle with God, from what is referred to as 'his unchallenged domain'. The struggle, it is to be assumed, has been going on since the beginning of the world. God and the devil are seen as co-eternal—an ancient heresy which ravaged the Church in the early days, and which now after so many centuries would appear to have made an astonishing re-appearance in Sanford, Florida.

Evil remains undefeated, and therefore God is less than all-powerful. If there is nothing extraordinary to the missionaries' thinking that God should graciously arrange for their canoe to be untied and afloat when pursued by the Macu, it must appear equally unremarkable if Satan had sneaked back to tie it up again. There is no small piece of mischief overlooked by Satan in his campaign of harassment, from delaying a plane to provoking infection in a cut finger. Ken Springsteen in West New Britain describes the long persecution thus suffered: 'Our adversary is diligent to oppose us, and he does all he can to discourage our efforts to penetrate his dark domain. We had storms at sea, a shipwreck, thieves and deceivers to contend with . . . I lost a finger . . . infection and blood poisoning followed.'

On the psychological front Don Schlatter reports little success against Satan's crafty campaign to induce the Lawa of Thailand to have a good time. 'Satan is trying his best to get them to follow worldly amusements, worldly pleasures . . . However, God is also in action.' A more subtle piece of diabolism is the whispering in the ears of the Lord's unmarried people. 'You're single and you're a failure'—thus undermining missionary self-esteem and resolve.

At least there is one piece of good news from New Guinea from converts who have inflicted a defeat on Satan by turning their backs on pleasure:

THE REASONS FOR FORSAKING SATAN'S WAYS

1. *We want to stop killing pigs and spending money for this.*

2. *Our custom of buying brides.* We could buy them for this price (K600) and later God can show us what to do. If God says Okay, it can be the price.

3. *Some more talk on marriage.* When we get married we do not want to dance, shout or be proud.

4. *Things that harm the body.* These things are smoking, betel nut chewing and beer. We want to quit all these things.

5. *Social Nights.* Galatians 5:19–20. These verses tell us that social nights is the place where a lot of sin takes place. We want to quit.

6. *Giving presents to children.* God tells us we have to work hard to get our food. Our children need to know how to work. We want to stop giving gifts to them.

Worst of all, according to missionary thought, in so evenly matched a contest between good and evil, is the news of Satan's own world evangelization programme. 'We are not told how he will finance the operation . . . (but) the most dynamic and effective conquest of people and history (scheduled to take 3½ years) is yet to come.'

We laugh, turn away and pass on, dismissing what may seem to us to be mere ravings from our mind. This the tribesman in his jungle clearing cannot do. When the missionary arrives he may never even have seen a plane before. Then suddenly a missionary air fellowship Cessna—which may even boom an amplified message to him in his own language—drops out of the sky. What he is about to hear is no more than an extended version of the doom promised on the sandwich board, but in this awe-inspiring setting it will take huge courage and strength of mind to resist.

10

In between the early journeys I lived for some years in Banchory, Kincardineshire, where to my amazement and delight it turned out that the local doctor, Stanley Lindsey, had had—for a Scotsman—an almost unique connection with Latin America. His father, an engineer, had settled in Paraguay and married a Guarani Indian; Stanley being the offspring of this highly successful union. The mingling of Nordic and Indian strains had produced an interesting result. Although somewhat swarthy in appearance in an environment of pink-cheeked Highlanders, Stanley would have seemed otherwise, by a comparison of photographs of the two men, to be very definitely his father's son. Yet temperamentally the two were in all probability poles apart. One assumes the father to have embodied the characteristics and virtues of the Scottish people. The son may have possessed these, too, but if so they were submerged beneath those of the more vivacious sort. He was mercurial, full of explosive enthusiasms, and set apart by sensitivity and charm of an unfamiliar kind that I suspected could only have been inherited from the non-European side of his ancestry.

We became the closest of friends. Stanley jumped at the chance to talk to anyone of his Paraguayan childhood, which had been extraordinary enough, for he had lived the kind of life that other boys of his day could only have read of in the unlikeliest of adventure books. The boys attended school for two days a week before being released to glorious freedom. Indians taught them to use the bow and arrow, to manage a canoe through the rapids, and spear fish. They were expected to play at least two musical instruments, one of these being the obligatory harp, with which they serenaded their *novias* in courtships that began at fourteen.

So, too, did vendettas, and at puberty a boy was likely, through no fault of his own, to find himself enmeshed in one of those inextinguishable quarrels left over from so many wars and revolutions. At a coming-of-age ceremony a father would disclose to his son the names of a whole list of hereditary enemies, among whom one or more of his school friends might be included.

Feuds were passed down through the male line, thus leaving Stanley free from the deadly obligations they entailed. He had once come across the corpse of a man shot in ambush sprawled by the side of the road, and in accordance with local custom had picked flowers and laid them on his chest. His memories apart from that were of music, laughter and love. Paraguay as he presented it was the archetypal South America, just as Charles Darwin had seen it, untamed, barely subjugated by law, and littered in this case not only with the fossil remains of animals but those of archaic custom.

I was deeply influenced by Lindsey's accounts of a tropical paradise seen through the eyes of a boy—so much so that it became for me that part of the unknown world I most wanted to discover for myself. Some years passed before the opportunity to do so arose as the result of the chance reading of an article by a German anthropologist, Dr Mark Munzel, published in 1973 by the Danish Society International Work Group for Indigenous Affairs. This described his horrendous experiences while engaged in anthropological fieldwork in the eastern forest region of the country.

Some years previous to this the international road leading to the Iguaçu Falls and Argentina had been completed. The new road bisected a dense forest inhabited by the Aché Indians—sometimes called 'white' due to the extraordinary pallor of their skins. The price of land shot up as the lumber extraction firms, the farmers and ranchers moved in, and the inevitable clearance of the Indians began. Small-scale Indian hunts had always been a feature of this area, these being normally mounted by specialist hunters who offered their services to farmers moving into a new forest area or wishing to extend the boundaries of their current holdings in the forest. The hunters employed 'tame' Indians, known as *señuelos* to track down their free kin. There are accounts of the old persons taken on such raids being cut up and used to bait jaguar traps, the young girls being sold to houses of prostitution, and the rest disposed of as slaves. Some of the most able hunters achieved a macabre celebrity, as in the case of Pichin López who, having murdered the aged and enfeebled Achés on one of his expeditions in the year 1949, took the survivors to the town of San Juan, where—naked and in chains—they were exposed for sale in the local square. Pichin's lieutenant at that time was none other than Jesus Pereira in charge of the camp at Cecilio Baez—a settlement where Münzel happened to be working when the new, big-scale hunts began.

Pereira had become a government official and had transformed his farm, worked by a nucleus of slaves already collected in the jungle, into a reservation, first under the title of the Camp of Blessed Roque Gonzales of the Holy Cross, but then renamed National Guayaki Colony. To this were brought the jungle survivors, many of them dying there in a matter of days from starvation, and common sicknesses against which they had built up no immunity. Münzel says that food and medicines were consciously withheld. In March and April 1972, to quote Münzel's figures, 171 Achés were captured and deported to the reservation, bringing the number there to 277, of which only 202 were left at the end of July. The Congressional Record of the House of Representatives of the USA, following the subsequent enquiry, confirmed that 48.73% per cent of the reservation's population had vanished.

Münzel noted an extreme disproportion of the number of young girls in camp, but then learned that these were given by Pereira to visiting government officials. 'I was myself offered first an adult girl,' he says (the offer being made in a disguised way by a government minister—and more directly by Jesus Pereira), then, as I showed no interest, I was offered an immature girl of 11.' In other cases, Münzel says, captured Achés wives were taken from their husbands and given to the 'tame' Achés who had captured them, this policy being used by Pereira to induce 'tame' Reservation Indians to go on his manhunting expeditions. Pereira kept order in the camp in drastic fashion, describing to Münzel

126

his use of the *tronco*, originally a Brazilian device used to discipline slaves, by which a victim was crammed into a species of wooden cage which prevented him either from lying down or standing up, and in this stood in full sunshine for a whole day. A few sickly offenders failed to survive this treatment.

Münzel's account and those of other witnesses underline the nonchalant acceptance of the average Paraguayan of what was going on. Truckloads of naked captives, screaming, bleeding, vomiting over each other came out of the jungle, and one reads of a village bus turning off its route to follow one, out of nothing more than curiosity. The Paraguayan zoologist, Dr Luigi Miraglia, was present at one such incident.

> *I was on the bus to Asunción when it made the usual stop at Arroyo Guasú. We heard that* señuelos *had just brought in a large number of Achés, and all the passengers got down to see them.*

They found the Achés guarded by the *señuelos*, bathing naked in the river. A passing car stopped.

> *A woman and her two daughters got down. One of them went down to the river's bank and took a child feeding at the breast from its mother, and went with it back to the car. The woman made no attempt to stop her nor even cried out. She seemed petrified.*

Dr Miraglia rushed after the abductress and took the child back. One wonders how many more such pathetic human souvenirs were taken when the hunters came in with their prey on that, and so many other days.

All these reports were concerned with Achés rounded up for delivery to the reservation, but these were probably in the minority of the victims of the hunts, for *ABC Color*, the country's leading newspaper, carried a report that the price of orphaned Aché children had fallen to the lowest ever: 'Due to the great supply it is said to be presently at about the equivalent of 5 dollars for a girl of around 5 years of age'. Mr Luis E. Pena, Research Affiliate in Zoology at the Peabody Museum, Yale University, who had recently travelled through the interior of Eastern Paraguay, was offered an Aché child. To this the writer added the convincing detail, 'the price quoted was above the normal one.'

The publication of Dr Münzel's charges provoked an international scandal. In March 1974 the International League for the Rights of Man, joined by the Inter-American Association for Democracy and Freedom, charged the government of Paraguay with complicity in the enslavement of the Aché Indians in violation of the United Nations Charter, the Genocide Convention and the Universal Declaration of Human Rights.

The response of the Paraguayan government which did not attempt to deny that crimes had taken place—was to dismiss Pereira from his post at the reservation, although no action was taken against him and he was said to have settled on his farm, now the master of fifty slaves of his own.

Otherwise the news was discouraging, for the reservation had been taken over by the New Tribes Missionaries, who were alleged to be 'attracting' the few Achés still at large in the jungle with methods only too similar to those employed by their predecessor. Back in Frankfurt Dr Münzel produced a new report, published by IWGIA as before: *The Aché: Genocide Continues in Paraguay*.

Münzel had remained in contact with his friends back in Paraguay, and the first indication that all was far from well was contained in a letter from his correspondent, the Jesuit Father Melia, showing concern in the mysterious fall in population at the reservation. At the end of Pereira's incumbency in October 1972, it was officially stated that there were 250 Achés in the camp. A year later, after the takeover by the missionaries, the figure was given at 100: 'a decrease due whether to escapes, deaths or the selling of Indians, we do not know'. On 23 August 1973, Münzel says a visitor counted less than 25 Achés, the grotesque situation being that the Indian reservation had more American missionaries than Indian inhabitants, as the missionaries with their families totalled some 30 persons.

With a following and final letter the bombshell burst: 'The New Tribes Missionaries are now hunting Indians by motor vehicle in the region of Igatimi, in order to integrate them into the reservation.'

My interest of old in Paraguay was now re-awakened and reinforced by the concern about what I had learned—so far at second hand—about the mentality and methods of the sect. As a result I approached a London newspaper who commissioned me to go to Paraguay to investigate and report. Two months later, in October 1974, I joined forces with the photographer Donald McCullin and flew to Asunción.

The Paraguayan capital was a calm and orderly place, a little stagnant even by South American standards, and endowed with an air of face-saving respectability suggesting a forgotten corner of the Victorian era. The hotel maid dropped a curtsey, there were no drunks and few beggars about, and the streets were full of women possessing a special kind of assurance rarely to be seen in Latin American women elsewhere. Wars, revolts and revolutions had drained away the lifeblood of the country. In 1870, after the three years' struggle against the combined forces of Argentina, Uruguay and Brazil, only 28,000 Paraguayan males were left alive, and cigar-smoking, gun-slinging women ran the country for decades. Before the balance between the sexes could be restored Paraguay fought Bolivia over the wilderness of the Gran Chaco. After that, in 1947 the Civil War broke out, and in the five years that followed a half million Paraguayans slaughtered one another. There were still not enough men to go round. Asunción was full of jack-booted women policewomen clumping up and down the street. We were told that there was no petty crime, and this was something we could believe.

We arrived without baggage, this having been off-loaded at Sao Paulo, and it was two days before it turned up, at which point a small, disquieting fact emerged. There was no sign of the lock on my suitcase having been tampered with, and when opened everything in the case was in order and intact, except a brand-new mosquito net in the makers' wrapping. This had been unfolded, then re-folded not quite as before. To one's first somewhat neutral impression of the city was added a whiff of secret manoeuvrings and a hint of menace. I began to suspect that we might be under scrutiny by unseen eyes.

It had been suggested that I should see Father Melía, and the anthropologist Chase Sardi, both active in the Aché Affair. Father Melía was 'away' and in reply to my letter I received a photostat copy of a letter of protest on the subject of the Aché he had sent to *La Tribuna*—a reaction suggesting that he felt a need for caution. Chase Sardi received me in a somewhat conspiratorial environment, and I was afraid that I might be placing him at risk. I told him that we wanted to visit the Aché reservation, and he said that we would require the permission of the Ministry of Defence, which almost certainly would not be given. In this case, he suggested going there by village bus, permit or no permit, adding the recommendation that we should hire two *personas de confianza* to see to it that nothing happened to us. 'Otherwise,' he said, 'you might disappear.'

The Aché reservation at Cecilio Baez was halfway across Paraguay in the direction of the frontier with Argentina. The last thirty miles of the road was no better than a forest track, negotiable, it was said, only by vehicles of the Land Rover kind, and then only in good weather.

The news was that no such cars were available for hire in Asunción. We went to the British Embassy in the hope of enlisting their help. The Chargé d'Affaires thought that something might be done and a meeting was arranged with a Paraguayan, Julio Mendoza, who worked for the Embassy in some unspecified way, described as always ready to help out when he could.

There was something unusual about Mendoza, a schoolteacher by profession with some time on his hands at this moment, when the children he taught only attended classes

130

on three days a week. He was a good-looking, unsmiling man in his forties, with a perfect command of English, who it was clear had the entrée everywhere in Asunción. What was singular about him was an exceptional, although unassertive, self-confidence of manner. The feeling he gave me was of a man saturated with power, and it was hard not to suspect that he was a member of the secret police. Julio said that he possessed a battered though serviceable Citroën 2CV, which he would be happy to place at our service. Although the sun still shone strongly enough in Asunción, the rainy season was beginning and on a long journey one ran the risk of being stuck in a quagmire. In a situation like this Julio found a 2CV better than a jeep because being light it was more easily hauled out of the mud.

We discussed our project to visit the reservation and Julio agreed that a permit was essential, and offered to arrange an interview with Colonel Infanzón at the Ministry of Defence. It seemed remarkable that a mere schoolmaster should have instant access to this important personality, however there and then Julio got on the phone, and within ten minutes an interview was arranged.

Next day we were summoned into the Colonel's presence. Paraguay was a place where stereotypes had to be cast aside. There was little in Julio's appearance and manner, and sudden, cool penetrating stare to suggest a high-school teacher. It was hard, too, to believe that the Colonel, a man of mild aspect, and outstanding courteous demeanour could have been the subject of serious allegations relating to the procuring of young Indian women, in addition to being one of the dictator's right-hand men.

He seemed uneasy at our request to visit the reservation, explaining his reluctance by the circumstance that a 'French couple' who had been there on what had been described to him as a scientific mission had filmed Achés engaged in sexual intercourse. Their film had been shown in Panama. We assured the colonel that we had no film cameras with us, and he seemed relieved. A trip might be possible, he said, but we should have to be accompanied by an officer from his department. He would also have to obtain the sanction of General Samaniego, the minister.

A wait of some days followed, which we filled in with visits to country towns in the neighbourhood of Asunción. Many of these—once early Jesuit settlements—were of great charm, and the grandiose churches of the seventeenth century remain. A superb example was that of Yaguarón, a building of such external severity as to be hardly recognizable as a church, yet which astonishes with the extravagant baroque of its interior, decorated by Indian artists.

The delay provided time for interesting interviews, notably one with the Bishop of the Chaco region, Msgr Alejo Ovelar. The bishop spoke of growing concern felt by churchmen and intellectuals throughout Latin America over the activities of 'certain missionary sects who seem indifferent to the spiritual—let alone material—welfare of the primitive peoples among whom they work, but subject them instead to commercial exploitation'. As a specific example he said that North American missionaries had set themselves up as middlemen in the Chaco region compelling Indians such as the Moros, who lived by hunting and trapping, to sell their skins through the mission. Traders who attempted to deal direct with the Moros had actually been threatened with violence. 'These missionaries,' the bishop said, 'are also implicated in the grave crime of ethnocide.'

In due course, Colonel Infanzón announced his decision. We could go to Cecilio Baez if we were prepared to give an undertaking that any article written about Paraguay would contain no evaluation of the situation of the Indians in that country. Since we proposed to avoid evaluations and deal in facts, not about 'the Indians of Paraguay' as a whole but about the Aché, it seemed possible to agree to this. The permit was then given, together with a letter of introduction to Mr Jack Stolz, 'American Missionary in charge at the Colonia Nacional Guayaki, Cecilio Baez'.

The permission in hand we saw Julio Mendoza again and arrangements were made to leave for Cecilio Baez next day. The morning started badly with a trivial local hurricane that tore the tops off a few palm trees and set the thatches

132

floating through the streets. Thereafter the weather settled unconvincingly, although the blue sky of the previous day had whitened and the horizons lost their edge. As we rattled eastwards on the paved highway to Brazil a haze spread through the landscape, and from time to time the wipers had to be switched on to clear the windscreen of mist. There were 120 miles of metalled road through the plains to reach the town of Caaguazú, and at this point we were rattling along in the old Citroën in grand style. From Caaguazú a dirt road to Cecilio Baez was in exceedingly bad condition and was expected to offer a challenge.

Julio proved a lively travelling companion, cramming the first hours of an uneventful journey through the plains with bizarre anecdotes of Paraguayan rural life. Much of this on first hearing sounded incredible but we were to learn that the incredible to us was the normality of existence in a remote country that had fallen in most ways a half-century behind the times. Paraguay had remained the poorest and probably the most violent country in Latin America. One subject Julio steered clear of; making no enquiry into the motive for our visit to Cecilio Baez. This seemed a little strange, and perhaps significant.

At Coronel Oviedo, 30 miles short of Caaguazú, solid-looking clouds bulged over the skyline ahead. Here we stopped at the Road Police post, where we were told that it was raining in eastern Paraguay, and that all the roads there were closed. This was a road junction with a main, although unpaved, highway to the south. Julio told us that his family house was at Caazapá, 60 miles down the road, and suggested that rather than return to Asunción we should press on and spend the night there in the hope of improved weather next day.

The next town on the Southern Highway was Villarica and here we found the road closed by an iron barrier. Here too we received a further demonstration of Julio's evident authority because, after a short discussion with the officer in charge, the barrier was unlocked and raised and we were waved on into a landscape veiled in pearly rain. We were now committed, Julio said, to a mildly precarious adventure.

133

If it rained in earnest we should be stuck indefinitely wherever we happened to be, in all probability miles from the nearest village. No attempt was ever made to rescue cars trapped in this way as long as the rain continued and this could be a matter of weeks.

Suddenly we were in another world. Here was all the Arcadian charm, the style and the swagger of South America, that had survived in its purest form. The streets of small towns like Caacayí (named after the call of a bird) had turned into a grassland cropped by mild cows, and diurnal bats fluttered from the windows of great sepulchral mansions, emptied by so many wars and revolutions. Aloof horsemen went thudding past under their wide hats, a palm always upraised in greeting. Enormous blue butterflies floated by. I had always believed that these *morphos* were confined to the shade of the rain forest, but here they planed down and settled on the road to suck at the juices of the horse-manure that had seeped into its surface. Julio said that they were never molested because the Guarani Indians, from whom so many of these people were descended, believed them to be the 'ears of God'.

The sun shone in fits and starts, and in-between the rain spattered on the windscreen in heavy summer drops, and slowly, as the water penetrated the skin of laterite on the road, it darkened almost to the colour of blood. The first rain of the year brought a sense of adventure. Laughing cowboys came galloping up through the scrolls of vapour, men at village street corners plucked at their harps and seemed to enjoy a small wetting, and girls with pre-Raphaelite faces scampered excitedly about, clutching yellow umbrellas.

Although shallow, the mud was extremely sticky, and we slid about in all directions. Sometimes Donald and I pushed for hundreds of yards on end, achieving a snail's progress, and splashed and stained like slaughterhouse men, while Julio drove flat out in bottom gear. The villages always produced eager assistance, although offers of aid were encumbered with over-formality, and sometimes even with polite requests to visit the house of the helper. As Julio said,

134

in these villages, spared by our times, every man was your friend apart from an occasional enemy whom you disposed of as soon as you could and in any way possible.

Although until this our friend had remained largely enveloped in mystery we began to learn a little about his background. By inclination, he was a poet, he told us, not only writing poetry on his own account, but translating the poetry of the Guaraní Indians of Southern Paraguay into Spanish. He had brought several bottles of strong red Paraguayan wine with him, and we pulled into the roadside in one village, left the car and slopped through the red mud into a café, to try the local meat pasties, drink a bottle of wine and talk poetry.

Like most Paraguayans from the south, Julio was bilingual in Spanish and Guaraní, the ancient Indian language of Paraguay, once spoken by the 130,000 Guaranís rounded up by the Jesuit missionaries and confined in the *reducciónes* until the expulsion of the Jesuits in the eighteenth century by order of the Spanish Crown. Julio spoke Guaraní by preference, feeling, he said, that no other tongue could rival its range and finesse in expressing the poetic experience. The Guaranís had never been able psychologically to impose hard boundaries on the flux of life, feeling as they did for animals and trees much as they did for men. As everyone knew, these Indians (and, as he later admitted, the Achés, too, who were a part of the Guaraní race) embraced, talked to, and even sang to trees. In the single word 'tree' their language was powerful and rich enough to embrace the concepts of living, growing, dying and turning to dust.

Of all the European poets Julio had read, the one that for him had come closest to Guaraní imagery had been García Lorca. It was the greatest possible fluke that this declaration should have led to a circumstance which revolutionized our relationship. We were relaxed now by the wine in our stomachs, the strong but strangely refreshing scent of unknown white blossoms stuffed into the dried-milk tins placed everywhere about the room, and the soft tapping of rain mixed with frugal harp music entering by the window. Julio quoted a *copla* from Lorca, 'The Spilled Blood', from

135

Lament for Ignacio Sanchez Mejías, which describes the impact on the poet of the sight of his friend's blood in the sand:

Que no quiero verla!	I don't want to see it!
que no hay caliz que la contenga	no chalice can contain it,
que no hay golondrinas que se la beban	no swallows can drink it,
que no hay escarcha de luz que la enfrie,	no frost of light can cool it,

Of the whole of Garcia Lorca's opus I could have hardly quoted ten lines, but among them I knew the two that followed, and was able to carry on.

no hay canto ni diluvio de azuzenas,	nor song nor deluge of white lilies,
no hay cristal que la cubra de plata.	nor crystal to cover it with silver.

Instantly everything changed between us. Whatever had separated us could not resist the knowledge that we shared Lorca, and we became friends.

Caazapá, reached at sundown—after pushing the Citroën through miles, it seemed to us, of slippery mud—was at the end of the road, and if there was any place in the world to get away from it all, this was it.

Ghostly, once opulent houses, built in florid Victorian style, stood in gardens that had turned to beautiful thickets. Both the streets and the railway line had become meadows, and a line of trucks abandoned thirty years ago were brightly ornamented with convolvulus. There were slow-moving indulgent cows everywhere, and girls in long, immaculate white dresses milking them. The rain had stopped and we found harpists offering their services as serenaders in the small square, and among them a number of dignified men

136

playing with tops. Girls sat in armchairs in the shallows of the river washing clothes among blue aquatic flowers. The velvet silence of this town was broken by the sweet tinplate hammering of a mission-church bell. In Caazapá the women dealt with the small-scale commerce and Julio introduced us to a girl seated at a nearby stall. Interbreeding was enforced upon Paraguayan survivors and most people in such small towns were related. This was Francisca, his cousin, who spoke freely, even with relish about her life. 'I'm seventeen years old, and sell eggs and honey. One child, as you see, but no husband. Our menfolk are incurably lazy. Why should I work to keep a man?'

Julio's house was in a nameless street in the outskirts of the town; a maroon-painted mansion enclosing three sides of a large patio in which bananas and pawpaws grew among the dense foliage of tropical plants, all of it coated with dew. The house was empty, serving as a *pied-à-terre* for members of the family who happened to be in the area. It was glutted with solid, dark, well made Victorian furniture. There appeared to be no locks on the doors. In Caazapá there was no longer electric light nor running water, although all the light fittings and the piping and taps were still in place, so the first task on arrival was to light the lamps, and draw water from the well. The English conception of privacy was unknown. While I was cleansing myself of red mud, people who seemed to be passing neighbours dropped in with a word of welcome, handled my personal belongings with good-natured curiosity, and went on their way. There was a moment of embarrassment when I lost my bearings in an unlit passage, opened the wrong door and found Julio in his underclothes in the act of buckling on an automatic pistol. He had a dagger strapped to his leg, just above the ankle. 'Why the gun? Julio,' I asked him. 'I brought it to show a friend who was looking for one,' he said.

We walked a few hundred yards to the town's centre for the evening meal, and I could only suppose that in Caazapá one stayed at home in the evening unless heavily armed. Nothing could have been calmer and more decorous than the atmosphere of the restaurant. The service was instan-

137

taneous, the waitress beautiful, and the food, like most things in this country, a little bizarre, featuring as it did a strapping waterhen, complete with head and enormously splayed-out feet, but otherwise delectable.

The night in Julio's house was uneventful. Famished beetles from the Chaco showered the streets during the hours of darkness, but we saw nothing of this. New experiences came crowding on the heels of dawn. At first light a man employed by neighbourhood subscription to wake householders up came into the patio, plucked a few chords on his harp and passed on to the house next door. This set up a piercing competitive outcry among the birds that had roosted among the bananas. Almost immediately the door of my room burst open, and an old woman came in selling hot meat pies, passing thereafter from room to room in search of trade. She was followed by a vendor of hot coffee, and thus roused and the rain having held off, most of the neighbours, still in their pyjamas, gathered in the street cup in hand, in sociable discussion.

Soon after this, possibly at six, a gaunt woman with streaming black hair and holding a long knife came striding into view. This was the butcher, who was followed by a boy pushing a handcart laden with the carcase of a newly butchered pig. A few yards to the rear the assistant butcher, a male, mounted on a piebald pony, wearing a fur hat, and holding up a small, red flag, trotted towards us. We followed the *cortège* to a corner shop, where a teenage girl stood guard, keeping in order unruly customers who tried to snatch up meat or sit on the counter, with light blows of her whip.

The morning remained fine although great saffron clouds laden with water threatened us from the horizon. We set out to see the sights of the town, first paying courtesy calls on several of Julio's friends. There are no door-knockers in rural Paraguay. Although sellars of pies, fruit and coffee seem to wander through houses at will, in the case of formal visits you stand under the window and clap your hands, whereupon if you are welcome the owner either comes out carrying chairs, or invites you in.

Within Julio's memory there had been Achés in the woods

138

all round the town, and it was hardly twenty years since the last of them had been cut up for the jaguar traps, or dragged away into slavery. Caazapá had suffered, as had few other towns, the huge calamity of five years of civil war ending in 1954 with the victory of the present dictator, General Stroesser. Julio took us to a shallow lake adorned with all the beauties of nature where 'Blues' captured in a battle with the victorious 'Colorados' had been ordered into the water and recommended to submerge themselves as best they could, and then, coming up for air, were picked off, one by one. The country in those days had been ruled by local bosses rather than any effective central government, and somewhere in the vicinity a minor 'Blue' boss had been buried alive, not only for his tyrannies when in power, but his offensive vanity.

We paid the customary visit to the local cemetery where so many victims of the war were brought for interment that the custom arose, owing to the shortage of hallowed ground, of 'borrowing' graves. Charitable persons leased or lent part of their family vaults sometimes over a period of years, until alternative space could be found. This temporary solution had been applied in the case of Matilde Villalba, chief political boss of Caazapá, ambushed and shot down with six of his sixteen sons.

Following these sombre events, Julio said, vendettas had dragged on for years. He quoted the case of a friend who had taken refuge in Argentina but had been tracked down after a hunt for several years by an indefatigable hired killer. This man entered his room one night, and with absolute calm and deliberation, stabbed him five times and left. The best part of a decade passed before his friend had fully recovered his health, returned to Paraguay and located his would-be assassin. Although the roles were reversed the circumstances resembled those of their previous encounter, except that his friend had lost faith in the knife as a weapon, killing his old adversary who awaited his end 'with impassivity' with a single shot in the stomach.

Remembering these things, our friend said, 'Thank God, we now have peace and tranquility.' No sooner had this utterance been made than we noticed several people running to get a better view of something that was happening in the next street, 'It is nothing,' we were assured, 'probably two men have challenged each other to a duel.' Since the showing of the film *High Noon*, he said, such confrontations had become the fashion, and whereas in the old days duels had been staged in a cleared space conveniently close to the cemetery, now that this was full a central street was usually chosen, at a time when the largest number of people were likely to be about. In one such episode some weeks before, both the duellists had shot each other dead.

As it happened the excitement this time was over an informally staged bullfight. A stockade had been put up in a matter of hours and when we arrived the proceedings had opened with clowns capering in the ring. Girls were whipping away a non-paying audience attempting to watch the proceedings through rents in the tattered curtains draped round the fencing. The bull was driven in, and Julio took one look at it and decided that we should go. About one bull in three, he said, crashed through the stockade and into the street, and then the best hope of survival was to lie down and keep absolutely still. It was the strong possibility of such a drama that drew the crowd—a case of anything for relief from the monotony of provincial life.

The rain clouds were building up, and the decision now had to be whether to make with all possible speed for Coronel Oviedo on the main Asunción highway or to continue to use up time very pleasantly in Caazapá, with the risk of being cut off for a week or more if the rains started in earnest. It seemed wiser to turn back, so we left Caazapá and drove northwards into the rain over officially closed roads, and making numerous detours to avoid collapsed bridges or bridges clearly on the point of collapse. Donald, as ever, was excited by the contrasts of stormy weather; the lurid light thrust at us from under the clouds, the strong, dour colours contained in wetness, the lanky, waterlogged palms scourged by the sudden gusts of wind. We caught his excitement and Julio thanked him. 'I have lived in Paraguay all my life, and for the first time I am seeing it. You have shown me so many beautiful things.'

The roadside streams were filling quickly with yellow water and in the outskirts of villages the boys were hooking out of them large catfish that had spent the dry season in a fish's coma, invisible in liquid mud. Now there were fish wherever there was water and we could see them splashing in the large pools forming in the fields. Predators of all kinds were out and about; delicately plodding storks, long-legged eagles up to their thighs in puddles, ash-blond foxes with fish-gore on their muzzles, and Paraguayan ostriches (rheas), singly and in pairs, running at the roadside to keep up with the car, which they were easily able to do, as our speed never reached 20 mph.

We reached Coronel Oviedo in the afternoon, a small town, patchily afloat in quagmires under a little sallow sunshine dispensed through small rents in the clouds, which then rapidly closed in. Julio suggested we might use up time by a visit to a woman known as Maria Calavera (Mary Skull), or otherwise *La Gran Payecera* (the Great Witch of Paraguay) who lived a short distance from the town. She was famous, Julio said, for the fact that General Perón of Argentina had made regular visits to Coronel Oviedo to consult with her on matters of personal fortune and national policy. Not only that, but it was well known that there were members of the government of Paraguay who still leaned heavily on her for advice. As further recommendation Julio mentioned that in a séance his father, a well-known doctor, had had with her, she had correctly predicted the date of his death – such mortuary information being one of her specialities.

Donald, not approving of visits to witches, would have nothing to do with this, accompanying us with some reluctance but refusing to enter the house. This was a large barn-like shack, standing alone and painted a lugubrious green. A veranda ran the length of the upper floor and on this perhaps fifteen women stood in a damp huddle awaiting their turn to be called into the presence. The rain streamed down. Two horsemen in soaked carmine ponchos went

141

splashing by. The witch's servant in gumboots and flowered frock appeared in a doorway to summon the next patient with a forlorn squawk on a horn. Whatever the sad and strange glamour of the scene Donald preferred to ignore it and settled as best he could in the cramped back of the car, and Julio and I left him to climb the stairs, shortly finding ourselves in the witch's consulting room.

I found Maria Calavera a woman of outstandingly pleasant appearance, about sixty years of age, comfortably shapeless, and seated behind a decrepit wicker table in a poorly furnished cell of a room. None of the familiar and often daunting bric-a-brac of the voodoo shrine was to be seen. There was no more of a satanic atmosphere than one would have found in the kitchen of a house in the run-down quarter of any local town. A small domesticated pig, its tail tied up in a blue ribbon, trotted in through one door, waited to be patted and trotted out through another. Julio introduced me, explained that we were passing and wanted to make a courtesy call. Maria Calavera nodded and gave me a welcoming smile. 'Does he wish to enquire about the future?' she asked. I noticed that she had the voice of a girl. It was as though she had possessed the power to hold back some part of her youth, and there was something a little eerie about this. Julio told her, no. He treated her with more respect than I had seen him pay anyone on this trip, and mixed in with the respect there was a touch of affection. He had warned me that it was better to leave the future out of this.

'Did you come here out of curiosity?' the witch asked me.

I admitted shamefacedly that curiosity had come into it, and she laughed and said that it was quite understandable, and it was evident that she was not put out.

She got up, reached in a shallow wall-cupboard and took out the skull after which she was named, and upon which her reputation was largely based. She put the skull on the table between us, placed my right hand upon the cranium, and hers—which was small and delicate, like that of a girl in her twenties—upon mine.

The skull began to move. This was the experience the

142

dictator of Argentina had described to Julio's father as an overwhelming one. The general had sat where I sat, possibly in the same roughly carpentered chair, and the skull had jiggled about as it did now, and this aimless reanimation of the bone, with its accompanying oracle had perhaps even influenced his policies, his successes and his mistakes. I was not overwhelmed; only affected by what I saw as a supremely skilful trick.

Suddenly the skull's erratic movements stopped but the witch's sympathetic smile remained. 'Are you suffering from some complaint?' she asked, determined as I could see, to give me something for my money. I said I was not, and now she was clearly puzzled. 'And you're quite certain?' she asked, and I could hear Julio quietly urging me to hold nothing back. 'Think again,' she said. 'Your right eye has given you trouble.'

I wracked my memory and then remembered that ten or fifteen years ago after experiencing some discomfort in the eyeball I had visited a clinic on the off-chance that this was the beginning of glaucoma, but nothing was found. Within days the pain passed off, and the thing had been dismissed from my mind. I admitted to the sore eye of so many years ago and she nodded her satisfaction. To cap this minor success she then gave details of an even more remote-in-time intestinal weakness which I had also done my best to forget. Did telepathy exist—but in any case was this telepathy? I was reluctantly impressed, but struck more by the triviality of these scraps salvaged—if in fact they were—from my past, than by the phenomenon itself. It had to be remembered too, that here I was dealing with no mere fair-booth practitioner with a crystal ball but the most redoutable exponent of the occult in all Paraguay.

Thereafter we settled to a friendly discussion of her profession. Paraguay was full of witches, she said, and there was a particularly powerful one in the next village, who was a good friend. This woman had a different area of specialization, being outstandingly successful in the treatment of phobias. When one of her patients demonstrated what was clearly psychotic fear, she would pass him (phobia

143

cases were nearly always men) over to her friend with a note that might say, 'This is a nice man who can't be convinced he hasn't a snake in his stomach. Do what you can for him.'

In exchange she would receive and deal with sufferers from affairs of the heart, and persons wishing to know the date of their deaths so as to be given good time in which to put their affairs in order.

'In Paraguay.' she said, 'there is too much love spilled over and wasted. Love is our downfall. Many women cannot marry because there are no men left to take them as wives. Husbands die young, and the country is full of widows. Almost all those who come to me for help are women. When they have used up all their tears they know there is nothing else for it, and they come to me.'

'And how do you help them?'

'I work to take the love out of their hearts, to make them forget the voices, the faces of the past. "Now you are my child," I say to them. "Now you will go to sleep and you will forget." Sometimes I sing to them a cradle song. The other *payeceras* give them *payé* made from white flowers, and they are happy for a day and then grief returns. When I cast out love it is gone for ever. I empty the mind. I destroy love and pain.'

'Do you use the skull?' I asked.

'Never with a woman. No woman can touch the skull. If a man comes to me, then I will use the skull.' The young, mild eyes in the old shapeless face watched me with sympathy and understanding. Down in the street in the gusting rain, Don, tired of waiting tooted the car-horn.

'Once a great general sat in that chair,' the witch said. 'I won't tell you his name. He had his problems, too, but I cured him.'

We turned eastwards down the main highway making for Caaguazú, where a last hope of the weather clearing up, thus permitting us to reach Cecilio Baez, had to be abandoned, and we decided to stay the night. It was near this town at the time of Che Guevara's fiasco in 1967, Julio told us, that Paraguayan guerrillas went into action. Che Guevara, his force split up and his immediate followers reduced to sixteen men, was wandering without purpose, lost and at the end of his tether in the Villagrande jungle just across the northern border when the Paraguayan revolutionaries opened their pitiful guerrilla second-front. The general charged with their suppression spread the rumour that they were carrying gold, and the peasants they hoped to free hunted them down to be able to get their hands on this. Those they caught and turned over to the Army were thrown from aeroplanes.

'Of Caaguazú,' Julio said, 'don't expect too much. There's an authentic country town atmosphere you might like.'

The streets were under water, and having found beds in a bleak-looking lodging house we splashed through shallow floods to the nearest *cantina* for a meal. The personality of this place was established by a model T Ford in a spanking state of preservation parked at the entrance and the patrons checking their guns, some imposingly antique, as they went in. Inside we faced once more the special bedlam of such public places in Paraguay with harp music turned up to the full and voices all round shouting to be heard. For supper there were outlandish portions of grilled meat served with mighty flagons of strong wine. After a moment the owner, who had been eyeing us protectively, came over and shouted into my ear, 'Drink up. The arrangements are basic where you're going tonight. Help you to sleep.'

Here, by purest chance, a boy of about eight, fetching and carrying in the *cantina*, was pointed out as an Indian who had been bought. In such cases the child will passed off as 'adopted', and given the family name, although he will remain in a subservient position in the family for the rest of his days. The boy admitted to being an Indian—the owner's family had rather absurdly denied that he was one — and he was clearly delighted by the rare experience of being for once the object of attention.

The owner had been right about the lodging house. Accommodation for all-comers was provided in a large room containing some thirty beds in rows, on which guests slept

145

fully dressed, some actually wearing their guns. There was a tremendous hammering of rain all night on the corrugated iron roof and as the path leading down to the latrine was submerged and the lights did not work, several vast pisspots had been placed outside the door.

Next day the weather showed no signs of improvement, so the only course was to turn round and drive back to Asunción. Julio told us we could count on a delay of up to five days, and suggested as a way of using up time that we should fly up to one of the northern towns where the rains had not yet begun. He expected to be detained in the capital on business of various kinds but recommended us not to miss the experience of life in the Mennonite colony at Filadelfia and Loma Plata in the Gran Chaco, to be reached in an hour's flight in a light plane. Here, he said, apart from the cotton processing factory and the spectacle of the occasional Mennonite daughter on a Yamaha, the pious and patriarchal calm of the Canadian Mid-West of the last century—from which the sect hailed—had been remarkably preserved.

The sect, which was of German origin, arrived in Paraguay in 1921 and established themselves in the Chaco, where they were able to buy a vast tract of land at a very low price. To avoid any stigma that might attach to forcible expropriation of the original Indian occupants, they conducted a second purchase of the territory, this time from the Indians. The price, according to their own account, for a 100–150 hectare plot was an old pair of trousers, a few metres of cloth, 'and some provisions'.

Cotton is the principal resource of this part of the Chaco and 6,000 once-nomadic Indians are now settled on small plots of land in the Mennonite colony. Many of those without land are employed in the cotton processing plant at Loma Plata. Payment is in tokens to be spent in the company shops. Workers are accommodated in *Arbeiterlager*, which from the photographs that have been published appear grim. The Mennonites share the viewpoint of W. Barbrooke Grubb, founder of the adjacent South American Missionary Society's relatively small holding of 3,750 hectares of land on which some 7,000 Indians are employed. Speaking of his converts Grubb said, 'While we impress on him (the Indian) that we regard him as a fellow man and brother, we at the same time leave him under no misapprehension as to his place in the world being a humble one, until such times as, in the course of evolution, he is qualified for a higher place.'

The Mennonite colony enjoys some degree of autonomy, and to go there permission had to be obtained at the Mennonite headquarters in Asunción. The official I saw asked me the purpose of the visit, and when I told him it was to see Indians he let out an incredulous bellow of laughter. Missionaries and the functionaries of semi-religous organizations seem often unable to repress their contempt for those whose lives they control. When Luke Holland of Survival International visited Loma Plata he found the Mennonites commonly referred to their Indian charges (German is the language of the colony) as *unsere schwartz arschlöche* (our black arseholes). The North American evangelists, primmer by nature, prefer the description 'savages', 'naked savages' —or in the case of those who resist contact, 'treacherous savages'—all of which terms are repeated endlessly in their publications.

To visit Loma Plata certificates of good conduct were required from the British Embassy. I obtained these and submitted them to the Mennonites for their consideration and then went back to the search for a vehicle capable of tackling the road to Cecilio Baez, should Julio decide that the 2CV was unequal to the struggle. At this stage we faced a severe disappointment, as Julio announced that through the pressure of business of various kinds he would be unable to come to Cecilio Baez. We were not only disappointed, but surprised at the sudden change in the plan, and it was not hard not to wonder whether there was more in this than met the eye. My suspicion that Julio had been assigned to us to keep us under surveillance had been constantly reinforced by numerous small indications that had arisen on the trip. Nevertheless there was no doubt that he enjoyed our company as much as we did his. We had struggled together over the terrible roads; Don had opened Julio's eyes to the great beauty often concealed in the commonplace; I had striven with mediocre results to put Guaraní poetry, via his Castilian, into English; and we had drunk together great quantities of excellent wine. Now our excursions were at an end. A possibility that occurred was that, as a result of the bonds of friendship that had developed, he had asked to be excused from going any further with whatever he had been instructed to do. For all that, we never failed to share an evening meal together for the rest of the time we were in Asunción.

Two days later the permission to visit the Mennonite colony came through but before we could book our seats on the plane a young English veterinary surgeon called Nicholls said that he had heard of our presence through our Embassy. This man told us that he was engaged in a scientific project in Asunción, and had the use of a Land Rover. He had had little opportunity until this to see the country outside the capital and would be very glad to drive us round if we agreed to pay for the petrol.

Thus were our problems solved. Rather unusually Mr Nicholls was interested in Indians. We suggested a trip to visit one of the old Jesuit reductions but he excused himself from this, offering the proposal of a visit to the Macas, who were established in a camp on what was literally a desert island in the Paraguay river a few kilometres from Asunción. The story of this tribe was a tragedy in traditional Indian style. They had been uprooted forty years ago from their home in the Chaco and dumped on this arid reserve, with no way of obtaining their livelihood apart from becoming a tourist attraction. They offer one of the few instances of a tribe who have resisted all missionary efforts at conversion. Despite the intense degradation to which they have been exposed, and the loss of their culture, so that the day's food for the family depends upon a daughter's willingness to strip off her clothes and paint herself in absurd and meaningless designs for the tourists' cameras, they have still retained the strength to force the missionaries to leave.

The visit would have been an interesting one, because it was rumoured in Asunción that the missionaries had succeeded in maintaining a commercial link with the reservation and, as the newspapers alleged, that this was the principal outlet for the illicit trade in jaguar skins and parrots' feathers collected by Indians under missionary control in the northern Chaco.

This small but doubtless interesting excursion could not be undertaken because of strong winds with the waves running too high for the ferry to make the crossing. Cecilio Baez then came up, Nicholls saying that he would be interested to visit the camp. It was there and then arranged that, weather permitting, we would leave early next morning. Nicholls made the proviso that we should arrange things so as to be back in the capital before dark. On this he was very insistent.

Next morning, by the greatest of good fortune, the rain had stopped, and we set out at six under clear skies and over the road that had dried out in the night. Nicholls had brought his wife, an extremely attractive young girl, for the ride. She, too, had seen little of Paraguay, and was excited by the many novel experiences it provided. Halfway between Coronel Oviedo and Caaguazú a notice proclaimed that we were entering the National Guayaki Reserve. It was an area of trim, well-managed woodlands with an occasional rich man's country house built to harmonize with the surroundings. We stopped for a coffee at a country club decorated with well made native artifacts, in particular handsome baskets, from other parts of the country. The Achés were represented by excellent framed colour photographs of utterly naked men and women, eyes wide with fear, running towards the camera. The manager had no idea at all where they had been taken, but thought that it must have been many miles away. In the ten years he had been there there had been no sign of an Indian anywhere in these woods.

Caaguazú, once again, came next, and here at last we were able to make the turn northwards along narrow and constantly branching tracks to Cecilio Baez. We found ourselves quite suddenly in a wide clearing at the end of which, from its size and style, was clearly the mission house. The huts were recognizable from the many photographs taken of them by Mark Münzel and of their Aché inmates of his day, who in their last extremity through starvation and dis-

ease had glued birds' feathers to their bodies in ritual preparation for death. The first thing I noticed, apart from the
presence of several Indian women in near rags mooching
about in the neighbourhood of the huts, was the smell of
human excrement. A white man in mechanic's overalls had
been tinkering with a piece of machinery and now he
straightened himself and came forward, with a look of suppressed anger. This was Mr Jim Stolz, the missionary-in-
chief. He took Colonel Infanzón's letter, glanced at it and
asked in a hostile tone where we had been, adding that he
had been expecting us for the past three days. It was clear
that Colonel Infanzón had been in touch with Cecilio Baez
by radio. Later it was evident, too, that he had made a call
that day, having learned of our departure with Mr Nicholls,
for encumbered as he was by so many things that called for
explanation, Mr Stolz had clearly made last-moment efforts
in stage-management. These only strengthened suspicion
that there was much to hide.

The moment seemed a delicate one by reason of Mr
Stolz's unconcealed hostility. This was no mild-mannered,
ingratiating Mr Fernley, but a tough-looking man with the
appearance and authority of manner of a top-sergeant in an
American combat unit. I realized that he would have to be
regarded (as missionaries often were in Latin America) as
a functionary of the government, empowered to run us off
if he thought fit. He wanted to know the purpose of our
visit, and I told him I hoped to be able to dispel certain
rumours that had been circulated about the camp's function,
by asking him some questions, while Donald would take
photographs. I assured him that we had no intention of
making indecent movies of the Indians. At this point it
turned out that Mr Stolz had never heard of Colonel Infanzón's 'French couple'.

Mrs Stolz now came out of the house. She was what we
would have thought of as the typical missionary wife; modest
yet brisk, resolutely smiling, and calm in what might have
seemed to her a crisis. She invited us into the house which
was pleasantly furnished without being luxurious, and
devoid of the ranks of labour-saving gadgetry commonly

150

found in such missionary establishments. A moment before several hefty-looking young Americans had appeared as if from nowhere, and were closing in on us, and, a little nervous at the way things might develop, I warned Donald to get away and take what photographs he could while I engaged Mr Stolz. Nicholls had followed me into Mr Stolz's office where Mrs Stolz handed out the coffee. Although I would have preferred to talk to the missionary alone I wished to avoid the embarrassment of asking him to go.

I asked Mr Stolz how many Indians there were in the camp, and he replied without hesitation that there were three hundred. This would have meant that at that moment the camp's population was the highest it had ever been, yet there were only twelve small huts to be seen, as there had been in Münzel's day, when half this number had seemed to Münzel to be grossly overcrowded, and for that reason all the more exposed to infectious disease. Most of the inmates, Stolz explained, were out working on the land, and, when I asked whether I could see them at work, he glanced at his watch and said that they were on their way back to camp and would be coming in soon.

I tried to pin him down. 'An hour. Two hours?'

'It would be an hour, maybe more. Some have to come from one place and some from another.'

'On foot?'

'If they can't get a ride.' Suddenly I realized that Mr Stolz had become vague, and suspected that it might be a defensive vagueness. I was not prepared at this stage to dismiss the possibility that the Achés would be coming back. It was now nearly noon. In Paraguay the working day starts soon after dawn, and the whole country knocks off for a siesta at midday. Work then recommences at three and continues until sunset. I asked Mr Stolz what the Indians were paid, and after a little hesitation he said they received 100 guaranies (about 33p) a day. 'They have no sense of trade or money,' he said.

What did they spend their money on? I asked, and he shook his head a little hopelessly. 'Could be jam,' he said, 'when there is any in the store.'

In view of the camp's striking increase in population since the visit of the *New York Times's* correspondent in the previous January I thought it reasonable to enquire where the new arrivals had come from. Mr Stolz's vagueness and evasiveness increased. 'They just came in from time to time,' he said. 'In the night.' The last group had arrived some weeks previously. He agreed that no 'wild' Aché were to be found anywhere in the vicinity, and those recently arrived had come from a long way away. What made them come? I asked and Mr Stolz said, 'Maybe they heard this was a good place to be in.' It was roughly the explanation Mr Depue had offered to explain the presence of his Ayoreos captured in the Bolivian Chaco some fifteen years before, and therefore abandoned to the limbo of his compound. Refuge in the mission had been depicted as a good thing.

The area surrounding the camp and for many miles in all directions had been cleared and planted with crops, and the farmers, as Mr Stolz admitted would kill a 'wild' Aché on sight. There were many enslaved children in the neighbour-hood. Four, he said, had been taken at Kuruzu some twenty kilometres away, one dying from a blow with a gun butt received at the time of his capture and the three others from measles shortly afterwards—a disease against which forest Indians have built up no immunity. 'It's the smart thing to own an Aché round here,' he said. 'I guess it's a kind of status symbol.' It was hard to believe that Indians would have faced these terrible hazards to reach what had been frequently described as a death camp. It was only after I returned to England that I happened to pick up a copy of *Brown Gold*, the New Tribes Mission publication, for 14 September 1974, in which Mr Stolz wrote of his jungle experiences.

I was sitting with another of the new Indians one day and we were reminiscing about the time Paul and I had made the trip into the woods and brought them to the colony. He looked at me seriously and told me that it was a good thing I hadn't come in without the Indians (the hunters) from the colony or they would have killed me. For a year

Paul and I had worked in that area around Codeteque trying to make contacts with them and other groups in the area. Several times we came on fresh camps. Only God's faithfulness kept us ever from meeting them face to face, and we were certainly trying our best to do just that.

With these words Mr Stolz explained the manner in which the Aché had been induced to leave their woods.

A further two years were to pass before someone sent me yet another copy of *Brown Gold* (dated April 1974) throwing more light on the horrors of Cecilio Baez, as revealed in a brief account by Mrs Jim Stolz. There was no vagueness or evasion about Mrs Stolz, no talk of Indians drifting in from time to time in the night because they had heard it was a good place to be in. On the contrary, this was the place where a lot of Indians died, and she makes no bones about it. Her contribution is entitled, 'Too Late!' By this she seems to mean that the missionaries were too late in their translation of the Gospel into Aché, although laying the blame on the Indians for this, and suggesting that God does too. The article is subtitled, 'In her culture, "Dressed for Death" in a large teeth necklace. She had not heard of being "Clothed in His Righteousness". She is in hell today.' The illustration is of an old woman, who had died in the camp, in her shroud.

The account had been written in the autumn of 1973, within two months of the receipt by Mark Münzel of a letter to say that, out of 250 Achés stated officially to have been confined in the camp a year before, only 100 remained. A second letter received—a matter of weeks later—said that the number of survivors had been reduced to 25. It was the period referred to in his press conference by General Marcia Samaniego, when he admitted that crimes had been committed against the Indians while refuting allegations of genocide, 'since there had been no intent to destroy them'. Nevertheless it was generally agreed that Indians had been hunted down in the forest and exterminated like vermin, and the newspapers were full of the accounts of able-bodied men sold into slavery, of nubile women forced into prostitution and of their children being sold for a few dollars, or even given away.

Mrs Stolz embarks by wondering

> how many more of these Guayakies [the word is a contemptuous epithet meaning rats] will meet their death with never 'a ray from above'? In September when a group of new Guayaki Indians were brought into the colony I thought perhaps this old woman would have the chance to hear the Gospel in her language before she died. So close, yet so far!

The colony, she said, had been stricken by a measles epidemic. The account is laced with unintentional irony. 'We couldn't believe the state in which it left these Indians, so recently introduced to civilization.' However 'Granny' responded to treatment. 'One night Jim took her a piece of raw pig meat to help fatten her up, and she eagerly licked the juice and blood off . . .' Next day death had claimed her.

Before she died she had told her family that she wanted to be cremated according to Aché custom. This created some difficulty with Paraguayans—presumably police or army officials in the camp—but the matter seemed unimportant to Jim Stolz.

> The hole was dug [in which she was to be burnt] and they carried her off on a pole, the body tied by a cord.
>
> As they were about to put her in the hole, a younger woman jumped in ahead, crying that she wanted to go to the sun, the Guayaki heaven where the grandma was going. It took four men to pull her out of the grave so the burying ceremony could continue.
>
> Again we were faced with the knowledge that these people have no fear of death. In fact, many have welcomed it. We have now begun to lay a ground work for the Gospel. They have no conception of hell that we can tell . . . Will they believe that a fire hotter than anything they could make to cremate a body is waiting for each one who dies without Christ?

154

Donald was anxious to photograph Achés playing their musical instruments; their flutes and above all a species of one-string fiddle with which a range of about three notes is obtained simply by bending the neck, and thus varying the tension of the string. Mr Stolz said flatly that there were no musical instruments of any kind on the reservation. Did the Indians perform any traditional ceremonies? I asked. No, he said, none. Were there any chiefs? No. Any medicine-men? Absolutely not. The only thing the Achés ever seemed to do was to sing, he said. The words of their songs were 'not too interesting'. The men were always trying to build themselves up as great hunters, and the women sang those terrible groaning, belly-aching songs. The Achés blamed everything on their ancestors.

At this point I decided to ask Mr Stolz what was the function of the mission and he replied that it was to bring salvation to those who were in a state of sin. This was to be done, eventually, by baptism after the converts had accepted Christ in their hearts and by 'admission through the mouth'. He thought it was a good thing that I should write down his replies to these questions on topics of faith and conversation and this I carefully did.

How many Achés had he baptised? I asked, and Mr Stolz said, none. 'Before I can bring them to Christ I must first understand what they believe,' he explained.

'And do you?' I asked him.

Mr Stolz said, 'Vaguely.' He had a problem with the language, he added, but at least he knew that they believed in three gods: the tiger (jaguar), the alligator, and the grand-father. 'This makes things difficult. When we talk of God's son they think of a tiger's son. It's hard to get across the idea they can be redeemed from sin by a tiger's son nailed to a cross. None of these Indians can make the admission, because they do not know what to admit.'

I asked Mr Stolz what progress, if any, had been made towards conversion, and he replied that most of them at least realized that they were living in a state of sin, particularly in sexual matters.

As by Mr Stolz's own estimate it would be many years

before any of the Achés were brought by his efforts into the fold of Christianity, it was supposed that meanwhile many would die, while a few, at least, would probably remain beyond reach of the missionary effort. What in the view of the New Tribes Mission, I asked, would be their spiritual fate?

Mr Stolz was on firm ground now. 'There is no salvation,' he said, 'for those who cannot be reached. The Book tells us that there are only two places in the hereafter: Heaven and Hell. Hell is where those who cannot be reached will spend eternity.'

It seemed to me unreasonable that divine retribution should be visited on the Achés because Mr Stolz had been unable to learn their language, but the missionary shrugged his shoulders. Such things were beyond his jurisdiction, he suggested.

In 1973 a visitor who counted 25 Achés in the camp had noticed the presence of some 30 missionaries with their families, charged with their spiritual welfare. Even now there could have been a dozen. In view of his admission of what sounded like conspicuous past failure and dismal future prospects I asked Mr Stolz to explain the large concentration of missionary effort in this unpromising area.

He thought of it as a testing ground, he said. 'Brothers and sisters new to the mission field ask to be sent here to gain experience by working with the unreached. This is where they find all the problems. And naturally they hope that God in his faithfulness will designate them as the instruments of spreading the message of his gospel to those who are lost.'

Soon after this he excused himself to return to stripping down an electrical generator some parts of which had to be got away to Asunción that day, and I only saw him briefly again before we left.

I now joined Donald at his photography, noticing that several young missionaries, not in evidence before, had come on the scene. We investigated small huts in the immediate area of the mission house. These averaged some 15ft square and it was difficult to imagine how as many as three hundred Indians could have been sheltered in them. We saw about thirty-five Achés in all, roughly half of them the possessors of skin of the waxen whiteness for which anthropologists have been able to offer no explanation. All of them were extremely mongoloid in appearance, and many could have passed for Eskimos. At a rough estimate about fifteen of these were women, several with babies. There were a half-dozen boys between eight and twelve years of age, and two young girls in this age-bracket, all with the distended stomachs and decayed teeth suggestive of malnutrition. The rest of the visible population was made up of adult males.

All the Achés, with the exception of two or three men wearing pseudo-military uniforms, were in dirty cast-offs. There appeared to be no sanitary arrangements in the camp area, which smelt vilely as a result. We noted that the uniformed males had access to bows and arrows with which they showed off their skill to the missionaries. The fact that these men were not at work, and that the missionaries fraternized with them in an affectionate manner suggested to us that these were the notorious *señuelos*, the Indian hunters trained from childhood, indoctrinated and some-times bribed to accompany the missionaries on their man-hunts, and track down their own people hiding in the forest. In common with all other visitors to the reservation one observed an extreme disproportion in the sexes of its popu-lation. If there had ever in fact been three hundred Indians—and presuming women were not compelled to work with their menfolk on the farms—men would have outnumbered women by 15 to 1. There were no young girls, no girl babies, no female that we could see younger than in early middle age. Where had all the girl children gone?* We found it

* It has been alleged that young girls from Cecilio Baez, and girl victims of manhunts in other parts of Paraguay, were sent to child brothels reported as a speciality of Asunción. In December 1977 the *Washington Post* published a harrowing account of such establishments catering for the 'sexual depravity among high government officials'.

strange that we should have seen no old men. These were the unutilizable remnants of a plundered community.

About half the Indian adults were lying on the ground in their huts in what seemed a condition of total apathy, giving no evidence of awareness of our presence as we came and went. There were gaps of up to six inches between the planks from which the walls of the huts were made, and, as these had failed to exclude torrential rain, the floors had turned to mud, over which an occasional board had been laid. We saw no signs of food anywhere in the huts—no scraps or left-overs.

Outside, little boys with distended stomachs under their filthy shirts who came running up to stroke our hands and caress our fingers (the Achés are the most affectionate and outgoing of the Indian races) showed us their tame lizards. Indians everywhere—certainly among the twenty or thirty tribes I have visited—have an ingrained affection for animals, taming them effortlessly with skills we do not understand. Every child to be seen had one, or more, animal or bird. There were coatis, raccoons, a baby fox, a fledgling vulture, and one came running proudly to display a hen perched on his shoulder. We wondered where this livestock came from since the children would certainly have been separated from their pets at the time when they had been tied up and dragged from the jungles after the hunt.

Mr Stolz made a final appearance. He had decided that we must see the store where the Achés' money could be spent. He unlocked this and pointed to several tins of jam, and to some popcorn which he described as the Indians' enduring favourite. The store contained a large collection of Aché bows which were for sale at low prices, but he admitted gloomily that there was very little demand for these. It was now three o'clock and I asked what news there was of the working party, and he said they had probably been held up by the state of roads but would be arriving at any minute now.

Having finished his photography in the central area of the camp, Donald had strolled off towards two huts on the

158

outskirts, followed by Mr Stolz's son, a friendly and clearly intelligent boy of about twelve who was by now carrying his tripod and who told him with reasonable pride that he was the only member of the missionary group who had been able to master Aché. A smiling young missionary overtook them and barred the entrance to the first of the huts, saying that there was nothing there. Donald pushed him aside, went in and came back to call me. I followed him into the hut and saw two old ladies lying on some rags on the ground in the last stages of emaciation and clearly on the verge of death. One was unconscious, the second in what was evidently a state of catalepsy, because although her eyes were wide-open she did not move them to follow my hand as I moved it from side to side close to her face. The fingers on her left hand were covered with the black mud scrabbled from the floor. There was no food or water in sight. In the second hut lay another woman, also in a desperate condition and with untreated wounds on her legs. A small, naked, tearful boy, sat at her side. Mr Stolz's son, happy to help with the tripod and handing up spare lenses, gave us a matter-of-fact account of what had happened. The three women and the boy had been taken in a recent forest round-up, the third woman having been shot in the side while attempting to escape.*

Donald took his close-ups, focusing down to within inches of the death-mask faces of the women. The missionary's son did his best to make himself useful and chattered on cheerfully. He liked the Achés, particularly the children, who let him play with their animals, and he hoped that they

* The shameful secrets revealed in the photographs have been a source of continuing embarrassment to the NTM for thirteen years. In May 1987 the European headquarters and training centre of the sect at Derby Road, Matlock, Derbyshire issued a bulletin containing the following bewildering falsehood: 'It is true that the lady had been shot but this was about 20 years before the missionaries were there.' The sect's hope of clearing its name in this way must be abandoned, for the original transparencies from which this picture, and many more taken at the missionary camp at the same time, are in the possession of the *Sunday Times*.

would all be saved. At that moment a small boy came in cuddling a monkey, and he went off with him.

There was something in the atmosphere here—the smiling young missionaries, more and more of whom had appeared, gathering in the background to sing what might equally have been a hymn or a cheerleader's song, the stench of excrement, the suspicion that there might be many hidden graves in this place—that made this the most sinister experience of my life. It was impossible not to be reminded of Jonestown, Guyana, and the deadly fanatics of the People's Temple. Beyond doubt Stolz had been lying, blundering from lie to lie in an attempt to cover sickening facts. It was quite clear that the Aché field-workers would never return—neither on this or any other day. But where were they?

I carried in my pocket a photostat copy of correspondence between a Paraguayan planter, Arnaldo Kant, and Nelido Ríos, Stolz's assistant. Stolz had stormed over the Kant's farm to complain that Kant had not paid for the Aché labourers who had been 'gathered' for him.

I explained to him that I had them at your request, and only to prevent them from being used as slaves . . . I was struck by the fear that this man inspires in these Indians. When they noticed that he was there to return them to the reservation they started to run away into the forest . . . The administrator claimed payment for the work the Achés had done, and I gave him the sum of 2,500 guaranies, [about £8], as proved by the enclosed receipt . . .

The details of this transaction were passed to Dr Münzel after Kant's father confessor had urged him not to burden his conscience by implication in crime.

It would have been the moment to confront the missionary with this irrefutable evidence of the practice of slavery, but in doing so I saw that I would risk jeopardizing the success of our mission. Mr Stolz was a man entrusted with the implementation of government policy, and this government happened to be the firmest and most ruthless of the dictatorships of Latin America—a continent where as a whole it is

160

dangerous to press inconvenient questions. Paraguay does not bother with Habeas Corpus; those who cause trouble are likely simply to disappear. The least that could happen to us if things at the camp of Cecilio Baez suddenly took a turn for the worse would be to suffer the loss of Donald's incriminating films. By now the missionaries had drawn apart from us in silence, and Mr Nicholls, previously affable enough, had become cold and hostile. Looking at his watch, he announced that it was six o'clock, and time to go.

We were just about to set out when another missionary family, a man, his wife and two sons, whom we had not seen until this time, came running up to ask for a lift to Asunción. The man said that they had been stranded by the rains for four days at Cecilio Baez, adding with absolute conviction that God had sent us in answer to their prayers.

Just like Mr Stolz, and Mr Fernley before him, this man failed to correspond in any way to my preconception of the missionary image, being in appearance practically the double of W.C. Fields, with an immense floppy straw hat, a Southern colonel's black bow-tie, and a quick, scornful laugh. He was immensely interested in trade and talked with endless vivacity of the thrill of picking up bargains, particularly antique weapons which he collected in the markets of such fairly backward towns as Asunción, where their true value was not fully appreciated. He was also interested in photographic equipment, owned seven cameras, and offered Don 'a good price' for any apparatus surplus to his requirements.

The Chaco missionary—he preferred not to give his name—turned out to be incredibly frank. Mr Stolz had told us that the Indians received 100 guaranies a day (spendable at the mission's store). This with a peal of incredulous laughter he dismissed as absurd. The farmers they worked for *promised* them 200 guaranies (66p) a week but more often fobbed them off in the end with an old shirt or a worn-out pair of pants. I showed him the copy of the receipt sent to me by Mark Münzel for the money paid to Stolz by Arnaldo Kant for Indian labour supplied. The Chaco missionary asked, What about it? If there was any money changing hands, that was where it went—into the mission funds.

161

There was no secret about Mr Stolz's activities as an Indian-catcher. He had been out several times recently 'to make contact', he said, and grinned knowingly at his use of the euphemism, and once, indeed, had narrowly been missed by an arrow.

Jim Stolz, said the missionary, had his problems but fortunately in the Chaco stations these were at an end, and all was quiet. An American firm in the tanning business had paid one million dollars for a lump of territory half the size of North Dakota, and had given the mission a fair slice of this in token of its appreciation for their help in various ways. Right now it was more than they could handle and anyone going up there with cash in hand could probably pick up the odd thousand hectares very cheaply. He wondered if Donald and I might be interested, and was amazed when we said that we were not. It was a once-in-a-lifetime opportunity, he said.

On this journey the Chaco missionary did all the talking. Mrs Nicholls was as agreeable as ever, but her husband had little to say. I was beginning to wonder if he could be a mission ally, or even, in a wholly unsuspected guise, the government official Colonel Infanzón had insisted must accompany us to Cecilio Baez.* The stipulation that we should leave the camp before dark now gave rise to troubling speculations.

That evening we met Julio—in my case for what was to be a last meal together—dining as usual under the imposing tower of the Guaraní hotel which, probably in honour of some convention, flew the flags of all nations with festive effect. There were few cities in which better to relax in comfort after a day in the jungle, offering as it did all the pleasures of civilization in its decorous way. It was clean and well lit, and nobody bothered you on any pretext. Cadil-

---

* An account of the meeting with Stolz, allegedly written on British Embassy notepaper and signed by Nicholls, was later used by the NTM in a successful dispute with an American newspaper. All knowledge of this was denied by the British Embassy, as of a statement, also used in the action, claimed by the NTM to have been issued by the Embassy in commendation of the mission's work.

lacs crept by with an occasional murmur of warning on a 'courtesy horn' specially fitted for Asunción. Harp music lilted softly over the restaurant's system; hallucinogenic payé flowers spread their fragrance from the table tops; a raised finger brought a waiter's instant attention with a cheerful cry of *a sus órdenes*. Mini-skirted policewomen paraded in pairs, and Julio said that if you winked at one she would sometimes wink back. All that was necessary in Asunción was to refrain from inquisitiveness and from any urge to look behind the scenes. And this applied to the country itself, and in particular the certain special areas of the Gran Chaco, and the eastern forests approaching the frontier with Argentina, now in the process of urgent demolition.

This was a relaxed and congenial occasion. Julio knew perfectly well where we had been but nothing was said about our journey. Apart from that, we talked about every subject under the sun, and then I told him that I would be leaving to go back to England next day, and I could see that he was sincerely sorry. Donald wanted to stay a little longer, and, with that, Julio's spirits revived. Once again giving an outstanding demonstration of his power to pull strings, he said that he would see to it that Donald got an invitation to the President's birthday party, to be held later in the week. This, as I later learned, duly arrived together with the further offer of a presidential launch for a fishing trip on the Paraguay river. Donald took this up and, even allowing for the conventional angler's hyperbole, seems to have caught some memorable fish.

11

The trip to Venezuela was planned as a kind of spiritual antidote to the creeping depression produced by the experience of tribal people, either—as in Vietnam—under attack, or when reduced by one means or another to the ultimate degradation and misery of the missionary camps. Unreached tribes still existed and television producers like Brian Moser had produced spell-binding films of them leading their traditional lives. With every year they became fewer, and rightly enough such reserves as the Xingu in Brazil had been closed not only to the missionaries, but to such casual visitors as myself, who—however innocent the intention—could wipe out a village by spreading among people without immunization the germs of even the common cold.

In 1982 the BBC showed an exciting short film of the visit by one of its teams to the Panare of the savannah of Venezuela. The cameramen were taken by the tribe on fishing and hunting expeditions, and took part in lively and memorable feast. Their hosts were handsome, well-formed people, with bodies displayed to advantage by the absolute minimum of clothing, and kept in good shape by an excellent diet of vegetables and fish, and a highly energetic life-style. They were first-rate artists, weaving decorative baskets in demand all over Venezuela, and even the possessors of a robust sense of humour. On a hunting expedition in which the Panare were shooting at monkeys with their blowguns, one hunter, exasperated at having missed three times, said, 'If I don't get the next one, I'm going to shoot the photographer.'

The expedition was led by the anthropologist, Paul Henley, whom I later met in Cambridge. It had been Paul's unique experience to have lived among these attractive people for some years, to have been formally admitted to membership of the tribe, and adopted by one of the women as her son. He was planning to return to the Panare area to continue his field studies there early in the following year and it was agreed that we should join forces in Caracas. Donald McCullin was to be included in this venture and Paul hoped that he would be able to photograph Panare ceremonies largely conducted at night, which he himself had been unable to do through lack of suitable apparatus and the somewhat specialized experience required to handle it.

We were now about to confront the soul-destroying procedure of the battle with Venezuelan bureaucracy, and only after some months decided that the struggle to obtain visas should be abandoned because it was clear that these would never be forthcoming. In the end we simply got on a plane and went, as presumably most travellers to Venezuela eventually do. No one in the Immigration Department in Caracas seemed surprised when we arrived without them, although technically we were there illegally. Dizzy with success, we now entertained the huge misapprehension that our trouble with red tape was at an end, little realizing that every working hour of the next ten days would be spent waiting in the anterooms of the ministries, edging hour by hour towards the time when—if we were luckier than most—all the necessary permits would be issued for our travel in the interior.

In these glum surroundings we saw the same faces each day, of the hopeful, the disillusioned, and the desperate, some of whom had been coming here for weeks. Applicants were called upon to supply letters of support from institutions and persons of standing, embassy certificates of good conduct, and short essays describing the applicant's intended action if ever allowed into the interior. These had to be taken to an office for notarization some miles away which was usually closed for one reason or other. If open it was crammed with persons awaiting the notary's attention until, without warning, the doors were closed again, and applicants were ushered out and told to return next day. Thus one profitless day followed another. We heard of one man, at the end of his tether, who had gone off without a permit and had been picked up by the National Guard and thrown into the *calobozo* in some nameless village in the back of

165

Venezuelan beyond, and held there for weeks while it was decided what was to be done with him.

The Ministry's offices were full of Venezuelan anthropologists who ran into the same difficulties as we did in the matter of permits, and they complained that only the missionaries, who abounded in the interior, were able to travel at will. One of the Venezuelans had been involved in the recent congressional investigation into missionary activity in Venezuela. 'We'd give anything to get them off our backs,' he said, 'but there's nothing we can do about it if the State Department wants them here. Even if they're kicked out, they come back again.'

He added an extraordinary piece of information. Down in the south near the Brazilian frontier the missionaries had established a hold on the Yanomami Indians, and had let it be known that anthropologists, who were lumped together with undesirables of all kinds as communists, should stay out. 'If I go down there to work,' he said. 'I'll have to employ Yanomami bodyguards to look after me. The missionaries are taking over the country.'

While assuming that there would be missionaries in plenty in Venezuela, and among them representatives of the North American sects, I had mistakenly imagined that their impact at this stage was slight—a misapprehension strengthened by the BBC film. Now to my consternation I learned that the NTM was strongly entrenched, and that a tentative establishment of a husband-and-wife post in the Colorado Valley had taken hold and showed signs of expansion. By way of consolation the anthropologist cited the Panare's record of resistance. They had come on the scene in the 1800s to fill a vacuum in the area which they now occupied, left by the over-zealous labours of Catholic missionaries. These had completely eliminated the original Indian population. The Panare had shown themselves almost uniquely able to cope with modern times. Whatever was of value to them, such as metal tools, they took. The rest they turned their backs on. For once, in his opinion, the NTM would find they had bitten off more than they could chew.

*

To add to delays, uncertainties and discomforts, Venezuela had decided on the very day of our arrival to devalue its currency, and the banks remained closed so that no traveller's cheques were cashed for the whole of our stay. The small amount of cash we had with us went rapidly. Caracas is expensive. Apart from other expenses, taxi journeys to and from the ministries alone, at £15 a time, came to £60 a day. It was not the most endearing of cities in which to be condemned to an enforced stay. We had put up at an average three-star hotel in a traffic-glutted boulevard which possessed no restaurant and, when we asked at the reception for suggestions as to where to eat, the manager recommended a 'pizza-parlour' just down the street.

We told him we had been thinking of something more adventurous and he said that if it was adventure we were in search of we had come to the right place. An excellent Italian restaurant, he said, was twice as far away as the pizza-parlour, and therefore the chances of being assaulted on the way there or back were exactly twice as great. He mentioned that local muggers used knives or guns.

The permit arrived and we set out the same day in Paul's Land Rover, driving eastwards along the coastal road to Barcelona where we stayed the night. Next day we headed southwards to cross the Orinoco at Ciudád Bolívar, thereafter taking the western highway following the upstream course of the river to Caicara, a brash and exuberant settlement in frontier style, serving the needs of an area possibly the size of one of the larger English counties. Here we bought presents for the Indians with whom we hoped to stay, and articles of prime necessity for ourselves, hammocks, mosquito nets, cooking equipment, beer and many other useful articles we had forgotten in our hurry to pick up in Caracas.

At Caicara, roads, as most of us understood the word, came to an end, and now we struck out across the savannah towards Colorado, where Indians had established themselves. Once again we were in an utterly untouched landscape, which, mysteriously, could never have been mistaken for any of the primeval areas of Mexico, Guatemala or

Paraguay. The savannah had always been as it was, free from the cropping of grazing animals and intact from the plough. Clumps of trees, now in flower, had planted themselves at exact intervals, and a thin scroll of gallery forest across the landscape marked the course of an unseen river. Through these trivial variants in the scene grass spread like a limitless lawn in three directions to the horizon, and only to the south the misted escarpment of the Sierra de la Cerbetana overshadowed the plain.

The Colorado Valley lay under its foothills, and coming down the trail the communal houses showed among the trees by the river like delicately woven straw hats. Panare women, wearing only g-strings, tassels and beads, were moving about with busy, strutting steps. The first male Panare who came into sight was a handsome lad of about eighteen, naked except for a splendidly woven red loincloth, astride a battered bicycle on which I was shocked to see that the message had been painted, *Christ Saves Us*. He pedalled away out of view among the communal houses. At the edge of the settlement was the building of the New Tribes Mission, a four-square uncompromising structure of breeze-blocks and corrugated iron at the head of its landing strip. In the calm, self-effacing outlines of the Colorado Valley it typified another world.

The Indians trooped out of their houses to welcome us. Paul Henley presented us to the thirty-two adult men and women as the extended family who had adopted him and to his fictive mother. We had brought gifts for them all, and in accordance with egalitarian principles each man received an identical nylon fishing line, and each woman a garishly decorated enamel bowl. In addition we handed over a sack of rice—in return for our share in the communal meals we might be invited to join. We were then directed to hang our hammocks in an empty house at the highest point of the village, recommended to us as being relatively free of mosquitoes. It was a traditional thatched construction, of the kind that the Panare built in three weeks, well swept, and free from litter of any kind. Following a perfunctory inspec-

168

tion to make sure that there was no rattlesnake in residence, we installed ourselves.

Soon after, Panare of all ages and both sexes began their visits, examining and commenting in soft, low clucking monosyllables on our persons and our equipment, dropping into unoccupied hammocks, and just standing about in companionable groups long after darkness had fallen, trying clearly to make us feel at home.

I noticed that the Panare either kept quite still, forming graceful Gauguinesque groupings, or tended to move in a rapid and purposeful way. The elderly men and ladies who visited us walked in the brisk and springy manner we associate with youth, and held themselves bolt upright. Girls came tripping in with the quick, delicate steps of typists on high heels over polished floors. This being a formal occasion, one or two nubile girls had tied a few square inches of cloth across their pubic regions, but others had not bothered. All had gone to the effort of tying pom-poms to their g-strings. These dangled in a provocative way over their buttocks. Possibly in nothing more than a polite pretence of interest they examined the uncovered parts of our bodies, drawing each other's attention to irregular skin markings, or scars. The little girls permitted themselves more liberties than the little boys, and were delighted to be allowed to tug at the hair on Don's forearms—a phenomenon producing undimmed curiosity and pleasure throughout the whole of our stay.

The missionaries had made a start with their inculcation of a sense of values by the provision of almost every toddler with a piggy-bank. The older children showed us padlocks and keys from the same source. At this stage in Panare evolution, when there were no doors to keep locked, they remained purely ornamental, incorporated occasionally in necklaces. A demure girl who had borrowed a friend's waist-cloth approached us with what was clearly a request. Paul translated. It proved that she was begging softly for one of the torch-batteries on which she had become dependent.

*

169

The working day in these countries starts at first light, if not before, and as soon as I could force my eyelids apart I saw that a number of Indians were back. Some of these had propped themselves in their gracefully inert poses against the sections of tree trunks supporting the roof, a few had slipped into vacant hammocks and the rest were going through our belongings. Each object after close inspection was carefully replaced where it had been found.

The settlement below, brushed lightly by pink mists arising from the river, was full of activity. Paul had mentioned that the Panare were free from the despotism of clocks, got up and went to bed at no particular time, and if minded so to do would often work through the night on any task that happened to have engaged their interest. While I attended to innumerable mosquito bites and Donald cooked himself the morning porridge for which he is famous, Paul had gone down to learn from his Panare family what tidings there were of the expected *katayinto*, the boys' initiation ceremony we were all much hoping to witness, and for Donald to be able to photograph.

It seems likely that most of the tribes surviving in undamaged form celebrate in one form or another their version of the *katayinto*. Fifteen years before, when in Brazil, I had come to hear about the great Quarup ceremony of the tribe known as the Cintas Largas. It had received tragic publicity because this had been chosen as the one day of the year when the whole tribe was certain to be concentrated in its village, and could be most conveniently wiped out by the aerial attack synchronized by that of the overland expedition.

The annual ceremony of the ill-fated Cintas Largas lasted (as does the *katayinto*) for a day and a night, and was an occasion for prolonged feasting, the drinking of ceremonial beer, and all-night dancing to the music of flutes and pan-pipes. Far more importantly the Quarup was a theatrical representation of the legends of the Creation interwoven with those of the tribe itself. It was both a mystery play and a family reunion, attended not only by the living but the ancestral spirits who appeared as dancers in masquerade, to be consulted on immediate problems, to comfort the mourners and to assure them that not even death would be allowed to disrupt the unity and the continuity of the tribe.

Many features of the Quarup as celebrated in remote Brazil corresponded to those of the *katayinto* in Venezuela. It cannot have been accidental, but perhaps the evolutionary process took a hand so that ceremonies of this kind, developed over the millenia, contributed to survival. They can be seen as a device for passing on accumulated tribal experience in the palatable form of dramatic entertainments to non-literate people. The *katayinto* provides a good time for all, but there is a solid core of instruction.

The ceremony embodies the initiation rites of boys about to enter manhood, and for good measure it provides a suitable opportunity for piercing the ears of infant children. These operations are enveloped in a cocoon of symbolical activities, all of which are bound to be mysterious to the onlooker, and some probably to the performers themselves. Ritual clothing is worn, ritual food eaten, ritual music played and ritual dances performed. The ceremony abounds in protocol as to who may or may not do what, and when. Some episodes are inscrutable, as when the boys who must be dressed in the loincloths of manhood by someone who is a stranger to the village receive a light thrashing on the backs of the legs at the hands of yet another outsider.

From this symbolic labyrinth a single dramatic interlude stands out. This is the sudden incursion of a group of threatening and aggressive strangers who angrily demand to be given beer. No one is under the slightest delusion that this is anything but a piece of theatre, because the newcomers will be recognizable to all present as Panare from a nearby settlement who have agreed to play this particular role. While the young initiates look on, their elders join heatedly in the argument that ensues, but gradually voices are lowered, reason returns, and the visitors, finally pacified, are invited to join in the general merriment.

Paul suggests in his book, *The Panare: Tradition and Change in the Amazon Frontier* (from which all of this information is drawn), that this episode which is central to the

171

ceremony symbolizes the young initiates' necessity for arriving at a peaceful arrangement with a potentially threatening outside world. The conclusion seems impossible to refute.

In 1981 Paul was told by the Panare that they had been obliged to cut this part out of the *katayinto* 'because God did not like it'. How singular—and how revealing—that the sect should have specifically objected to that part of the ceremony that seemed to us all to advocate conciliation and the peaceful settlement of disputes. In the following year, 1982, there had been no initiation ceremony at all, and Paul had assumed at first that this had been no more than a postponement. Now he returned with a discouraging report. We were to hear that God had again raised objections and the *katayinto* would not take place once more, although it 'might' be held next year. It seemed likely that the missionaries' strategy was to encourage indefinite postponement.

It was an astonishing state of affairs. The Panare offered the phenomenon of an Indian tribe that had been in close contact with non-Indians for at least a century, yet had succeeded in retaining their aboriginal culture intact. They had shown, according to the Venezuelan anthropologist Maria Eugenia Villalón who had devoted some ten years to a study of them, 'an almost incredible imperviousness to the influences of the Western World'. Now suddenly having withstood so many pressures for so many years, it seemed as though they were on the point of capitulation, and about to surrender their ethnic identity, their 'Indianness' by renouncing the most important ceremony in tribal life, that in which the boy assumes the rights and obligations of a man.

Although in Indian style the Panare displayed no sign of any emotion, save perhaps curiosity, they were clearly delighted at our visit, all the more so because they knew that the Land Rover would be at their service when there was heavy fetching and carrying to be done. Among their garden produce they grew sugar cane and heavy root vegetables, raising the cash they were coming more and more to need by selling a substantial amount of this to non-Indians, the *criollos* living in the neighbourhood. The *criollos*, who raised cattle, and fed themselves otherwise somewhat monotonously on their own meat, bought all the fresh vegetables they could get from their Indian neighbours. In addition the Panare made decorative baskets for which collectors of Indian handicrafts paid high prices. These baskets, which they did not use themselves, they sold cheaply to *criollo* dealers acting as middlemen. With the cash raised on their vegetable produce and their baskets the Panare had begun to buy such consumer goods as record players, soap, aspirin, dentifrice, popcorn, scent, old bicycles, and above all torch batteries from the missionaries. The missionaries no longer gave desirable things away, as Mr Halterman had at first done, but charged for everything, cash on the nail, although their prices, Paul said, undercut those of the local traders who naturally showed some resentment over this incursion into their trade.

The *criollos* lived in small, scattered villages in the vicinity. They and their fathers before them had remained in close contact with the Indians, and had nothing much against them. In this backwater of Spain's dominion of old where *compadrazgo*—a formally established friendship between males—still existed, some Indians had *compadres* among the *criollo* population. This was the case on the village of Maniapure where we took a half dozen Panare in the Land Rover, loaded up with their produce for sale.

It was a lively if slatternly little place of a few wooden shacks and a couple of *cantinas*, where cattlemen, briefly released from the boredom of their lives in the saddle, relaxed in exuberant fashion. Two unnecessarily sophisticated-looking tarts preened at the bar in the place we chose, in surroundings otherwise homely and dishevelled. A flower-decorated wall-ikon commemorated a notable murder; the barman had one eye, the chairs offered either a back or a seat—but not both, and most of the customers carried a gun.

They were all genial and polite, happy in each other's company, and delighted to meet strangers. Sitting as best

173

they could in their ruined chairs they played dominoes, throwing each domino down like a challenge to a duel. Whatever they had to say was suppressed by the uproar from an old juke-box, looking like part of a crashed car. Our Indians had already unloaded their produce, had accepted soft drinks from their *criollo* friends, and now stood together, in an absolutely motionless group, having each of them automatically fallen into the inevitable Panare martyrdom of San Sebastian posture.

We took our drinks outside. Parakeets squabbled like sparrows in the trees all round, and a boy who had managed to catch a few offered them in plastic bags at 25 cents each. The sky was curdled with birds, among them being two majestic vultures with white wings and tails, spiralling under a cloud like a meringue.

A horseman rode up, a guitar on his back, and a spur in some way attached to a single, naked foot. At our gesture of invitation he sat on the edge of our table, accepted a beer and began to play. At this moment a tourist car stopped on the bridge at the end of the village and the occupants emptied some rubbish into the river. This was snatched up by eagerly awaiting catfish.

'There's a pool down there,' the guitarist explained, 'the fish get trapped in the dry season. The otters go after them.'

'Don't they eat fish in this place?' I asked.

Our friend seemed surprised at the question. 'In the whole of my life I've eaten nothing but steak and rice,' he said. 'I long to eat beans, but they make you fart, which is ridiculous. As for fish, I've never even tasted it, and I can't say I want to.'

The Panare lived well, their diet was varied and excellent, and their life expectancy was considerably longer than that of the *criollos*, yet Paul had noticed a certain change for the worse, the first sign being that their food intake was diminishing. Until 1974 their principal settlement and their communal houses had been in the mountains where they had lived close to their main source of food. Since then, and

174

shortly after the establishment in Colorado of the New Tribes Mission, they had begun to move down the plain. It was clear that the mission's policy of 'attracting' and settling the Indians was taking effect, and the time the Panare expended on cash cropping or making baskets for sale had increased at the expense of the time devoted to procuring food for their own consumption. Now that they had abandoned their settlements in the mountains it became tiring and irksome to undertake a day's journey to the areas in which they had previously hunted—and there was no game in the nearby savannah. Meat supplies, then, were running short. Another contingency—although they were unaware of this—threatened them. Venezuela, most enlightened of the South American countries in the treatment of its Indians, did its best to defend their rights in their traditional territories, but would find it difficult to intervene once for any reason the Indians withdrew, and invaders moved in. Should this happen the Panare would be committed for good to the plains where, apart from the vegetables they grew, and dry-season fishing, food would be in short supply. And there would be no going back.

The missionary strategy foresaw and worked for this conclusion. It was showing signs of success in another direction. The whole Panare concept of society is based upon an abundance of food, contributed by those who have procured it to a pool, which is then shared equally by every member of the community, whether they have been able to play a part in its procurement or not. Should a food shortage arise, or be for any reason provoked, Paul said, the principle of sharing might be irrevocably damaged by the necessity imposed on those who had provided the food of feeding themselves, and therefore ceasing to contribute to the pool.

Moreover, such festivals as the *katayinto* had always been organized on the assumption that there was meat to spare, and this, obtained by hunting in the mountains, was smoked and stored until there was enough for the *katayinto* to take place. Settlement of the Panare close to the mission in the plains meant a fall in food supplies, and with this the missionary goal of total dependability would be in sight.

We visited Guanama, one of the small Panare communities in the neighbourhood, having a population of about half the size of that of Colorado, although compared with Colorado it was a hot place, sweltering at the end of an unfinished dirt road that faltered southwards in the general direction of the Amazon. A half a dozen Panare males came out of a communal round-house, moving springily like ballet-dancers with offerings of hot mango juice. As in Colorado they were dressed in no more than scrupulously woven loin-cloths and armlets of blue and white beads. Their average height would have been an inch or two taller than that of the cattlemen of Maniapure, but a long ancestry of nomad-ism had shaped them, and by comparison their nearest *criollo* neighbours, who spent their lives on horseback, or in cars, seemed awkwardly put together, even a little mis-shapen. The Panare, who could walk or run fifty miles in a day across the savannah if put to it, were lean, lithe and supple, coming close in their bodily proportions to the classic ideal.

Guanama was spruce and trim, with everything in place, a little like an anthropological model in London's Museum of Mankind. It communal houses, each of them sheltering two or three families, were masterpieces of Stone Age archi-tecture, built for all weathers and marvellously cool under their deep fringing of thatch. It was a quiet place as Panare settlements are wont to be. The dogs remained silent and respectful, the children—as ever—did not cry, and the adults, back from hunting or work in their gardens, slipped into their hammocks after greeting us, to resume soft-voiced discussions on the topics of the day. Only one thing seemed out of place in this calm and confiding atmosphere. This was the new barbed wire fence—the first we had seen in the great openness of rural Venezuela—a symbolic intrusion, as we saw it, of an alien point of view.

We made a point of this visit to Guanama after a report of extraordinary happenings by María Eugenia Villalón, with whom I had corresponded before a meeting in Caracas. She had been in Guanama about eighteen months previous to our visit to record Panare songs and, returning to the area

176

this year while engaged in a census of the Indian minorities, she had proposed to entertain the villagers by playing these back to them. No sooner had the tape recorder been switched on than the Indians leaped to their feet in a state of panic, running in all directions, their hands clasped over their ears. The Panare explained to María Eugenia that what they had been compelled to listen to was the voice of the Devil speaking through their mouths. Now they had found Jesus and henceforward would sing nothing but hymns. They lined up to oblige with one of these, a Panare version of 'Weary of Earth and Laden with My Sin', the first line repeated *ad infinitum* to Mexican guitars, and the rattle of maracas. It was clear to Señora Villalón that the New Tribes Mission had moved in, but the question was how they had brought about this instant conversion, for there was no mission post in the vicinity, and it was known that the missionaries rarely ventured far abroad. The only conclusion was that this was the work of one of the trained native evangelists — the 'deacons' — they were beginning to employ.

But apart from the barbed-wire fence Guanama was free from the ugliness too often associated with the disruption of custom and belief. We preferred not to abandon hope and Paul now put the fatal question. 'When is your initiation ceremony to be held?' The reply was a depressing one, confirming our worst fears. 'There will be no ceremony. God is against it. We have turned our back on all these things.'

It was dark when we got back to Colorado. We established ourselves in our house, lit the lamp, scanned the dark corners for possible intrusion of noxious company, unfolded our mosquito nets, heated the contents of a couple of tins for supper, then settled ourselves for a nightcap of rum and a chat under the stars. Shortly we noticed two very faint tentacles of light reaching out towards us from the dark silhouette of the village, and understood that the Indians had been awaiting our return, and now proposed to pay us a visit. It turned out that they were all young children and nothing could have been more poetic than this scene as they came closer up the two winding paths, clad in little more than bracelets and necklaces, all of them pushing their bicycles, the little girls shining their torches, and the boys with their hands full of fireflies which lighted the path for a few inches ahead.

Soon they were with us. The bicycles, all bearing the inscription *Christo Viene* (Christ is coming) were carefully parked, and the children swarmed in to pore over the pictures of pop stars in Venezuelan magazines, to be entertained by Donald's conjuring tricks (which produced the first smiles I had ever seen on a Panare face), and to climb into our hammocks in search of any articles of any interest that might have been hidden there to keep them safe from tribal mischief.

There was always a father or two in the background with a baby round his neck and perhaps another under his arm. As soon as a baby was weaned its father lost no opportunity to grab it up, often managing to carry on with whatever he might be working at—in one instance tightening a bicycle chain—and controlling the child with another hand. Until the hyperactivity of late childhood set in, parent and child would be hardly separated. Linda Myers of the NTM, writing from the Panare mission at this time, said,

Why is there so little outward expression of love . . .? Everyone is so detached. These are the answers I got to my questions: 'Why learn to love someone who may die soon?' 'Why develop precious memories of someone you may have for only a short time?' . . . In the Panare old ways of life before the Gospel was shared with them everything was bad.

Where we saw every possible manifestation of parental love, it was clear that the NTM could not.

To Donald's great dismay the Panare made it clear that they did not wish photographs to be taken. This became evident

178

next morning. We had awakened with the first light, by which time numerous children had arrived to continue their investigations broken off on the night before, and a number of adult men had placed themselves like pieces of gilded statuary at the entrance to the house. Presently we heard the putter of a motorcycle engine and an Indian on a Yamaha came up the path with two bead-festooned babies astride the petrol tank. Donald reached for the camera; consternation broke out, and in a moment we were alone.

On all sides there were marvellous shots to be taken, but Paul thought the camera should be kept out of sight, even counselling Donald to avoid the temptation to take tele-photo shots of Indians engaged in any of their routine activi-ties, or of the impressive assembly of the whole community for the ritual of the evening meal, in which we had so far not been invited to join. In Paul's opinion the only time when discreet photography might be feasible was when the Indians were involved in some activity, such as hunting, that engaged the whole of their attention. The problem here was that they never announced in advance their intention to go on a hunt, which was more of a spontaneous impulse when a number of them suddenly decided that the time had come for pleasurable relaxation after the relative boredom of an extended period of making baskets for sale.

Then again, the further problem for all concerned, as always happened, was that as soon as the missionary policy of 'sedenterization' showed signs of success the pressure on the game in the immediate vicinity of any settlement increased to a point where it began to disappear. I found it disappointing that I saw no interesting animal life at Color-ado, having hoped at least for an occasional glimpse of a giant ant-eater, an armadillo, an agouti—or even a fox. Three years before Paul had gone off on a monkey hunt with the Indians to stock up with meat for the *katayinto*, and the Panare had used their blowguns with great success. Now there was no longer a monkey to be seen.

Not only that but, through a break in the chain of cause and effect, the blowguns, too, had been put away and I never saw one in use. This, Paul explained was by no means

179

through any voluntary change in the Panare hunting technique, for not only had the game become scarce, but the guns were wearing out. The Panare were unable to make blowguns themselves but obtained them in deals with the neighbouring Piaroa Indians who were the accepted specialists in their manufacture, and who were accustomed to go on trading expeditions during the dry season. In exchange for the guns the Panare supplied curare of the finest available quality, prepared from the ·bark of a local tree. Now, suddenly, the trade was at an end, for the Piaroa had been missionized both by the fundamentalists and the Catholics. These had turned them into wage-labourers, so that the days of Piaroa trading expeditions were at an end. A few of the Panare had been able to buy old shotguns but did not care much for them owing to the excessive damage they inflicted upon the quarry—so often birds, hunted for their plumage.

The best hope for photography lay in an alligator hunt in the river running through the settlement, where we often went to bathe and wash up the plates after a meal. This unimportant tributary of the Orinoco was on the whole shallow, with numerous sandbanks and rare pools in which a small alligator might be expected to lurk. It was beautiful in a weird sort of way. Its bed had been cut into laterite rock, but shining through the pale sherry-coloured water it seemed quite inexplicably to be plated with gold leaf. Great, pointed, black leaves lying on the bottom were being shifted, slowly downstream by the current, like a flotilla of miniature war-canoes, going into the attack. There were numerous small fish here, not more than two inches in length, which, although bearing no relationship to the legendary piranha, darted in constantly to nip at bare flesh. It was *de rigueur* here to bathe in the nude, and although we made a point of keeping off the scene when the tribal maidens were about, overpowered by curiosity they rarely returned the compliment. The shallows where our bathing and washing up took place were haunted by innumerable humming birds. Unaccountably, in our opinion, they were attracted by the special fragrance of the Fairy Liquid we used, and gathered to buzz excitedly in our ears and to dive on the rinsings as soon as we appeared in sight.

Fortunately we had not long to wait before an alligator hunt took place, but little time to prepare for it. Gallery jungle hardly more than twenty yards wide covered the river banks for a mile or two outside the village, after which the course of the river divided to form a number of islands, some of them wooded. Here, in reduced form, we were in an Amazonian environment. At this point we all took to the water, although—warned by Paul of the possibility of treading on sting-rays ensconced in the sand—we were slowed down by extreme caution. The Panare raced about in all directions, chasing fish into shallow blind-alleys of water where they could be speared. Unfortunately there was no catching up with them. The Indians moved as fast through the shallow water as we did on dry land, and wherever there was action it took place out of reach of the camera. Distantly we saw an arm raised, a lance go into the pool, a movement of agitation in the water and a fish flapping on the bank. The capture of a single undersized alligator was seen as a series of small watery explosions. It happened a hundred yards away and by the time we had splashed and floundered to the spot it was all over, and the animal, no more than four feet in length, had been dragged away to be cut up. The Indians' verdict at the end of it was that it had not been a success, and once again it showed the way things were going. It was months since a substantial alligator had been killed. Not a single monkey remained in the gallery forest and with every such expedition fewer and smaller fish were caught. Paul promised the Indians that we would take them in a fish-poisoning expedition to one of the rivers deep in the savannah, and normally beyond their reach, as soon as they could go to the mountains and collect the liana from which the poison was made.

12

Next day María Eugenia Villalón and her husband Henry Corradini arrived unexpectedly. Now that the census of the Indian population that had kept them busy for some months was at an end, they were hoping to take a few days' rest. Characteristically this was to be spent among the Indians, and they had chosen Colorado which they had known over many years, and for which they had developed a deep affection.

The Corradinis were professionals of travel for whom a journey into the Venezuelan savannah was hardly more than a casual outing, and settling into an Indian *maloca* no less convenient than checking in at a three-star hotel. In a matter of minutes they had hung up their hammocks, and arranged the floor space beneath with their equipment like army-kit laid out for inspection. Everything necessary to sustain life had been fitted neatly into their motor-home and was instantly accessible. They were furnished with that supreme armament against tropical discomfort, iced drinks—which they shared with us as we sat outside on their camp chairs looking down on the settlement and admiring the overlaying profiles of the night. Donald and I, still condemned by inexperience to rough it, slept in our clothes under our suffocating mosquito nets. The seasoned travellers slipped smoothly and unobtrusively into their night attire, and had provided themselves with nets which although excluding the tiniest of flying insects, allowed the passage of air. Perhaps the Panare had caught a sniff of discipline in the air, for this was the first night when their customary invasion failed to take place.

Conducting the census must have provided extraordinary interest. Such exercises in a Third World environment rarely amount to more than a partial success, and when, as among tribal societies, people refuse to stay in one place the difficulties encountered must be overwhelming. The Corradinis were carried by helicopter, but in Venezuela, in the past, some Indian groups could only be reached after days and weeks of foot-slogging journeys, at the end of which pitfalls were plentiful. Tribes might be highly fragmented. The Panare, numbering in all just under two thousand, were split up into thirty-eight communities, any of which, as the Corradinis discovered, might decide at any time to pull up sticks and go somewhere else, encouraged in any such move by the knowledge that, if pushed to it, a new village could be built in as little as two weeks.

Language was a problem. In the case of the Hoti, the Panare's nearest neighbours, only one man—a missionary—had been able to master the local tongue. Even then, realizing that single-handed he would never succeed in translating the Gospel into the language, he had withdrawn. Consequently there was no way of explaining to the Hotis what was expected of them when the helicopter finally landed in their midst.

Both the Corradinis were dismayed at the inexplicable progress made by the evangelists among the Panare communities, and by the ease with which the missionaries assumed a kind of dominance in such places as Colorado, where the governmental presence was hardly noticeable. They reported the alarm felt by Venezuelans in general, and their frustration and perplexity that despite their huge unpopularity not only in Venezuela, but in Colombia, Peru and Brazil where great efforts had been made to expel them it had only been possible at most to debar the missionary sects from certain areas. To these they had always found the means to return.

They had brought with them a great deal of printed information about the two Congressional investigations into missionary conduct, the latest of which, opening in 1979, remained in session for two years, filling the press with bizarre accounts of evangelical goings-on. Naval captain, Marino Blanco, charged with keeping an eye on the doings of foreigners in Venezuela's remote regions, spoke of scientific espionage (the allegations had been made in several Latin American countries). He noted that the missionaries

183

inevitably installed themselves in areas known to contain strategic materials, such as cobalt and uranium, and claimed to have proof that they were in the pay of American multinationals. They had been in trouble in Colombia, suffering temporary expulsion for 'damage to national interests', and for 'assisting illicit exploration carried out by transnational companies'. The captain had found missionary baggage labelled 'combustible material' to contain military uniforms, and 'other articles'—this being taken by the press to refer to geiger-counters. The uniforms were explained away by the missionaries as intended to impress the Indians. Captain Blanco said that the head of the New Tribes Mission had tried to bribe him.

A Ye'cuana Indian, Simeon Jiménez, speaking defective Spanish with much eloquence, appeared to describe the prohibitions imposed upon his people as soon as the missionaries had taken hold. They included the drinking of fermented juices, dancing, singing, the use of musical instruments, tribal medicines and tobacco, and the tribal custom of arranging marriages within the framework of kinship groups.

Jiménez stressed the psychological terror to which the Ye'cuanas were subjected to force them to become converted. In particular he cited the appearance of a comet, described by the chief missionary in the area as heralding the end of the world. The missionary had gathered the Ye'cuanas together and given them three days, on pain of suffering a fiery extinction, to break with their wicked past. They were later warned by the same man of a communist plot to drive the missionaries out of the country, saying that if this were to happen US Airforce planes would be sent to bomb Ye'cuana villages.

I was unable to see Simeón himself while in Caracas and listen to an account of their traumatic experiences from his own lips, because he was seven days away by canoe in the Orinoco jungles. Instead I called on his wife, Dr Nelly Arvelo, a distinguished anthropologist who had set the seal of her approval on the lifestyle of primitive hunters and gatherers by marrying one. She confirmed all her husband had had to say, including an incident when Simeón's aged grandmother had come to him in tears, imploring him to give up his struggle before they were all reduced to ashes.

Terror apart, Dr Arvelo said, the missionaries had worked out a new kind of punishment for those who resisted conversion. 'Indians,' she said, 'like to do everything together. They share everything, particularly their food. They're very close to each other. The missionaries understood this so they worked out that the best way to punish those who didn't want to be converted was by isolation. As soon as they had a strong following in a village they would order the converts to have nothing more to do with those who held out. No one, not even their own parents, was allowed to talk to them, and they were obliged to eat apart from the rest. It was the worst punishment an Indian could imagine, and often it worked.'

Simeón Jiménez's testimony was followed in the Congressional hearing by the appearance of a plane-load of converts with short-back-and-side haircuts, baseball caps and bumper boots flown in from the jungle, but their offer of a hymn session was turned down by the commission. Some embarrassment in the missionary camp was caused by the arrival of a supportive Indian group from the frontier area with Guyana—a stronghold of the competitive Seventh Day Adventists. Finding that several of the delegation had been infected by heresy, they were hastily dismissed.

The cause of evangelism seemed weakened by the showing of a highly praised film (*Yo Hablo a Caracas*) of life among the Makiritare Indians by the Venezuelan director Carlos Azpurua, with a lively commentary by their shaman Barne Javari. The shaman denounced missionary interference in the life of his people with extreme fervour, and a little of the flavour of his attack, delivered largely in incantatory style, may survive in translation.

Wanadi made us all from good white earth.
He made the good and the bad. Spanish, French and now the Juduncu (missionaries).
He gave the whites iron, that's where the trouble lay.

They invaded, they attacked us with iron. We couldn't resist.
We claim no more than the headwaters of three small rivers.
We are neither Catholic nor Protestant. Go, leave us in peace.
In return we promise never to invade you, or interfere with your customs.

A group of foreign anthropologists, three of them British, wrote a letter to a Caracas newspaper calling for the Mission's expulsion, and two American signatories were immediately summoned to their embassy to receive an ambassadorial rebuke. According to Captain Blanco there was at least one other intervention by the US Embassy in support of the New Tribes Mission. 'I ordered the arrest of two American engineers named Ward and Curry, who were carrying out (illegal) scientific investigations . . . Later it was proved that James Bou (head of the New Tribes Mission in Venezuela) had organized their journey . . . Mr Bou telephoned the US Embassy, and the Counsellor of the Embassy then called me, asking me to release the two men.'

The feelings of the Venezuelans as a whole were summed up by the Apostolic Vicar of Puerto Ayacucho, the Amazonian capital, who said: 'These people have created a terrible confusion in the Indian's mind. They have no conception of Indian culture. When you forbid the Indian to dance, drink his yarake or eat the ashes of his dead one, you destroy his culture. One doesn't spread God's message by terror. The New Tribes Mission relies on force and if the native allows himself to be converted he does so not out of conviction, but fear.'

The creation of fear, in the opinion of Marí Eugenia Villalón, was the most powerful weapon in the missionary armoury—more potent even than the establishment of dependency upon goods which, without becoming wage-earners, the Indians could not procure.

In government service María had been in contact with

186

sixteen Venezuelan tribes and had arrived through her study of them at the conclusion that in all essentials there was little to differentiate them in matters of lifestyle and beliefs. They had evolved in a relatively benign climate in which the seeds could be grown and harvests gathered all the year round; the forests provided an abundance of game and the rivers were full of fish. These were the pre-conditions under which a competitive society never developed. The Indian groups in Venezuela—and so far as she knew, elsewhere in the Amazonian territory—had no chiefs. The communities worked together, lived in communal houses, took decisions at tribal discussions—in which the old men perhaps carried a little more weight than the rest. It was a peaceful and enjoyable life, with a good deal of feasting, ceremonial occasions, and some drunkenness. Paul Henley said that, in the five years of his association as a tribal member with the Panare, he had only heard of one crime, the author of which was regarded by the Indians as demented. There were no punishments.

With these advantages—of which the Indians were well aware—Indian tribal society presented a tough and resistant front to disruption from without. No one could convince them that what was on offer as an alternative existence was likely to be an improvement upon the one with which they were familiar. Then the missionaries moved on to the attack with their horrific picture of what awaited them as non-believers in the hereafter.

> 'The fearful and unbelieving . . . shall have their part in the lake which burneth with fire and brimstone, which is the second death.' We hear much these days, especially as related to the heathen, about the large hope, which according to the word NO must refer both to this present world and the next. So then the heathen, in spite of their religious philosophy, altruism and negation of self, are in a hopeless state. This, as God sees things, is being utterly lost. (Brown Gold, May 1981.)

The horror of burning everlastingly in the after-life was

dinned constantly into Indian ears by powerful airborne evangelists, who went so far as to encourage the belief that they were in regular radio contact with God. They built fences round their converts to isolate them from any possibility of rescue through more liberal religious teachings from the outside world.

Henry Carradini, who had prepared a study of the NTM's publications for presentation to the Venezuelan Dirección de Asuntos Indígenas (Indian Affairs Office) when their expulsion from the country had been under consideration, had taken note of books of scripture stories translated by the sect, which he suspected might have embodied manipulations of the holy text. In April 1972 Mr and Mrs Price of the NTM had carried out an aerial survey of the Panare region and decided on establishing a mission in the Colorado valley, where an easily accessible Indian settlement had been observed. A Jeep was sent to the spot, where they were well received and generously treated by unreached Indians so often referred to as savages. 'The Lord provided us with a Panare guide, without whom we could not have known where to go.' Although they had been told before that the Panare never worked for anyone, such was the native hospitality that 'the Indians seemed willing to have us come to live there and build a house for us . . . the Panare fellows pitched in and worked really hard.' Clearly there was satisfactory human material for the missionary labours here, and only a small note of disapproval obtrudes. 'On the other side of the clearing could be seen a large, hollowed-out log in which they had their drink, made of mashed corn, sugar cane and sweet potato. The tracks where they had danced were still visible.' However, when Mr and Mrs Price had arranged for the levelling of an air-strip and it was time to return to base, they left in a happy mood: 'I had grown attached to the valley and the people, and hated to leave, although we had been there only 8 days.'

Thereafter progress towards salvation went at a snail's pace. The Indians were helpful and friendly in every way but they had had contacts with missionaries—Jesuits and Franciscans—in the past, and had clearly not enjoyed the experience. Five years after the Lord had 'impressed upon the hearts' of the original three missionaries to settle where they did the Panare continued to lead their same old easygoing lives and remained as wary and unreceptive as ever. As late as March 1972 a brief report revealed that things were still not as they should have been. 'On the surface, it seems as though they (the Panare) have not the least interest in spiritual things.' This despite the fact as the report mentions that in addition to the missionary groups six trained native evangelists were at work in the tribe.

Up to this point the process of establishing dependency had failed in Colorado, so now, at quite an early stage in their activities in the valley the missionaries turned to their second weapon—fear. Two books based on what purported to be stories from the Bible were produced in translation, the first, *Learning about God* (1975) and the second, *The Panare Learn About the Devil* (1976). The creation of these had presented certain linguistic problems, solved in the end in resolute fashion.

Difficulties arose from the fact that, as in the majority of Indian languages, there are no equivalents in Panare for many words held as basic to the concepts of the Christian religion. There is none, for example, for sin, guilt, punishment and redemption. There are many other pitfalls. The concept of a universal God runs contrary to all the processes of Panare thought, and in any case he cannot be thanked, but only congratulated. 'God is love' may be translated 'the Great Spirit is not angry'. The Panare mentality and character were established in a relatively protected forest environment over thousands of years. In this famines were impossible, plagues are not recorded, and the wars that shaped our history were reduced here at most to a ceremonial skirmish. Consequently the Indians can only grope after the meaning of words coined in a more stressful society. The biblical dramas become hardly more than shadow plays. How can the walls of Jericho fall down for a man who has never seen a brick? How can an Indian, who has never

189

known dearth, be urged to store up treasure in heaven? What point can the parable of the talents of silver have to a Panare whose language possesses no word for profit? Most of the biblical animals are missing in the rain forest, so 'the Good Shepherd' may have to be translated as 'the food-sharer who looks after the pigs'.* Redemption is explained as a trading bargain after the arduous rigmarole of cash payments, debts and credits have finally been made clear. Adam and Eve and the fall of Man are omitted from Panare translations owing to their horror of incest.

But the basic sense of guilt was at the heart of the missionary problem and it was something that had to be manufactured, before repentance and salvation—both equally obscure concepts to the Panare—could be reached. The translators may have decided that the best way of tackling this was by re-editing the Scriptures in such a way as to implicate the Panare in Christ's death. Henry Corradini soon discovered that the New Tribes Mission's version of the Crucifixion as arranged for Indian consumption was at striking variance with that of the Bible. Gone were Judas's betrayal, the Romans, the Last Supper, the trial, Pontius Pilate turning away to wash his hands, and the crown of thorns. He read on:

The Panare killed Jesus Christ
because they were wicked
Let's kill Jesus Christ
said the Panare.
The Panare seized Jesus Christ.
The Panare killed in this way.
They laid a cross on the ground.
They fastened his hands and his feet
against the wooden beams, with nails.
They raised him straight up, nailed.

* To some the image seemed inappropriate, so elsewhere small numbers of sheep were imported and raised in an unfavourable environment, so that this could be put right.

The man died like that, nailed.
*Thus the Panare killed Jesus Christ.

If this could not create feelings of guilt, nothing could. Now there was talk of God's vengeance for the dreadful deed.

God will burn you all,
burn all the animals, burn also the earth,
the heavens, absolutely everything.
He will burn also the Panare themselves.
God will exterminate the Panare by throwing them on the
*   fire.*
It is a huge fire.
I'm going to hurl the Panare into the fire, said God.

The comet had come and gone but the frightening memory of it remained. God had relented once but might not a second time.

God is good.
'Do you want to be roasted in the fire?' asks God.
'Do you have something to pay me with so that I won't
roast you in the fire?
What is it you're going to pay me with?'

The nature of the payment demanded is a foregone conclusion; unquestioning submission to the missionaries' demands, the abandonment of their traditional life and their customs, their culture. The pressure proved too much even for the well-tried nerves of the Panare, and within months the first results began to come in. The following, headed 'Panare Breakthrough', is quoted from *Brown Gold*, dated 1977:

* It seems common practice among the missionaries to accuse Indians of killing Christ. David Stoll, writing of the SIL in Peru, describes a missionary teacher calling his Amuesha congregation Jews 'because they did not have faith and were killing Jesus'.

*I finished stressing the need for each one to ask God for
the payment of their own sins . . . A few hours later Achen
[a Panare woman] came by the house, she said, 'I asked
God like this: I want my payment for my sin [sic]. I don't
want to burn in the big fire. I love Jesus.'
. . . Here we had sat for almost a year teaching one
believer and nothing else happening and then all of a
sudden, WOW!*

On the whole Paul kept his proper scientific distance in this
conflict, content to record the effects of missionary pressure
as dispassionately as he would have recorded changes in
rainfall through deforestation. Venezuelan anthropologists
made a burning issue of it. Henry Corradini had arrived
from Caracas in the hope of being present at the *katayinto*
and, hearing that it was to be postponed again, stormed
down to the missionary's house with the intention of confronting them. Just as in my case, no one answered his
knocking on the door. The missionaries were there but they
had decided to keep out of sight, and in the time we spent
in Colorado they appeared never to leave the house. Henry
blamed them, too, for the Panare's sudden aversion to photography. He and María Eugenia had been told by Panare,
in other communities they had visited to carry out the
census, that the missionaries had assured them that the 'flu
from which so many had died had been brought on 'through
taking photographs'. They were also warned of any contact
with the outside world, the words used being, 'Tell the ugly
stranger to go away unless he comes with words of God in
his mouth.' It now occurred to us that we might be to
some extent included in this interdict. Although it had been
previously understood that we would join in the activities of
the community's life and take part in the evening communal
meal, it now appeared that this was not to be so.

Henry and María Eugenia had had many strange experiences in their journeyings to count the Indians. In one
remote Panare community a native evangelist, trained perhaps by Mr Stucky at Colorado, was at work with the children trying to inculcate the principles of Christianity. 'The

village children were made to kneel down in a row. No one could understand what was going on, nor could the Panare evangelist make them understand. In the end he said, "Every time I say the word Jesus, you must bang your head on the ground," and this they did.'

Henry had listed some of the missionary recommendations and prohibitions—all issued in God's name—they had encountered.

God wants us to wear pants. He wants us to use money. He tells us that we have to work hard to get our food. He does not care to see us lying around in hammocks. He does not wish us to plant sugar cane any longer. God wants us to use soap. He wants us to eliminate unpleasant odours; to wash under the armpits and around the anal area.

The sales promotion for soap and detergents particularly infuriated Henry Corradini. 'The Indians are never out of the water,' he said. 'Without exception they're the cleanest people in the world. How dare these gringos tell them they stink?'

Ugly strangers or not, the arrival of Henry and María Eugenia was always a source of great excitement to the Indians, and in addition to the young Panare who were always with us, the grown-ups soon arrived on the scene not only to make courtesy calls, but to enquire whether they had brought beads.

Of all the trade goods the white man has had to offer the Indians, beads have had the most enduring appeal and remain in constant demand in all parts of Latin America. The Indians are discriminating in their choice of colours. In the north of Guatemala the wives of Germans who bought coffee *fincas* and settled there in the twenties wore amber necklaces, which the Maya in the area of Copán would sell themselves into semi-slave labour on the plantation for months on end to possess. The Germans soon found out that the Indians coveted the beads for their colour, not the rare substance from which they were made, and so imported yellow glass beads in great quantities from Czechoslovakia, the use of which within a year or two became general in all the Guatemalan north.

The Panare are prepared only to take blue and white beads, and remain perpetually starved of the embellishments they make from them because the *criollo* traders have never bothered to track down a source of supply. The missionaries refuse to deal in adornments reflecting the taste of what they see as the bad old days, and supply only bracelets and necklaces made from plastic or sea-shells. As ever, the small, well made beads came from Czechoslovakia, and Henry bought them by weight, a kilo at a time in Caracas. The Panare lined up as they might have done at the check-out in a supermarket, and, employing a glass of the kind used with medicine, Henry measured out the beads. No money ever changed hands, although the Indians were under strict instruction to abandon the ungodly practice of barter. Instead Henry accepted the small woodblocks incised with traditional designs which the Panare inked before a dance and then used to print decorative patterns on their bodies. Of these, since there were hardly two designs that were the same, he had made a large collection.

This was the best of the day, the fresh evening hour when all the strong colours leaped out at us again from the monotones of heat and high noon, and a light, scented breeze stirred with the cooling of the sun. We had carried our camp chairs outside the house and looked down on the cooking smoke arising from the village, and listened to the soft domestic clatter. Innumerable small butterflies had come drifting in to settle as they always did at this hour, mysteriously selecting a huge polished boulder in the vicinity from which to hang like polished scales; and a line of cranes crossed the sky, making for their roosts in the sierra. It was the moment for the day's supreme luxury of rum taken with iced water from Henry's large vacuum container, and now with this last drink the ice had come to an end.

In a few days Henry and María Eugenia would be obliged to return to their work in the city. This time they were more reluctant than ever to go, knowing that although from where we sat this small paradise showed no signs of change, an internal disruption of the most convulsive kind was happening, and that with every year that passed its end came closer.

After the bead distribution the Panare seemed disinclined to return to their houses and lounged comfortably in the vicinity, rode their bicycles up and down, or climbed into our hammocks for a chat. One of the Indians, speaking of a small festive event they had recently been allowed to get away with, mentioned that the missionaries had said, 'Jesus Christ has agreed to let you have this one dance.' This seemed the moment to suggest the possibility of holding what the Panare call a 'for nothing', a watered-down version of the *katayinto*, devoid of any of the ritual significance certain to have called down the missionaries' ban. The Panare stage a 'for nothing' whenever they can, purely because they like to drink and dance, and they can normally be induced to go through a full repertoire of dances if provided with a sack of sugar with which to brew the very mild, sweet beer obtainable from only three days of fermentation. In preparation for this a day or so is spent in cutting down a tree and hollowing out from it the 'canoe' to contain the beer—in itself a traditional community exercise in which everybody takes part, and seen as contributing to the fun. We asked if a 'for nothing' could be arranged, and the Panare thought that it was possible, and they would see what could be done. There was always doubt in our minds that this would be allowed to happen. In a warm climate the first sign of fermentation can be detected in any sweetened juice only hours after it has been exposed to the air. We had heard of native 'deacons' keeping watch to see that all such drinks were jettisoned as soon as the first bubbles appeared on the surface. Whether the Panare would feel in the mood to dance on the basis of sugar and water where no encouraging bubbles were present, remained to be seen.

The Corradinis thought that we should in no circumstance miss the experience of a visit to the hostel in Caicara run by the Catholics for destitute Indians, who flock into such towns when they have been dispossessed of their land, and

195

with the destruction of their tribal culture are reduced to begging and scrounging, and picking through refuse tips in order to stay alive.

In Caicara six evangelical temples fought each other over the conquest and division of souls. So bitter had the struggle become while we were there that one sect broadcast deafeningly amplified pop music—including old Beatles tapes—for no other purpose than to drown the calls to salvation of its nearest rival. At the end of the day it is to the Catholics that the demoralized and dispossessed must turn for refuge.

The hostel was vast and gaunt with a stained and rancid bleakness of a special tropical kind. This must once have been an army post, with stalls for horses and barrack-rooms lined up round a square. The Indians had slung their hammocks everywhere over the urine and the vomit smeared on the cobbles. They were all drunk, and those on their feet were laughing and colliding with each other and falling in heaps. In the ordinary way Indians giggle softly, no more than that, but raw alcohol had taught these remnants from a half dozen different tribes to laugh uproariously in Western style. Crows hopped round them picking at unidentifiable messes. The men and women who had taken refuge here were dressed in anonymous mission rags and only a single woman stood out as being a Panare, because she was half-nude in tribal style, and had managed to hold on to her blue and white beads. Her expression was one of desperation. These Indians had suffered to the full the processes of what is now spoken of as acculturation. They had walked with the Lord, and come to the end of the road. The nuns came and went, dodging silently through the shadows with averted faces. There was some sort of infirmary on the upper floors to which entrance was resolutely barred. We were told that Puerto Ayacucho was peopled with thousands of Indian derelicts existing in these conditions.

To the missionaries it was without importance. Nothing had any point of purpose but salvation and, once saved, a soul could never be lost. The Indians who picked through the refuse heaps in the slums of these towns, living otherwise on the prostitution of their womenfolk, had still 'grown

196

in the Lord', while multitudes of the unreached, however blameless their existences, would burn forever in hell. Almost any means, therefore, justified the ends of conversion.

The citizens of such old trading posts and frontier forts are here on a short-term basis. To live in such surroundings is like serving out a sentence. The hope is to make a little money and get out. 'Ten years of this is enough, after that I'll be on my way,' they say. 'I've got my eye on a little place down the coast.'

The town is full of outcry and urgent appeal. Its walls are covered with religious texts, stuck on everywhere, usually in rows like savings stamps. The missions crowd together in a single street, attempting to attract custom with a roaring medley of revivalist hymns and rock. None of the big names in evangelism is present. These are second-liners with a few hundred adherents and titles like 'The Congregation of Jesus' and 'Holy Crown'. They have no illusions about making converts but have resigned themselves to the recycling of human waste. Indians who wander or stagger in are welcomed with a firm handshake and receive some promotional present of supreme uselessness: a disposable razor with which to scrape hairless Indian cheeks, cotton mittens once favoured by drivers over dusty road; perhaps an old anatomical chart demonstrating blood circulation and the functioning of the kidneys. A principal attraction in some cases is a glass of Coca Cola. In this the recipient may secretly stir a pinch of ground-up, noxious bark which provides a brief paralysis akin to extreme intoxication.

Adversity covers faces here with its own special mask. The Panare in their savannah homeland bear a strong tribal resemblance to each other. This, after a year or two in Ayacucho or Caicara, is lost. The last members of four or five tribes, who roam the streets of the town in their anonymous rags, are no longer distinguishable from each other. One—pointed out as a Panare—lounged on a corner. His relative prosperity was advertised by the flowered shirt, jeans, trainers, short haircut, and the cigarette in a long holder. This he waved about between puffs in a manner copied from an old film. His wife, who crouched in an angle of the wall just out of sight, was for sale for a cupful of sugar. His prosperity I was assured, would be short-lived, for he was in an advanced stage of tuberculosis.

Quoting the materialistic *Brown Gold* on the subject of unreached Indians:

> *It is fair to say that they sit in darkness. While we cook on fancy stoves they cook over open fires . . . while we ride in cars, they have never owned a pair of shoes. While we sleep on nice mattresses, many of them sleep on split bamboo floors. While we struggle to keep our computers going, they are still rubbing sticks together to make a fire. While we perform heart surgery, some of them have never seen a band-aid. I'd say that God is right when He says that they sit in darkness.*

These in Ayacucho and Caicara are the reached. Where is the light they were promised?

13

The argument is persistently advanced by the Summer Institute of Linguistics that the integration of all Indians as wage-earners and consumers into the national life of any country in which they may be found is inevitable. This being so, the argument runs, every effort should be made to prepare them for the transition from a classless society to a class-structured one, in which it is generally admitted that their place will be at the bottom of the social pyramid.

It is a proposition with some attraction for the sect's educated supporters, who are inclined to be repelled by Bible-Belt rantings aimed at a less sophisticated audience. The missionaries agree, too, with the governments that they have been called in to serve that it is unreasonable and uneconomic that relatively small tribal populations should be left in peace to enjoy the resources of the large tracts of forest they require for the maintenance of their way of life. What is conveniently ignored is that such forest areas have little direct impact on national prosperity. The clearing of the forest—usually by burning—provides a quick, once and for all profit for a small number of beneficiaries, but the soil is too thin for the ranches that replace the trees to remain in business for more than a few years. After that the desert takes over and the surviving Indians will join the unemployed and the unemployable in the slums of the towns. It is a situation that has become a commonplace of the development of Brazil, where nevertheless the destruction of the trees continues at such a rate that the Brazilian Department of Forest Ecology has estimated that the Brazilian rain-forest, once larger than Europe, will have disappeared in its entirety by the beginning of the next century.

The missionary sects have made it clear that it would suit their book from the point of view of ease of conversion if the Indians could be induced to surrender their racial identity, but is it really true—as they contend—that this loss is in any case inevitable, and that Indian and non-Indian societies cannot co-exist? The fact is that, despite the terrible abuses to which they have been subjected, this is not so, as witness the situation in the savannah of Venezuela where no significant clashes would appear to have occurred between the *criollo* population and a half dozen Indian groups. Records dating back a century suggest that the Panare have got on well enough with their neighbours, and have probably increased their numbers during that time.

A recent example of peaceful and mutually beneficial co-operation between the two races has been seen in the unlikely environment of the mining township of Tiro Loco. In 1971 a rich field of diamonds was discovered in the valley of the Guaniamo about fifty miles south-east of Colorado, provoking a diamond rush of exceptional proportions. Prospectors had found the diamonds in dense, trackless jungle, and almost within days miners and their camp-followers (women outnumbered the men) began to stream like ants from Venezuela and three adjacent countries towards the area of the *bulla*—as these explosions of speculative excitement are named. The profession of diamond prospecting calls for toughness of a special kind. Most of these men and women covered the whole distance involved—sometimes hundreds of miles—on foot. The contingent from Brazil—known as *garimpeiros*—would have been organized in a species of blood-brotherhood under a captain exercising powers of life and death. All these semi-desperadoes from Guyana, Colombia and Brazil were illegal immigrants, but the police took care to let well alone.

With the arrival of the mining bands on the banks of the Guaniamo all hell was probably let loose. The name Tiro Loco means 'Crazy Shot' and there is no doubt that there was a good deal of crazy shooting until a batallion of *Cazadores*, a crack anti-guerilla force, moved in to disarm the trigger-happy miners.

The Indian group living nearest at the time of the first invasion, when the *garimpeiros* were still staging their ambuscades and shoot-outs over rival claims, were a settlement of possibly 150 Panare. One would have thought that as soon as they had news of the gunplay they would have thought it prudent to withdraw further into the jungle. Instead they came closer, first to a point within a half day's walk from the mines, then probably deciding they had nothing to fear, setting up house at the very edge of the mining community. They went there in the hope of coming to a trading arrangement with the miners, by exchanging the vegetables they grew for steel tools.

An agreement was immediately reached. The mining population numbered 8,000, and the normal miseries of living in a shanty town in the tropics were accentuated by an absence of fresh food. Supplies flown in cost three to five times the normal price, and miners forced to live for years on end on jerked beef and beer developed a range of complaints attendant upon vitamin deficiency. Nothing could have been more attractive to them than to have these Indian market-gardeners set up in their midst. In return the Indians got their axes and their machetes. The arrangement worked without a hitch. Even before the disarming of the miners there had been no single hostile incident to disrupt the relationship between the races.

It seemed to us that a visit to Tiro Loco was not to be missed, and we accordingly drove there over what was undoubtedly the worst road in the world, reaching the mining settlement after many hours.

The scene confronting us was one of macabre desolation. The soft contours of the rain forest, spread over low hills, had been ripped apart. Unnatural precipices, sombre ravines and caved-in hillsides had been left where the earth had shed its entrails, with men crawling in and about them, disappearing with their shovels into black caverns and barrows. This was a free-for-all—mining in its most primitive form, with nothing evident in the way of machinery more than high-pressure hoses squirting water into black lakes of mud. Miners starting here with no capital to buy equipment were given ten square metres to do what they liked with, and many of them went to work with pick and shovel. Paul

201

said that no adult Indians could be induced to work in the mine, but that there were a few adolescent boys who had been through the mission school, who had been persuaded to do so. Sheets of corrugated iron lay everywhere over this scene like an awful industrial manna dropped from the skies.

The central, administrative area, known as Milagros (miracles) had been built on a solid stratum of crushed beer cans. A toucan, eyes closed, possibly in a coma, had perched on the roof of the police station nearby. We were on a low hill, and from this slightly elevated point of vantage we counted 82 wrecked cars. The wheels from these, and many others, had been built up into several ziggurats intended perhaps to provide the town with architectural interest.

Standing here, I saw, for the first time in my life, the swing doors of a saloon fly open as they do in the old Western movies, and an unwanted customer pitched headlong into the street. We went in and were immediately approached by a young man with a German accent who told us that his name was Wolfgang, and he was one of thirty-two brothers. There was a simplicity and an urge to communicate about him, often found in men who live adventurous and dangerous lives. 'We work the alluvial deposits all the way up through Brazil and Colombia to Guyana. Sometimes we're rich and sometimes we're poor. My brother picked up enough dough in a couple of days to pay a half million bolivars for our father's operation. The police in Guyana shot him as a spy. Half the guys here are on the run. They take your gun off you as you come into town. This is a quiet place. You have to work hard to get yourself shot.'

The saloon was full of hatchet-faced men and attendant whores, many of them absurdly dressed, and most alternately exhibiting the defiant mirth and lurking melancholy of those condemned to a perpetual semblance of gaiety. Despite the considerable heat one wore a mauve feather boa, dabbing constantly with a wad of cotton wool at the beads of sweat breaking out on her cheeks. These were mining camp regulars, who spend the whole of their lives trudging from *bulla* to *bulla* on their prodigious Amazon-Orinoco beat. They were muscled like athletes and some were literally Diamond Lils, frequently rewarded in gems by the customers who engaged them on a contractual basis.

It was a film set from Chaplin's *Gold Rush*, with all the posturing, the macho display, the mock violence and the threat of real violence. Innumerable cockroaches like small, plastic toys were scurrying about the floor. An added, exotic touch was the presence of a tribal Indian girl from the Mato Grosso with a great tousled mane of black hair and a face with something in its expression of a Jivaro shrunken head. This was the *companheira* of some prospectors from Brazil with whom she now drank beer, serving their sexual needs as well, it was said, as supplying the fresh female urine regarded as a certain cure for infected sores. The Mato Grosso group stood apart, arguing vociferously in Portuguese between long gulps of beer which they drank in ceremonious fashion, almost like a gathering of German students. About 17 tons of beer per day were consumed in Tiro Loco's score or so of saloons. Beer was expensive. It cost the equivalent of £30 to get mildly drunk.

In another two or three years all this would come to an end. The last, slightly discoloured diamond would have been scraped from the alluvial mud, and the miners and all their womenfolk of whatever occupation would turn their backs on this apocalyptic scene, and begin the long trudge towards the new *bulla* beckoning somewhere ahead along the meandering course of the Orinoco. Meanwhile there were diamonds in plenty. If you knew what you were doing, Paul said, you could pick up a good one for a song. But a knowledge of diamonds was something none of us could lay claim to. Shown what looked like small fragments of yellow glass we pretended amazement. It was certainly impressive to learn that a man holding three or four of these dull little crystals in the palm of his hand who, as he told us, had reached Tiro Loco on a worn-out horse, would leave it at the wheel of a new Plymouth shortly to be delivered from Caicara. It was a profession in which you could borrow the money for your first morning run and end the day a Croesus; nevertheless, three miners out of four were penniless at the end of their days.

The Panare had established themselves on the town's outskirts on the top of a low, rounded hill, and here, reclining for the most part in their hammocks, the representatives of the far past looked down upon the goings on of those of the present. Some primeval instinct seemed to have assured them that they had nothing to fear from the miners, but that there was every chance of being able to bargain with them for articles of prime necessity, in particular, steel tools. Game was vanishing in all places within reach of those who hunted for sport, and the Panare were obliged by this shortage to compensate in their search for food by increasing the size of their gardens. This, in turn, called for more and better tools. The deal they managed to strike with the miners was that they would keep them supplied with fresh vegetables in exchange for machetes, axes, shovels and the like. These the miners easily made up from materials supplied by the wrecked cars.

They had built a road—the only well-surfaced one in Tiro Loco—that wound round the hill up to the Panare settlement, and here at the top we found the Indians living in the most splendid houses we had so far seen. Relieved of outside pressures of any kind—due perhaps to the fact that the missionaries preferred not to expose themselves to contamination by Tiro Loco—they had practised all the old building skills in purest form. The houses had been put together with an evident passion for regularity. So much so that there was something in the result almost to suggest a very high-quality factory product. All the bamboo poles were of matching length, and the main poles were tied to the supporting ones always in the same place with economy and style, with indigo string and a single knot. The eye was taken everywhere by symmetry and the most scrupulous alignment. The Panare had built a fanciful porch at the entrance of each house, decorating this with an interlacing pattern of fronds and leaves. In a similar way decorative fringes employing a number of leaves of different shapes had been added to the thatch, reaching almost to the ground.

Inside the house inevitably all the hammocks were lined up, and the mosquito nets suspended above them correctly folded, army-style. Garden tools and blow-guns were stashed away on wooden trays suspended from the roof, and from one of these protruded a blonde plastic doll provided with a Panare g-string, necklace and bracelets of blue and white beads. Fine white sand from the river bed covered the floor, patrolled by magnificent heraldic-looking cockerels on the look-out for insects. Whenever a cockerel deposited its droppings in these pristine surroundings, a Panare leapt from his hammock to clean them up. These the Panare keep as pets and they are never eaten; the eggs laid by the hens are left undisturbed or given to *criollo* friends.

Our visit was in the early morning hours after a night in our hammocks slung in the open air at the back of a saloon. We had been troubled by unseasonable showers and a glut of praying mantises which, although harmless, seemed repellent. Up on the hill it was surprisingly cool, and we arrived at the moment when a Panare woman had just snatched up a puppy to bedaub it with warm ashes from the fire 'to keep the cold out'.

The men, who rolled out of their hammocks to greet us, wore traditional loincloths, but the lady with the puppy had hastily covered her ample form (although certainly not from reasons of modesty) with a model gown from Caracas, dyed since purchase an unsuitable Panare-red. This was clearly a gift from the mining camp, as was her small daughter's lace party frock, with frills, and the baby's necklace of silver coins collected in five countries.

The sun came up. We drank mango juice together and then set out for a stroll in the jungle to view the settlement's newly cut garden. The jungle still within sight of Tiro Loco was superbly Amazonian. Fifty miles away as the crow flew, in Colorado, not a drop of rain would freshen the savannah grass for months, but here the great trees drew the rain towards them. Down among the corrugated iron of the valley the sun temperature by this time would not have been less than 120 degrees F. In the forest cool air moved with a soft and mysterious turbulence as if breathed in and out by a colossal lung. The rain-forest was different in every way from the narrow gallery-forest of Colorado which had been almost as familiar and comprehensible as a woodland in England. Here there was alien grandeur, a touch of menace and the unexpected. Trees had taken over and organized their environment for millions of years, and animal life was dependent, parasitic, and subordinate to them.

Where their trunks soared from the earth, great muscled roots reached out to explore the earth in all directions in search of leafy detritus to digest. The trunks were smooth and pale and slender, branching out only when they reached the forest canopy hundreds of feet above. Each tree claimed its own living space, able in some unexplained way to liquidate competitive growth within its territory. As a measure of defence against destruction by natural catastrophe such as forest fires, each species had devised the means of spreading its seed thinly so that the possibility would never arise of every single tree of one kind being wiped out. For this reason on our jungle walk we never saw two trees of the same species growing side by side, and it was said that as many as 200 varieties grew in a single hectare. Lianas roped down, some of them dangling weird flowers, to within feet of the ground, and looking upwards into the tangle of greenery the impression was a kind of forest in reverse growing down to join the upthrust of vegetation.

Animal life in the forest was on the whole nocturnal so nothing stirred among the crumble of humus strewn on the forest floor, but where there was rapid decay fungus flaunted gaudy colours. We saw anthills built into red sculpted pyramids up to 15 ft in height but no ants. Innumerable birds whistled, piped, shrilled on trumpets and banged gongs in the canopy above. A few bewildered moths flapped about our faces. The jungle was full of the smells of childhood, of earth probed and turned by worms, of ferns, raindrops splashing on warm surfaces and the spiritous vapours of gum arabic, camphor and benzoin.

The Panare flitted through the trees on both sides and ahead, and presently the jungle opened out and we found ourselves in the garden they had just cut. Fifty or so trees had been accurately and tidily felled, all pointing in the same direction, and we surveyed them as they lay among the deep litter of their branches with proper solemnity. It was customary among some tribes to perform ceremonies of conciliation when they cut down trees or killed animals—a practice vigorously opposed by the missionaries. Enough orchids lay among the shattered branches to stock the florist shops of a city.

We walked back to the settlement on the hill and rested for a while looking down over Tiro Loco. The long narrow trail of corrugated iron twisted like a metal dragon through the valley. Here and there workings had bitten into the forest and then been abandoned, and the places were now lightly brushed-in with the green of sprouting vegetation. In five years at most the mines would go and in ten a rampant form of convolvulus would cover with its vast blue flowers all that remained of their shacks and their abandoned machinery. What would the Panare do when these changes came about? It was a question they were unable to answer. Such tribal peoples hardly concern themselves with the shadowy prospects of the future.

Paul thought they would follow the miners and grow their vegetables as before, as long as they stayed within reach of some suitable forest.

14

We went back to Colorado eager to discover whether the Indians had reached any decision as to the possibility of holding a 'for nothing'. The response to our enquiries seemed ominously cautious, and when pressed the Panare put us off with unconvincing excuses. So far no one in Colorado had been prepared to tell us that *all* such social activities were displeasing to God but we felt the day growing nearer when this would happen. None of us had set eyes on the missionaries, although Henry Corradini had endlessly patrolled the mission area in the hope of a chance confrontation. Henry had been identified by the sect as an agent of Satan; a deceiver, along with a miscellany of members of the World Council of Churches, anthropologists and liberal journalists gathered together under Satan's banner in preparation for Armageddon, now perceived as just round the corner.

Finally, after many wasted trips down to the mission, we heard a plane coming in. Before we could get down to the landing strip, it was down. Two missionaries came out of the house with a third brought by the plane, and the three hurried away. Within five minutes they were airborne.

Following this unexpected departure we felt entitled to hope that the situation might have eased so far as we were concerned, that the ban on photography might have been lifted, that we might have been invited to join in the communal meal, and the 'for nothing' might have been comfortably arranged. This proved not to be the case, and it was soon evident that a man who had been their first convert, and their only supporter for several years, had been able to assume the missionaries' authority, and maintain their prohibitions in their absence.

He was a Panare who walked with some difficulty having been lame from birth. Henry Corradini said that his rise to power illustrated a process inevitably following the discovery

208

of a handicapped person in a tribe where the evangelists had established a foothold. Although certain missionaries such as those who had helped in the enslavement of the Achés are prepared to lie in defence of criminal activities, others such as Mr Halterman of La Paz stick to the truth and can be breathtakingly frank in their discussion of their methods. An NTM missionary in Caracas had described the strategy in selecting any handicapped person found in a tribal resistance. 'They say that all's fair in war,' said the missionary, 'and for us this is a war for souls.'

'When we come across a man with some physical defect,' he went on, 'let's say a club foot, or a withered arm, we concentrate our energies on him. We see this man as having a grudge about the way life's treated him. He's an outsider who harbours resentment against those who are more fortunate. We know that this is the guy who's going to let us in if we play this right, and we start off by giving him the best of everything; smart clothes, rides in the plane—maybe we let him fiddle with the transmitter, anything to build him up, make him feel like he's one of us.'

'Let's say there's some kind of important figure in this community. It could be just the oldest man, or maybe some sort of a witch-doctor who's been called to witness for the Lord. We can say for certain that it's only a matter of time before our man takes over. He builds up his own following of guys who see the way things are going and like to be around for the handouts. The next stage is that these people who are working for us and who have grown in the Lord decline to associate with the ones who want to keep going the way they always have. That's the way it always goes, and it's natural that it should. Trouble is there aren't too many guys with withered arms around, but where we see one we know we're on a winner.'

The man we supposed to be the missionaries' deputy in Colorado was always in sight about the village. There was no way of knowing how many Panare had accepted the Word, or were on the point of conversion, because with the sole exception of this man, they had refused up to this to be parted from their ceremonial loincloths and their trinkets of blue and white beads. The missionaries' man wore the kind of trousers which seem inevitably in such surroundings to be grubby, and with them on special occasions a T-shirt, training shoes, dark spectacles and a baseball cap. He never, so far as we knew, took part in the evening communal meal, so presumably lived on canned food from the missionaries' store.

In Tiro Loco Donald had gone round taking all the photographs he wanted to, and it was galling that in Colorado, presenting as it did such an incomparable panoply of tribal life, photography should have remained a strict taboo. Paul's suggested remedy for this impasse was to devise some means of enticing the Indians away from Colorado and the lame man's censorious eye, and thereafter involving them in strenuous activity in such a way that they would be too absorbed in whatever they were doing to notice that photography was going on.

This was the end of the dry season when the rivers of Venezuela everywhere were full of fish of many varieties, some of enormous size. Some years before, Paul had gone on a small-scale trip involving fifteen men when 75 kgs of fish were caught in an hour or two in a knee-deep creek. In the rivers further afield, hundreds of fish became concentrated as the water shrunk in pools where they could be seen circulating just below the surface like trout in a farm. This angler's paradise continued to exist, because only a few Indians were there to fish. The Creole population ate little but meat, and if they ate fish at all insisted upon the imported frozen kind.

In previous years at this time the Panare had been accustomed to turn a fishing expedition into a major fiesta. All the village men, women and children accompanied by numerous pets such as tame parrots, dogs, ducks and pigs made the long trek to the Tortuga river, a tributary of the Orinoco, and there on the banks built a makeshift settlement where they stayed a week or two, returning home only when the unrelieved diet of fish began to pall. Such great tribal excursions, preceded by the brewing of beer, and accompanied by a great deal of dancing and merry-making had come to an end. The first essential in missionary policy was to settle the Indians permanently in what amounted to a colony under their close control, and such trips, Harry Corradini informed us, were debarred wherever they had established their rule. Without transport it would have been difficult to reach the fishing ground on the Tortuga river, and return in a day, and when Paul offered to take a fishing party in the Land Rover, the opportunity was clearly too good to resist.

Traditionally most Indians poison rivers on such a big-scale fishing expedition. The method is less gruesome than it sounds, for the Indians have mastered the art of conservation. The effect of the poison is confined to a small area, and does not spoil the flesh, and the fish that are not taken recover. Indians never fish or hunt for sport, thus year after year abundance is perpetuated.

For small-scale fishing in which only two or three men work together as a team the Panare use a plant, *kayin*, produced as a garden crop, but this is too weak in effect for employment in a substantial river. In this case a trip is made into the mountains to collect a liana called by them *enerrima* which is pounded up and then washed into the water. We had wanted very much to be able to go with them and photograph the collectors of the *enerrima* at work, but they left without warning at about dawn on the day before our fishing expedition, possibly under the influence of some taboo in the matter.

Next morning we took nine Panare aboard the Land Rover and headed out across the savannah in the direction of the Tortuga river which at its nearest point could have been ten miles away. Once again I was struck by the savannah's landscaped appearance—that of a park laid out by men. Although no rain had fallen for months it had remained remarkably green and fresh, and the short grass reaching barely halfway to the knee was clear of any scrubby invasions. The ground was level, and there was hardly any limit to the speed at which we could have travelled had it not been for frequent and often sudden encounters with creeks. These, although no more than 12–15 ft in width, and at this season quite shallow, could only easily be crossed at

211

fording points where the bottom was hard, and these were relatively few. This area had seen the beginnings of the first serious quarrel between Panare and *criollos*, when a small rancher had put a fence across Indian tribal land. So far the only casualty had been a single cow, but the episode warned of the possibility of worse to come. The Indians had kept the upper hand because notwithstanding missionary support, the rancher had been obliged to take down his fence.

We zigzagged at high speed across the low grass on the look-out for safe fording places. The Panare had armed themselves with 6 ft wooden lances with steel barbs, and a couple of bamboo poles were carried in the hope of knocking down a few mangoes if any ripe ones were seen. Once again I was disappointed at the absence of animals. The Panare hunted deer, agoutis, armadillos and tortoises in the savannah, but at the best of times these were only present in the rainy season.

Bird life was spectacular and abundant. The positioning of springs was marked in the savannah by somewhat regular and evenly spaced clumps of trees, most of which were either in flower at this season, or bore fruit. They were visited by vast flocks of birds, among them parrots, toucans and macaws. These the Panare ignored unless they were in search of macaws' feathers or toucans' beaks for ceremonial purposes, and never took more than they required for any specific ritual. We stopped near some promising trees and the Indians took their poles and ran from tree to tree beating the branches within reach and picking up the ripe mangoes that showered down. The birds, unaccustomed to humans, would ignore our approach and go on feeding, and then, when an Indian struck at a tree with his pole, it seemed to shatter like glass, exploding hundreds of flashing fragments into the sky. Humming-birds of a half dozen varieties buzzed sullenly in our ears and poised in mid-flight to inspect us within inches of our faces. A few feral pigs grubbing among the fallen mangoes went scuttling away, but these were of no interest to the Panare, and were ignored.

We reached the Tortuga, found it much shrunken with no apparent flow except in the shallows linking the deep pools, where a multitude of fish were trapped. At most it was 40 ft across, low in its bed and bordered by the usual sparse and untidy gallery-forest. A number of fishing eagles perched in the trees to watch the water in which an occasional swirl was produced by some large fish manoeuvring near the surface. The backbones of their catch littered the bank. Bones retaining shreds of flesh had attracted the attention of numerous sulphur-coloured butterflies, as had also the damp earth on the margins of pools left by the receding waters, at which they sucked, twitching their wings.

The Indians, who at all other times had appeared calm and phlegmatic, had suddenly been possessed by excitement at the prospect of the fishing, and scampered up and down the banks in search of the most suitable stretch of water to be poisoned. The impression they gave was of a domination by a group-attitude so engrained that a consensus had to be sought before any action could be undertaken, and that the conceptions of leadership and personal initiative were foreign to this community. Nevertheless, as with the termites, the group could function as an individual when the occasion demanded and decisions were rapidly taken, and without evident dissent. Shortly after our own arrival we were the spectators of the extraordinary scene of some forty Panare pedalling furiously towards us across the savannah on their missionary bikes, *Christ Is Coming* painted on each mudguard. Moments later bikes were parked, and they had ranged themselves with the contingent we had brought at equidistant intervals for two or three hundred yards along the water's edge. There was no apparent discussion. Word came back to Paul that a site had been chosen and the fishing was about to begin, and we hurried to the spot.

The pool chosen was about one hundred yards in length, a bulge of water bottlenecked at each end with sand banks, and shallows through which only a ray could pass. Paul thought that the water in the pool could have been six to eight feet in depth, and that in all probability some hundreds of fish could be trapped in it to await the coming of the rains. The wildlife of the locality paid little attention to us. When we arrived kingfishers as big as starlings were splashing into the water, an elegant long-legged eagle went mincing past, and a spectacular flycatcher continued to hawk among the butterflies within a few feet from where we stood, in no way perturbed by our presence.

Three Indians had stationed themselves on some large, water-smothered boulders carrying the baskets with ground-up *enerrima*, which they now doused in the water and from which a milky whiteness began to spread. I had expected a longish wait until the poison had reached all parts of the pool for it to produce any effect, but this was not the case. Within two minutes of the baskets' immersion and before the cloudiness they released had even reached the middle of the pool a tremendous subaqueous commotion began, a whirling Catherine-wheel of tin-plate reflections in the depths. This agitation spread instantly to all parts of the water and, impelled as if by centrifugal force, big fish shot outwards, dorsal fins cutting the surface towards the shallows. Occasionally a fish broke surface, hurled itself into the air, to splash back or even thump down on the bank, thereafter propelling itself in a series of leaps for a dozen feet or so across dry land.

The Panare, each one in his place, chattered excitedly, lances upraised, waiting for reasonable targets to present themselves as soon as the fish began to slow down. After their first frantic outwards rush, driven by the need to break out of the confines of the poison, the fish fell into incoherent movement, swimming still at high speed but without direction; spinning in tight circles, zigzagging, scrawling flashing curlicues just beneath the surface, turning over on their backs, flinging themselves into shallows only inches deep in which they scuttled with gaping mouths and violent oscillations of the tail. Among them went the corpse-white rays, flapping with their wing-like fins, and the smallest of these escaped. The Panare stood in motionless lines along the banks like statues produced in the atelier of a single sculptor. There was no warning of action. They seemed all to throw their lances at the same moment. As far as I could see every lance struck a fish and as the Indians pulled their fish on to the banks I could see why there had been no fight; they

214

were all speared through the head. From the moment when the fish was speared until it was released from the barb and the Indian went into action again it took a maximum of three minutes.

Paul who had stationed himself in the line a few yards away was taking fish with great expertise. He had had several years' practice with the lance, and although he was a little slower than an Indian and less ambitious with the length of his throw I never saw him miss. An Indian passed a lance to me but in a single attempt I covered myself with ignominy by entangling myself with the line. I noted with interest that in a society almost devoid of a sense of property, each of the Panare was most careful to keep his own catch separate from that of the rest. This although all the results of individual effort were due shortly to be amalgamated with the inclusion of the catch as a whole as part of the community's food reserves. Paul, who had enjoyed the fishing as sport, would present what he had caught to his fictive Panare mother, but as she would certainly pass this on to the community it was hardly more than a ceremonial gesture.

The fishing went on for about two hours after which the pool had been emptied apart from several exceptionally large fish continuing to twist and turn in its centre. Suddenly, as if by common consent, the Panare seemed to lose interest in these, and all the lance-throwing stopped. I had seen them unerringly spear fish through the head at up to thirty feet. It seemed strange that these monsters only a few feet outside this range should have been spared, and I was inclined to wonder if prestige entered into this restraint, and whether no Panare was inclined to risk public failure.

Several hundred fish had been taken, among them several 25-pounders, and the total catch could have been in the neighbourhood of a ton. The Panare said that the fish they had left would recover in about four hours, and that as soon as the rains started there would be as many as ever in the pool, although thereafter they would have to be caught by line. As the Indians set about cleaning their fish on the spot, the eagles dropped around us like parachutists from the trees, and began to clear up. I was sorry to be unable to recognize any of the fish, and that no examples of the legendary piranha had been present.

The expedition had been a phenomenal success—by far and away, Paul said, the most exciting he had accompanied. Don had secured an outstanding and perhaps unique photographic record of a sensationally productive Stone Age operation, and no Panare had shown the slightest sign of disquiet. The Panare had stocked themselves and now they congratulated each other in their soft, clicking language. As originally planned the fishing would have been on a smaller scale, and therefore less satisfactory in its impact on the Colorado economy. It seemed both ironic and extraordinary that the bicycles bought through the mission should have contributed to this success.

The fact remained that everything had turned out well for all concerned, and at this moment of general satisfaction a Panare, who had arrived on a bicycle but not taken part in the fishing, pushed to the front. This was a convert, but unlike the missionaries' deputy, he was well-formed and athletic in appearance, but marked down for what he was by the fact that he wore a shirt. Taking a tract from the folds of his loincloth he thrust it towards us. It was printed in English. The heading asked, 'Has life nothing better to offer than this?'

Perhaps the great success of the fishing had made the Panare a little reckless, or perhaps as they saw it, with missionary disapproval to be faced, they might as well be hung for a sheep as a lamb, and that night we were invited to join in the evening meal. It was prepared just in the way Thomas Harriot, official historian of the first English colony of Roanoke in Virginia, had seen the Indians of the island smoke their catch of fish in 1585. 'They stick four stakes of equal length into the ground with a number of posts across them. The fish are laid upon the platform, and a fire built beneath it.' And—exactly as the Panare did: 'after the platform is full of fish and will hold no more, the rest of the catch is hung at the sides, or on sticks close to the fire.' This would have been a familiar scene, too, to the engraver De Bry who illustrated Harriot's book, for so much of the scene

216

at Roanoke must have resembled our surroundings at Colorado: the face painting, the hair cut into a fringe, the armlets, the bead necklaces, the g-strings worn by the young girls.

The 25-year-old Harriot, an intimate friend of Sir Walter Raleigh's, spent a year at Roanoke, and with the colony's collapse he returned to England with the first samples of the potato and the tobacco plant, together with material collected for Raleigh's *History of the New World*. He was enchanted with the Indians of Roanoke Island. In the book he wrote describing his experiences, he gives an account of their methods of catching fish. He says of them,

> *It is a pleasing picture to see these people wading and sailing in their shallow rivers. They are untroubled by the desire to pile up riches for their children, and live in perfect contentment with their present state, in friendship with each other, sharing all those things with which God has so bountifully provided them.*

Certainly Harriot would have spoken with equal enthusiasm of the engaging and pacific Panare.

This was our last evening with the Indians. We sat with them on fallen tree trunks to form a hollow square round the hideous enamelled bowls we had brought and in which the food was served. A dozen or so adult males were present, most of them accompanied by young children who were exceedingly well behaved and rather grave. The women busied themselves with the cooking and serving of the fish, and they, with their babies and adolescent children, formed a separate group to eat their meal. There were no shirt-wearing members of the community to be seen.

We ate enormously, urged continually by our Panare hosts who groped among the bowlfuls of fish in search of particularly succulent morsels, which they passed to us. 'When they have feasted together to their contentment,' Harriot said of his Indians, 'they are wont to dance, an exercise in which they take constant delight.' There would be no dancing on this occasion, and it seemed likely to us that for the Panare the dancing days had come to an end. Nevertheless, whatever the rules had been against photography, it was clear that they had been suspended, and not even the children showed the slightest signs of shyness when the camera was pointed in their direction.

Soon we saw lights bobbing in the bushes nearby and heard soft childish voices, sounding a little like the clucking of contented hens. The older boys and girls having finished their meal had arrived with their torches, or their hands full of fireflies, and were waiting by the path leading up to our house, to which they would accompany us and renew their rummaging among our possessions in search of the exciting bric-a-brac of the West.

LATE NEWS OF THE PANARE

On 13 March 1987 *El Nacional* of Caracas revealed that missionaries of the Summer Institute of Linguistics had entered Venezuela illegally in August of the previous year and had been able to establish a base among the Panare Indians in the neighbourhood of Caicara. The newspaper noted that this missionary sect—following denunciation by the United Nations and the Organization of American States—had already had its contract rescinded or been actually expelled by the governments of Mexico, Ecuador, Brazil, Panama and Colombia.

It further pointed out that the Panare Indians were now the victims of a three-cornered struggle for their conversion between the New Tribes Mission, the Catholics, and the new illicit arrivals.

Simultaneously with this news an attack was launched upon missionary activity among the Panare by officials of the National Council of Scientific Investigations and the Venezuelan Ministry of the Interior, charging the missionaries with psychological terror, mental and physical cruelty, instigating panic, the division of Indian society by favouritism extended to converts, and monopolization of native handicrafts for the missions' commercial benefit.

Investigators of these national bodies reported an occurrence in January 1987 when an NTM missionary entered the Panare village of San Vicente—a settlement on the road to Tiro Loco—telling the Indians there to stop all work, get rid of their shotguns and fishing gear, and kill their dogs as the second coming of Christ was at hand, and only by uninterrupted prayer could they hope to save themselves from celestial fire. The terrified Indians did as instructed, and when they complained of hunger the missionary told them that God would provide for their needs. All they had to do was to abandon their village, congregate on the river bank, bibles under their arms and continue chanting and

219

prayer until by God's power the fish would be killed and float to the top. This they did for several days, and were only saved from starvation by the arrival of the National Police.

The government investigators discovered that a half of the total population of 2,300 Panare had been converted by North American fundamentalist missionaries. Following conversion they found that the Indians were obliged to pay dues to the mission, amounting in some cases, according to their informants, to 500 Bolivars (£9) a month. There were cases when Indians had been forced to sell all their possessions to meet what to them was an enormous sum. At the unhappy village of San Vicente defaulters were so terrified of God's punishment that two cases were reported of fathers prostituting their daughters to 'the foreigner' in exchange for the reduction or cancellation of their 'debt'.

On 25 May 1987 *El Mundo* of Caracas spoke of increasing demoralization of the Panare under a fanatical regime which might even lead to mass suicide as in Jonestown, Guyana.

. . . AND OF THE AYOREOS
14 November 1987:

> *Commenting on the news that a group of Forest Indians had been sighted in the Chaco, near Mariscál Estigarríbia, Father José Zanardini of the Silesian Mission urged that to avoid a massacre of the kind that happened last December there should be no immediate attempt at contact. 'Apart from the ideological violence of forcing them out of their environment,' the father said, 'they will all die of influenza or measles as happened in the case of the last group.' Father Zanardini hoped that as the Indians had been sighted on private land belonging to the Casado company, legal measures might be taken for their protection.* (Ultima Hora, *Asunción, Paraguay.*)

Ultima Hora added that the massacre of the previous year had caused intense dismay among those concerned with the welfare of Indians, and provoked condemnation of the New

Tribes Mission from whose camp the 'civilized' Ayoreos had gone out in pursuit of the others.

12 December 1987:

Survival International mounted a vigil at the European Headquarters of the New Tribes Mission, at Matlock Bath, to commemorate the death of five Indians, killed one year ago in a Mission manhunt. A letter of protest signed by Bishop Trevor Huddleston, Lord Avebury, Chairman of the Parliamentary Human Rights Group, Rabbi Richard Rosen and Survival International President, Robin Hanbury-Tenison, called on the Mission to halt its controversial activities and respect tribal religion and culture.

Arena

☐ The Gooseboy	A L Barker	£3.99
☐ The History Man	Malcolm Bradbury	£3.50
☐ Rates of Exchange	Malcolm Bradbury	£3.50
☐ Albert's Memorial	David Cook	£3.99
☐ Another Little Drink	Jane Ellison	£3.99
☐ Mother's Girl	Elaine Feinstein	£3.99
☐ Roots	Alex Haley	£5.95
☐ The March of the Long Shadows	Norman Lewis	£3.99
☐ After a Fashion	Stanley Middleton	£3.50
☐ Kiss of the Spiderwoman	Manuel Puig	£2.95
☐ Second Sight	Anne Redmon	£3.99
☐ Season of Anomy	Wole Soyinka	£3.99
☐ Nairn in Darkness and Light	David Thomson	£3.99
☐ The Clock Winder	Anne Tyler	£2.95
☐ The Rules of Life	Fay Weldon	£2.50

Prices and other details are liable to change

ARROW BOOKS, BOOKSERVICE BY POST, PO BOX 29, DOUGLAS, ISLE
OF MAN, BRITISH ISLES

NAME..

ADDRESS..

....

....

Please enclose a cheque or postal order made out to Arrow Books Ltd. for the amount
due and allow the following for postage and packing.

U.K. CUSTOMERS: Please allow 22p per book to a maximum of £3.00.

B.F.P.O. & EIRE: Please allow 22p per book to a maximum of £3.00.

OVERSEAS CUSTOMERS: Please allow 22p per book.

Whilst every effort is made to keep prices low it is sometimes necessary to increase cover
prices at short notice. Arrow Books reserve the right to show new retail prices on covers
which may differ from those previously advertised in the text or elsewhere.